BEHIND THE SUN

AMELIA SMITH

ISBN: 978-1-3999-1602-8

For Toumani and Chierno

Some of the events in this novel are based on real life

Between the sun and us is darkness,
and yet the air seems blue.

— Leonardo da Vinci

In the Middle East if a man sees himself walking behind the sun in a dream it's believed to signify his capture and imprisonment. The forcibly disappeared are put behind the sun, sometimes forever.

CHAPTER ONE

If you found yourself beside the slanting walls of the Old City, then looked upwards at Aleppo, you would have seen the turrets of the ancient citadel. From afar they were cream, much like the houses that surrounded it and climbed up the slopes and lined the potted roads, but up-close green grass seeped through the cracks and around the looped arches the brick gave way to a murky brown.

Shams never thought the citadel was the most beautiful part of her city. It's just that somewhere near the base of the castle was where she considered for the first time she might like to kiss Amin.

This morning, as she wound her way through the cobbled streets of the souq, past the plump roast chicken that hissed on spits and the dark blocks of olive oil soap that had been cut with a rough hand and pressed against the glass-fronted cabinets, she hesitated, her thoughts lingering for a moment on that encounter. She felt the corners of her mouth turn upwards into an involuntary smile, then checked herself as she rounded the corner and the familiar sight of the studio came into view.

Shams turned her key in the brass lock then heaved back the door, revealing the narrow staircase that led up into the darkness towards the studio. Pushing it shut with her hip, she locked it behind her and left the key in place. She wedged her phone between her ear and her shoulder and turned to the small shelf as she spoke.

"Rasha can you hear me?"

She flicked through the post as though it was a pack of cards and when she didn't hear anything, peered at the phone to check the call had gone through.

"Rasha are you there?"

"Sorry, had to shut the door. What's up?"

"Amin did it again last night."

There was a short pause, the sound of a zip being closed, some papers being rustled.

"Have you tried to talk to him?"

"Yes. Well, not specifically this time. What's the point? He obviously doesn't want to change. Rasha, do you think this is a normal relationship?"

"Shams there's no such thing as normal, it's what's normal for you that matters. Look, you can't live in this state of uncertainty forever - it will kill you. Make the list."

"Ok, ok."

"We'll talk about it next time I see you. I have to run; I'll be late for work. Big kiss."

"Love you."

Shams slid the phone into her bag and listened to the sound of her heels clicking against the narrow staircase. Was she burdening Rasha too much with her problems? Rasha was always there for her, she knew that, but there was always a hint of superiority in her voice. Rasha never seemed to accept her for what she was and it had not escaped her notice that the only other person in her life who made her feel that way was Amin.

It hadn't always been like that. She closed her eyes and recalled the first time she met Rasha. "All economics comes down to really is supply and demand." What was his name again, that student who had been after Rasha for weeks? Tahir, that was it. "Tahir, it's good that three years of studies can be boiled down to one such simple equation. I could have told you that and saved you a lot of time." Looking back, Rasha's comments didn't seem so funny, but at the time she thought it was hilarious.

About halfway into her ascent the smell of wood shavings hit Shams and she paused for several seconds and stood, inhaling slowly. They say the longest and toughest relationship you can have is with yourself, but she didn't agree. She found the contradiction of being comfortable with her personality, but feeling Rasha and Amin weren't, unsettling. Nothing will ever be perfect in life and the only way to navigate – or avoid altogether – feelings of disappointment is to accept that nothing is perfect from the start.

Naturally, she had often wondered whether it would be simpler to cut them out altogether, but she was convinced that these relationships defined her and that without them she may cease to exist as Shams. Perhaps she only existed by what she was in contrast to other people. That was a scary thought. Then there was her father and mother to whom she had struggled to relate for twenty-three years – nineteen, if our first memories start at four.

At the top of the staircase Shams unlatched the door. The floor was freshly swept, the wooden broom leant against the corner. There were six rows of boxes piled high on the table under the window and Shams straightened them with two hands to prevent them from falling. One knocked into the framed photograph on the wall and she reached over to adjust it.

'Abdullah Tibi and Shaimaa Rahman with the president and his wife, 4 October 2001.' She leaned in closer. She had never seen that line before. The four of them were in the centre, smiling, surrounded by twenty schoolchildren. "Just a PR visit to your mother's school," her father had told her when she asked.

Shams ran her palm over one of the boxes. When she first began to learn her father's trade it was her brother Yusuf who had shown her how to sand down the boxes, apply the design on top and then carve around the shape of the leaves, being careful to cut the stalks to exactly the right width. If they were too thick they detracted from the delicate nature of the design. If they were too thin the mother of pearl would seep out of the edges and the box would be ruined.

One Sunday Yusuf had taken her wrist between his forefinger and thumb and swept it across the box, tracing the line of the flowers and showing her how, despite the illusion of chaos, the shape of the flowers was in fact one fluid line. That evening he had flipped the box over and carved their initials in the bottom right-hand corner, tucked it into his bag, and told her he would keep it as a souvenir.

Now, Shams turned to the radio and hesitated: "Government forces step up bombardment of terror-strongholds in Homs and other cities. This morning the government announced the country is in a state of real war and stipulates the maximum penalty for dealing with terrorists..."

She snapped it off and rubbed her temples. She could feel a headache coming on. Shams looked across the studio, or their second living room, as she and Yusuf referred to it. Her father had once suggested she and Amin get married in here and Shams suspected he hadn't been joking.

She knelt to take her notebook from her bag. It was a present from her brother. She loved how it felt in her hands; how the smooth leather contrasted with the raised edges of the design. She rubbed her thumb against the spine and felt it catch on the edge. Over time she had developed hard pieces of skin around the tips of her fingers from where she held the chisel and scars on her wrists from where it had slipped, cutting into her skin. On one occasion bright red blood had poured over the box and though she scrubbed most of it away, she took great satisfaction in knowing that someone had a box at home with flecks of her dried blood between the cracks.

She let the pages run through her fingers until she found an empty one and wrote 'Amin – pros' at the top, underlining the text several times. 'Reliable, generous and kind.' She sat back to consider what she had written and scribbled out 'kind', replacing it with 'thoughtful.' That was better.

A noise directly below the studio interrupted her thoughts. She dropped the notebook and peered through the tiny window. A crowd was moving slowly through the street below. The people had formed a rectangle that tapered at the end but when the front swayed to one side the back went in the opposite direction which momentarily formed an s-shape. Shams could hear a certain rhythm to the chant but the exact words were obscured by the echo of their voices hitting the ancient walls of the souq.

The protester directly behind the leader was carrying the leading edge of a giant flag bearing the stars and stripes of her country, and a girl at the back had a firm grip on the other end. Through the sea of folds in the fabric Shams could make out 'Syria' written across the bottom edge.

She scanned the road. She didn't recognise anyone in the crowd, though that was unsurprising anyway since she could only see the tops of their heads. She liked the way the group moved from side to side, there was a kind of hypnotic quality to it. She had seen the images on the news, seen the protests across the region. Everyone had, even if they said they hadn't. Watching from afar is one thing, but when it comes to you, only then do you know what you will do.

She looked up as a few stray children ran to catch up

with the group. She watched their determined progress. Did she want kids of her own? Amin had asked her often enough, but she wasn't sure. She loved the fact that they were on a journey; they were a reminder of how we have to enjoy everything as it is rather than wait for the finished product. She liked to look after other people's children, but she also liked to give them back at the end of the day. No, she decided, she didn't want her own. Not yet.

The crowd turned the corner at the end of the street and she looked to the right, to see if there was another group coming, then tensed and felt her breath draw out of her with a sudden gushing sound. Directly in front of the building, a man was standing with his feet slightly apart looking directly up at her, a camera positioned over his eye. She saw the movement of his finger, watched in slow motion as the shutter went down behind the lens and back up again. She breathed in, twisted away and flattened her back against the wall.

Shams heard the door downstairs. Someone was shaking it violently. She slid down the wall and crouched for several minutes, feeling the pull in the muscle along the top of her thighs. The knocking sounded again, it was urgent, aggressive. She patted her pockets feeling for her keys. Had she locked the door on her way in?

She stood, shook her legs out, and prepared to go downstairs. If she didn't answer the door, it would make her look guilty and she hadn't done anything wrong, only looked out of the window to see what the noise was. She wiped the sweat off her forehead. It had been disturbing her thoughts, preventing her from working. Any reasonable person would understand that.

She secured her notebook with an elastic band, buried it between her father's books on the window ledge, and laid out a box and chisel on the worktop. She turned as something small fell from between the books, stooped and brought it up to the light to examine it. It was a plastic ball with one side flattened glass.

Behind the door she stood for several minutes, breathed in and out slowly and deeply, and then smiled as she pulled it open.

"Why did you lock the door?" His face clouded as he pushed the door and Shams stumbled backwards.

"Yusuf? What are you doing here?" She pulled the door open further, looked up and down the street but couldn't see anything. As she closed it, she caught the smell of used oil coming from the vent of a kitchen.

"I work here."

"Right." She pushed the door so that it clicked, then she turned. "But not on a Saturday."

"I've got a headache; can you draw the curtains?"

Up in the studio Yusuf was pacing up and down, rolling his fingers over his eyes in circular motions. When he pulled them away Shams could see red veins across the whites, angry red fissures like cracks of lightning.

"Yusuf where have you just come from?"

"Out. I was out."

"Yes, I can see that. Out where?"

"Just out. Shams."

"Yes?"

"The curtains. Please."

She moved towards the window and untied the rope that held the curtain away from it. Their mother had spent six months sewing the thick red material into a rectangle after it was given to her as a present by her sister. When it was finished it was so heavy their father had to drill holes for extra screws and spread them out across the curtain pole to make sure it was robust enough to take the weight.

That was what confused her about her father: he was

usually so detached, uncaring, but then he would spend hours completing a practical task for someone. Perhaps that was his way of showing his love; she had never thought of that before. Relationships with people aren't all hugs and kisses.

"Do you think Mum would even notice if we replaced the curtain? I can't remember the last time she was here."

Her brother's voice was somewhere in the distance, like he was talking through glass. He sounded exhausted.

"Shams you're taking too long, hurry up." He rubbed his eyes again. "Shams are you listening to me?"

Shams took her time pulling the curtain across. If she gave Yusuf some space he might calm down. She felt her chest wheeze as the dust clouded the air and she tried to bat it away with her hand. She felt guilty when she thought of how long it had taken her mother to make the curtain and how little they used it.

Shams' mother was good at sewing but she did have a tendency to exaggerate, she thought, looking down at the blue dress she had made for her. It had a square neck which plunged into the sleeves stopping just above her wrists. Towards the knees it flared out, which meant the material rustled as she walked and this annoyed Shams. From the front it looked quite simple, but when she turned there was a line of pale blue feathers sewn down the back and running all the way to the hem.

"Are you listening to me? Shams?"

"Yes, yes. Let's get rid of it."

"We'd have to hide it though. She'd go mad."

"Just tell her it was you. She'd forgive you anything."

There was a pause, a creaking sound as he lowered himself into a chair. "What do you mean by that?"

"You know what Mum's like."

Shams bent down and flicked on the light her father used

when he was working late. She stared at Yusuf's face in the orange glow.

It was white and there were beads of sweat running down his neck; she could see the outline of his stomach through his t-shirt where the perspiration had made it translucent. His jeans were streaked with black and from the palms of his hands up to his elbows were red cuts.

She opened the cupboard under the sink and held out her right hand as several boxes stashed there fell towards her. She retrieved a metal bowl, placed it beside him then placed a hand on the back of his neck. It was burning.

She reached out and turned his arm over so she could see the cuts. "Where did you get these? Yusuf, this looks really painful. Let me get you some bandages."

"No." He pulled his arm away. "Nowhere. Playing football with some friends. Stop fussing, you're getting like Mum."

She returned to the workbench, picked up the chisel and began to work away at the design, looking up every thirty seconds or so to check on her brother. The sun had found a crack in the curtains and she noticed how it caught the mother of pearl and gave the impression the lid was covered in fragments of mirror. She blew at the excess wood she had driven away with the force of the chisel.

"Hello." Shams spun round at the sound of the voice behind her.

"Amin. Right, of course."

He held up a blue plastic bag. "I brought some food."

"Right." She smoothed her dress and rubbed the small of her back where it had grown sore from bending over the workbench and walked towards him to retrieve it, bunching the handles together so that she wouldn't have to touch his skin.

"What's up with him?" Amin gestured at Yusuf.

"He's ill." Shams looked at Amin. She loved how his jaw

line formed an l-shape from the bottom of his ear and met his chin. He had perhaps two or three days' worth of stubble that cast a faint shadow over the bottom half of his face and contrasted with the depth of the colour in his eyes.

He is certainly handsome, thought Shams, her cheeks reddening. To counter the feeling it stirred in her she considered his hair – she hated the way he combed it to the side and applied too much product so that it always looked greasy. Moreover, she had been troubled for years by his tendency to start conversations with his mouth full and his lack of awareness when stray food was caught around his lips and chin.

Amin lowered his voice. "Is he asleep?"

She shrugged her shoulders. "I think so."

"Shams there's someone downstairs asking about you."

She felt her heartbeat quicken and she turned away. "Asking about me? What do you mean? What kind of person? I mean - who?" She busied herself with the boxes, stacking three on top of each other, then changing her mind and laying them out side by side.

"Middle-aged man, kind of husky voice. He stopped me as I was coming in and asked where I was going. He asked if I knew Yusuf."

She spun back round. "Yusuf? Why is he interested in Yusuf?"

"Well I thought you could tell me that. Look at him, he looks like a mess. Where has he been?"

"No idea."

"Come on Shams, he must have told you."

"He didn't," she could feel her voice becoming high pitched and she fought to breathe slowly, trying to readjust herself. "He just said he had a headache, and that he had been out playing football with some friends."

"Football. Right. Well anyway, whoever it was asked me to give you this."

He held out a brown padded envelope and she felt one of the bubbles in the lining pop as she took it.

"I'll open it later."

"Open it now."

She sighed, tore off the end then peered inside. "It's a photograph."

"Let me see." Amin tried to snatch it from her, but she pulled it away.

"I'm looking first. He gave it to me remember." She moved towards the light and turned it around in her hands. "It's a bandage, or a cast or something like that."

"A bandage? It can't be, why would someone give you a picture of a bandage. Shams let me see it." He took a step towards her. "Give it to me."

She gave a heavy sigh and handed it over. He screwed his eyebrows together as he concentrated on the image.

"You're right, looks like one of those casts they use in hospitals."

"This is ridiculous, let's put it away now. It must have been a mistake." She held out her hand. "Amin give it back to me."

He curled the photograph round so it formed a tube then held it above his head, just out of her reach. "What's Yusuf involved in, Shams? He's your brother you must know. Why would someone send you this? Why would they wait for you outside? It's creepy."

Shams looked down and realised she was still holding the bag of food so she placed it on the table next to the window and pulled out two chicken kebabs. The grease from the meat had formed dark pools on the light paper and shreds of lettuce sprinkled onto the floor.

"You know Shams, just because he's your brother, it doesn't mean you have to protect him. It's my job to protect you, and I don't want you mixed up in anything out of your control."

Shams bristled. "I don't need protecting from anyone, least of all from Yusuf. And nothing about our relationship should be described as a *job*."

She reached forward and peeled the paper off the top of her kebab, letting it hang down the side like a spiral. "How was work?"

"Shams why are you ignoring this?" He was standing opposite her now, his nostrils flared, waving the photo around in the air, flicking it against his other hand. "Why are you ignoring what was in that envelope? What's going on around you?"

"Stop shouting, you'll wake Yusuf." She looked down at her food and then up again. "I'm not ignoring it. I'm choosing to get on with my life. And right now, I'm hungry and I want to eat."

"You can't get on with your life; your life has completely changed."

"What do you know about my life? About the choices I want to make?" She stood up, then sat back down again. "I haven't chosen to be a part of this, therefore nothing in my life has changed. It's Yusuf's problem not mine." She lifted a napkin and caught some sauce on her right cheek. "So tell me, how was work?"

Amin circled around and eventually sat down. "Do you really want me to answer that?"

"I asked, didn't I?"

He rolled his eyes. "Utterly boring. I really don't think a desk job is for me."

"What is for you then?"

He paused, looked up at her and started speaking without swallowing the mouthful of kebab. "I'd like to work here with you. We could run a great business together." He reached out and held her hand. She pulled it away, pretending to catch a stray tomato that had fallen onto the table.

"Your father's getting older. It's a family business and he certainly has you in mind to take over one day. Yusuf's hardly interested."

He rested the bread on the napkin. "It would be a chance for us to spend more time together."

Shams tried to swallow her mouthful, but it caught in her throat and she coughed, then thumped her chest with her fist.

CHAPTER TWO

Before he started work Xr would take five minutes to smell the death in the room. Death was a void, a gaping black hole. Why, then, was the smell it created so thick and smothering?

He leant against the navy metal locker and pulled on his overalls, enjoying the click between his fingers as he fastened the poppers. The light blue covers slipped easily over his trainers. He stood for thirty seconds, staring at his feet. Today he would put on an extra pair to try and limit the damage to his new shoes.

He stopped at the hatch in the wall and exchanged pleasantries with Ahmed behind the counter.

"How's your wife?"

"She's well Xr. Much better, thank you for asking."

"And the kids? How did Magid's exam go?"

"Very well. He came top. Bouthaina and I are so proud of him."

"You should be. And he's lucky to have a father like you."

Xr had often wondered how a man of Ahmed's age had managed to keep both the hair on his head and on his face so black, unlike his father who had turned completely grey by the age of twenty. He couldn't remember exactly how many children Ahmed had, but he knew it was above seven. A number of times he had passed him on his lunch break or after school to find Ahmed fashioning gifts for them, whether it was origami swans or sketches of Aleppo's landscape.

"Are you well Xr?"

"Good, good." Xr took the camera, looped it over his neck and felt it pull as it swung loose. "See you later, no doubt."

At first, when his boss had assigned him the name Xr he found it difficult to get used to and when people called him from across the room, he often ignored them. Not out of rudeness, but because he wasn't used to answering to this name. Still, he could see the benefits. He was able to take on a different persona here at work from the one he bore outside in the real world.

He turned towards the grey corridor. It was always good to go through the motions, continue with work, get on with your life, even if the world you knew was crumbling around you.

Xr moved onto the office where the pathologist was bent over a pile of documents. He was a thin figure who always pinned his apron under the arms to try and encourage it to fit better. His wrinkles fanned out from the corner of each eye, like fingers from an outstretched palm. Without lifting his head, he raised his voice when he heard Xr enter the room.

"One to thirty," he barked, turning the page of his notes with his yellowed fingers.

Across the hall Xr still felt the chill around his wrists and at the nape of his neck, yet the smell was no longer quite as overpowering as it had been in the beginning. These days it took three or four minutes before the odour released by the rows of bodies began to hit his nostrils. He stood with his feet spread apart and his chin pointing upwards waiting for it to arrive. A sombre ritual.

Xr squeezed together the catch covering the camera lens and placed the cap in his pocket. He walked towards the first body and placed his fingers between the toes then released them, tracing a finger along the leg to where it joined the hip, over the chest which was covered in bruising and further up, letting it rise over the nose and eventually rest on the forehead. Just next to where his fingertips lay the number '24' had been written in black felt tip.

He took two steps back then photographed each stage of the journey his finger had made with his camera, zooming in on the bruising and lifting the back of the head to check for lacerations behind it. There was a cardboard notice tucked under the corpse's shoulder with the number 'one' written in blue biro. When he was done, he stepped to the right, took in the next body and began photographing again.

Xr moved his face close to the mouth. The front two top teeth were missing and the bottom two had only half remaining. He could smell burnt hair and when he put his hand behind the head it felt soft. When he withdrew it, the hair came away between his fingers and he brought his hand up to his mouth as he heaved. Wisps were caught under his nails and he made a futile attempt to wipe his hand on the corner of the table.

He had almost finished the entire row when he stopped at the end of one of the silver tables. A woman. He ran four fingers around the inside of the neck of his shirt and felt the heat arrive. He looked at the floor for a few moments then lifted her left wrist with the palm of his hand. The top layer of her skin had been torn off from her elbow to the tips of her fingers and her right arm was bent outwards in the shape of an L. Where the palm met the wrist was an inky sketch of a diamond.

Xr photographed the tattoo three times then moved closer to study her face. There was something familiar about the image, he thought, tilting his head to one side. He pulled at the plastic cap which covered her hair. A single curl fell out and came to rest gently on her shoulder. He stood for several minutes peering at her face, then stroked the lock of hair with his knuckle. It felt cold and Xr wondered how much colder it would get when her whole body was buried beneath the earth.

Xr often thought about his good fortune that all of his family were still alive. Of course, his grandparents had died before he was born, yet even though photos of them had been hung in a line in the corridor, he had no recollection of the moment they departed from this world. Working deep inside this morgue he wondered what grief felt like, how the relatives of the deceased he photographed every day coped with their loss at night.

There was a loud knocking behind and Xr turned to see the pathologist.

"Have you finished?"

Xr nodded, reaching inside his pocket and placing the cover over the lens. He turned, pressed his chin further into his chest and slipped through the door which his boss held open for him, holding it with his two hands out behind him so that it wouldn't slam.

Xr always compared the feeling in his shoulders in the icy morgue with how stiff they felt in the office. Despite the cold, he was relaxed amongst the bodies and his lungs breathed easily as a result. Back at the desk with its plastic chair he felt the familiar tightness in his muscles and circled both shoulders backwards to ease the discomfort. There was a muscle just next to his shoulder blade which always felt knotted. He crossed his right arm across his chest, hooked it over his shoulder, then poked it with his finger and tried to relieve the tension.

"What are you doing?"

He turned in his chair to face the pathologist, one finger still kneading his muscle. "I have problems with my right shoulder. Sometimes I wake up in the morning and I can barely move my neck."

"I don't pay you to come here and talk about your problems. You're here to work. Get on with what you're doing - there's not time for this." He walked over to Xr's desk and dropped a stack of cardboard at the corner.

Xr stood, retrieved the photos from the printer and one by one stapled them to the cardboard. On the back he wrote the numbers that were next to each corpse then added descriptions of the body – height, age, hair colour – then the cause of death. Heart attack, natural causes, cancer. All of them were dictated by the pathologist, his voice echoing coldly around the room. Xr nodded and recorded everything in careful Arabic script. When he had finished, he filed the records in a grey cabinet according to the number that had been marked on each forehead.

Eight hours after he first arrived in the morgue Xr stripped off his overalls and took out a black plastic comb from his locker to scrape his hair backwards. He rolled some aftershave behind his ears and retrieved a baseball cap from the bottom of his rucksack, pulling the peak away from his head so he could sweep aside the stray hairs. He peeled off the shoe covers and slid his feet out so he could inspect his trainers for blood. Nothing this time.

Not far from the exit he approached the checkpoint and stepped on the brake. The officer tapped on the window and he lent across and rolled it down, wondering, not for the first time, why the soldiers insisted on standing on the passenger side of the car.

"Identification."

The sun bounced off the soldier's helmet and he wore a belt of ammunition around his waist. His socks were pulled up out of his boots and over the army trousers. Had his mother washed them for him last night?

Xr reached into his pocket and pulled out his leather wallet, popped the fastening open with the same hand and retrieved his military ID. The plastic cover was coming away at the corners and he flicked it with his thumb nail. In those days his hair had been much longer, he observed, smiling at the photo of his head and shoulders in the corner.

The card bent towards him from where he gripped it, his thumb on one side and his four fingers on the other. He looked up. "Not my best photo." Xr couldn't see past the dark glasses but he stared into them.

"A photo's a photo, what does it matter." The officer snatched the card and stepped away from the car then turned it over in his hand.

Xr relaxed into his seat and considered the soldier in front of him. Do we all harbour within us the ability to commit acts of atrocity if the circumstances are right or if we are forced to do so, or is it simply that some of us are that way inclined?

He was distracted from his thoughts by the soldier's hand waving in the air. "Move along." He took the card back through the window, drew in a deep breath, restarted the engine, pressed his foot down on the accelerator and drove off into the darkness.

CHAPTER THREE

Snatched from sleep, Shams pulled the blanket over her head to block out the noises from the kitchen below, drew her legs up tight until her knees were touching her stomach, then rolled onto her back. She had slept in an awkward position which had left her with a sharp stabbing pain in the left side of her neck.

She thought of Yusuf, the cuts all over his arm, how aggressive he had been in the studio. How does the brain choose your first waking thought of the day? For several weeks now she had thought of little else but her brother, though she hadn't *chosen* to think about him. He was just always there in her mind.

She pulled back the covers and looked at herself. She had fallen asleep in her dressing gown again and the knot from the belt had left its tangled mark on her stomach. She stood, picked it apart, threw the gown over a chair and headed for the kitchen in her pyjamas.

Her "good morning," was met with silence. Her father sat with his back to her so she had to embrace him from behind. She felt him stiffen.

"You look terrible." Her mother said, gripping her shoulders with her arms out straight. The jarring sensation irritated her. It was too early for this. "Are you ill?"

"No Mum, you say that every day." Shams turned away. "Why can't you say something nice when you see me in the morning? Why do you always have to see the worst in people?"

"Don't speak to your mother like that." Shams turned to the table and rolled her eyes at her father's admonition. He had said a lot worse in the past; they had all witnessed it.

Laid out before her were boiled eggs, slices of cheese, fuul, olives and bread. Shams could see the rings left by hot drinks placed directly on the wood so, by force of habit, she lifted the coffee pot up and onto a woven mat. It was only on Sundays when she had to do that, the only day her father didn't go to work until late.

When her father was home you always knew in which room. For such a slight man he was unusually heavy-footed. Her mother, on the other hand, who had a penchant for sticky baklava and a generous waist to prove it, nonetheless moved everywhere gracefully. Her parents were a mass of contradictions which, when taken together, often balanced out.

He was about to start his tea and the leaves inside the rounded glass were still spiralling through the liquid where he had stirred sugar into it. A single boiled egg lay in the centre of his plate and as he cut through it the knife made a grating sound against the glass.

"You need to come to the workshop with me today." He paused to sprinkle salt and pepper on the deep yellow yolk with great concentration. "There is a lot of work to be done."

"Work? What work? There are already hundreds of boxes at the studio with nowhere to go."

"Hundreds!" her father snorted, dismissively.

"Ok not hundreds, but there's at least twenty extra boxes piled up and even some under the sink. There's no point in making any more. There's no one left to buy them."

"Shams, this is not just about money." He laid down his knife with the weariness of one who hoped but did not expect to be understood. "It's a craft. A trade. A livelihood. And besides, do you really think all of this madness is going to last?" He waved his hand towards the door trying to take in the chaos around them.

Shams stood up to open a window. She couldn't understand why Yusuf insisted on eating chicken for breakfast and why their mother insisted on cooking it for him every time. The smell was offensive at this time in the morning.

She sat back down at the table, and found her eyes drawn to her father's moustache. It spanned the length of his top lip, the hairs creeping up into his nostrils. When she was young, the wedge of hair was so dark it glistened in the sun but with age it had developed grey specks that she often mistook for food.

"Well?" he pressed.

"Well what?"

"Shams," her mother warned from across the room.

"Will you come?"

She looked over at her mother who was spearing the chicken with the point of her knife and turning it over in the boiling fat. Every so often she would jump backwards as the oil spat on her skin but she wouldn't turn and face the table. It occurred to Shams that her mother was weak, too eager to appease her father, and she hated her for it.

"Why won't it last?"

He took a sip of his tea. "Perhaps 'last' is the wrong word. Those people, the ones gathered out there on the street – they need to realise that what they're doing out there is pointless. They are risking their lives – and ours too – and for what? There is too much invested in this country, too much to lose. Nothing will ever change." He checked himself. "No - nothing *needs* to change."

"Dad I can hear you from all the way down the hallway. That's rubbish." They looked at the door, Yusuf was leaning against the frame. His jeans and t-shirt looked as if he had just snatched them up from the floor of his room. "It worked in Egypt, it worked in Tunisia. Why shouldn't it work here?"

Her father leaned back into his chair and crossed his arms. "Worked in Egypt. How did it work in Egypt? So one man stands aside and you think that's enough? You think you've changed the country? Let me tell you this: behind every tyrant there are layers upon layers that you can't see, layers that you will never get to, certainly not in this lifetime. You're so naïve – and blinded by idealism. Do you not realise that once you unpick something you can't put it back together, so why unpick it in the first place? You young people, you think you know everything, think you can click your fingers and change the world in a day, you have no idea. You have no idea what's ahead of you."

"You're wrong Dad." Yusuf walked over to the table and poured himself a coffee then stood balancing the mug on the palm of his hand. "Whatever happens, it's the mentality that's changed. Once people have tasted freedom, there can be no retreat. Once the lid of fear is lifted it's impossible to put back. You can't change how people feel about politics now, even if you try to tighten the fist of power. Look at us all, we were asleep. What did politics mean to us? Nothing. Now look at us."

Abdullah twisted his chair towards his son. "Yusuf, you have no idea how lucky you are. This generation has it all compared to the world I grew up in and now you just want to throw it away, and for what? All those people down on the streets, marching when they should be at work. Ridiculous. Earning money: now that's a route to your freedom."

He crammed half of the egg into his mouth and washed it down with the last of his tea. "I mean, yes, I inherited the studio from my father, that's correct, but look what I've made it into. A thriving business. Or at least it was until all this madness started. Then afternoons and Saturdays in the visa department to top up my salary."

"Yes, Dad, you tell us every time."

"And we never want for money." He stood and placed the glass plate beside the sink to show he was done. "And that is something you two will never truly appreciate, because you have never been without money." He paused for a moment, distracted by the view from the window, then turned to face them both. "This is Syria. It's our country and we have to protect it."

"Syria? Our country? Dad, what are you talking about?" Shams could see the veins in Yusuf's neck pulsating. "This country is called Syria, and we may be Syrians, but we know nothing about this country. We were never allowed to know anything about this country, it belongs to somebody else. And even that is vanishing. There is no Syria anymore, can't you see that?"

"That's enough." The three of them turned as Shams' mother span round from the stove still carrying the cast iron pan. She shook it over a bowl she had lined with kitchen roll and as the chunks hit the paper oil spread to the corners. "Have some more food. Sit down and eat, it's time to change the subject. Yusuf, I made all this chicken for you, you'll offend me if you don't eat it. Please, have some."

The velour of her nightgown was speckled with darkened, stiff stains which had refused to come out in the wash and Shams wondered whether all women of her mother's age wore nighties rather than pyjamas or if it was just her mother. And the gold hoops, they were a permanent fixture in her ears, no matter what her outfit was.

Wearing them all the time was the closest her mother had ever come to admitting she owned jewellery. Shams knew she did because her grandmother had told her about the vast collection stored under the bed, but her mother had never showed it to them and rarely wore any of it. One Sunday, when she was entertaining the family, Shams and Yusuf crept into her room and peered underneath the mattress. The darkness was filled with wooden boxes, embroidered purses, jugs and bowls, each overflowing with jewels. Directly below the pillows squares of fabric lay piled up, each folded down the centre to protect the bracelet or earrings inside. Towards the back there were rings that had been rolled inside silky material then secured with an elastic band.

Shams thought about the image of herself that her mother presented to her children, then the mother with all her secrets. She found the contradiction of loving her but not wanting to grow up to be like her unsettling. In the end all we ever want is to be ourselves – why, then, was it so hard to do this in public? She concentrated on her food so she wouldn't have to entertain the thought any longer.

"Have some, Abdullah," her mother tried again. She had turned to face Shams and her father and she pushed the heap of chickpeas and tahini towards him. He patted his belly to indicate he was full, reclined in his chair and pulled a cigarette out of his pocket, lit it and inhaled, tapping the ash onto the floor.

"Your brother will go first and open up the shop whilst you have a shower."

Shams spooned a forkful of hummus into her mouth and swallowed it. "We'll wait for you, we can all go together."

"No. I need to take your mother somewhere."

"Where?"

"She needs to get her eyes tested. Doctor says she needs glasses."

"Mum is that true?" She turned to face her mother. "You didn't tell us."

Shaimaa opened her mouth to speak.

"Your mother doesn't have to tell you everything. Now go and get ready."

Shams went quietly upstairs. She called her brother's name but heard no reply. She stood with one hand on the doorknob and pressed her ear against the wood. She heard him cough. "Yusuf?"

She knocked again and pushed at the door. He was spread out on the bed, his headphones on, his laptop resting on his knees.

She crept up behind him and placed two hands on his shoulders. "Yusuf Tibi."

He ripped the headphones off his ears and snapped the laptop shut. "Shams, what are you doing? You should knock before coming in here."

"I did. Twice." She walked around the bed so she was facing him. "Just wanted to see how you are that's all. What were you watching?"

"Nothing. A film."

"Can I join you?"

He rolled his eyes, smiled and patted the bed. "Sure. Like old times."

She climbed onto the bed next to him and he curled his arm around her. "Sorry I snapped."

From her position she had a clear view of the ceiling. Spread across it were tiny glow- in-the-dark stars, bursts of lime green against the white. In the right-hand corner, closest to the door, he had placed a moon.

"Do you remember when Dad stormed into the room with a metal ruler and threatened to tear down your solar system?"

"Yeah. I told him I had fallen asleep under it for fifteen years, I couldn't stop now."

"You were afraid of the dark."

He bristled. "No I wasn't."

"Maybe you still are."

Yusuf sat up and reached over her, trying to put his laptop on the side table.

"I'll do it." She turned and placed it on the white plastic. In biro he had scrawled all over the surface, cartoon characters with oversized heads and flames coming out of their heels.

"So, tell me about Amin."

Shams daubed her finger in her mouth then rubbed the edges of the sketches to see if they came away but Yusuf had etched them into the plastic. "What do you want to know?"

"Are you happy?"

"Yes. I think so."

"'I think so?' What kind of an answer is that? You should be ecstatic, feeling like your life is full of magic – not thinking and doubting."

She threw her head back and laughed. "I don't believe in magic."

She turned around to face him. "Do *you* like Amin?"

"It doesn't matter what I think."

"It does a bit."

He turned so he was resting on his hip. "Look. How does Amin make you feel? That's what you should be asking yourself."

"Of course I like him. But parts of his personality really grate on me. I often find myself asking if it's just human nature that we're not entirely compatible or if there is indeed someone more compatible out there." Shams pulled a piece of imaginary fluff off her jeans. "Come on, let's watch this film."

"No. I have to get to the studio, you heard Dad. Another time."

Yusuf swung his legs off the side of the bed and stood up.

"Yusuf you've got something stuck to your back. It's paper." Shams moved to the other side of the bed so she could pull it free. "14-year old tortured…" She looked up at Yusuf but he snatched it away from her.

"Hey I was reading that. What is it?"

"Nothing."

"It clearly isn't nothing."

Yusuf stood and folded the paper in half, then in half again and looked up at his sister. He thought for a moment. "Look Shams, I will explain everything to you, but you're not to share it with anyone, not even Amin, ok?"

"No don't tell me, I don't want to know."

He stared at her. "What? What do you mean you don't want to know?"

"I said I don't want to know. Yusuf, you heard what Dad said at breakfast, we shouldn't get involved. There's no point, it won't end well. It never does. We have a nice enough life here. Mum and Dad are difficult but we've carved something out under all this, we'd be crazy to throw it all away."

"Shams, stop acting like you have a choice. You can't just turn your back and say there's no point. You have to do something, we all do."

"It's not about choosing. I don't even understand why it's important."

"Shams, politics is everything. It's the roads you drive on, the school your kids will go to. How can you say it's not important?"

She sighed and threw her arms up in the air. "Do you really think we're all just suddenly going to get a choice in what happens to our schools? Or the potholes in the road outside the flat are suddenly going to get filled in just because a handful of people are marching through the streets? Yusuf, this is ridiculous, you're going to destroy our family. You and I both know nothing will ever change."

"I am not going to destroy our family. *They* are going to destroy our family."

Shams got up to leave. Yusuf had always been stubborn but these last few weeks he had been worse than ever. She turned at the last minute, her hand on the door. "Yusuf whatever it is you're doing, shut it down. Please. For us, for your family. Just leave it alone."

A few minutes later Shams was lying on her own bed on the other side of the wall listening for the click of the front door. When at last it came she crept back into her brother's room.

She could see the bed had been made, the sheet folded around the top of the blanket at a perfect right angle, then tucked under the bottom of the mattress. The surface had been smoothed with such care from the middle to the outside, it may as well have been ironed.

Shams turned her attention to the right side of the bed where his mahogany desk stood. The cable to Yusuf's laptop snaked across the top, the computer gone. She pulled back the drawers and sifted through the papers inside. Old college assignments, bus tickets, some notes he and friends had passed between each other at school, but nothing unusual. She wiggled the drawers one by one until they came off their runners, laid them out on the floor, and checked to see if anything had fallen behind. She found an old pair of boxers, some coins and three paper clips so she slid the drawers back in place, pushing the last one with her elbow to that it was smoothly in line with the others.

It was getting hot so Shams flicked the switch of the fan in the corner and listened as it whirred into action, enjoying the way it her made her hair swirl around her shoulders.

She turned to his wardrobe, which was already open.

Inside there were three sections – a row of vertical, square openings, a shelf running across the entire length of the interior and a metal bar the colour of gold from which his jackets and shirts hung.

Starting with the rail, Shams took every jacket and ran her hands down the length of his clothing before sliding them into the pockets. Nothing. She couldn't reach the clothes on the top shelf but she ran her hand along the length of it.

Shams turned to face the bed again and crossed her arms. Why was it so pristine when the rest of the room was in disarray? She slipped her hand between the mattress and the bed frame, ran it all around the outside, but found nothing. She walked to the end of the mattress and used all her force to flip it up and look into the space below but all she could see were Yusuf's socks.

Shams let the mattress drop with a thud then stood for a few moments to see if her mother would come to investigate the noise. She crept over to the door, pulled it ajar and listened, but all she could hear was the sound of the television.

Shams sat and bounced up and down. What was that? The sound of paper rustling. She pulled back the blanket and saw that towards the foot of the bed the surface was uneven, as though Yusuf's clothes were caught up under the bedclothes.

The sheet itself was pale yellow and had tight balls of fibre all over it caused by their mother's insistence on hot washes. Another exaggeration, thought Shams. She pulled at it from the centre and the elasticated corners popped off but even with the sheet dangling out of one hand she still couldn't see what was making it uneven. She ran the flat of her palm along the top of the mattress then let it drop down the back where one of her nails was suddenly caught in an incision in the foam. She reached her hand inside, grabbed with her fingers then withdrew her hand to reveal scrunched up balls of paper, which she released onto the floor. She picked one up and opened it.

'Aid worker shot in the head in family's living room' read the headline in scrawled handwriting. The paper felt flimsy in her hands and she ran her fingers over it carefully for fear it might rip, then placed it on the floor, her hands shaking. 'Twelve-year-old boy tortured for painting his school wall' she read before scanning the rest of the text.

Shams kneeled beside the bed to explore the rest of Yusuf's mattress. She found similar incisions at various points, never at the same level. All over the mattress she was able to put her whole hand inside and pull out pieces of paper.

She sat back, her head against the white desk, the papers spread in a semi-circle in front of her. What were they doing here?

She heard a noise and when she turned towards the source of the sound, she heard another one, this time louder. She stood, tightened the pieces of paper into balls and packed them back into the holes, all the time trying to keep the mattress as smooth as possible. When they were all inside, she picked up the sheet and let it sail over the bed before tucking the edges into the corners.

When the blanket was back in place, she crouched down to check if any of the papers had fallen under the bed. There was one – she reached for it, tucked it into the pocket of her cardigan, then stepped outside.

The bathroom was directly opposite, the door ajar. She slid through the gap. Through the crack in the door she could see the landing.

As a silhouette appeared in the hallway she panicked. It was her father. He must have left something behind. He would have to pass where she was standing to get to his room or he might be on his way to the toilet. Either way it would be impossible for him not to see her. She turned. Where could she hide?

She prepared to step onto the landing and offer some excuse, when she saw him pause, reach out his hand and push down on the handle of Yusuf's door to let himself inside.

CHAPTER FOUR

Sharif twisted the lens of his binoculars but couldn't focus enough to get a clear image of the faces. A sunshade had been placed over the back windows, the kind that keeps the sun out of cars for children, and it was obscuring his view. He was ninety per cent certain it was the target but he wanted to be absolutely sure.

The sound of the engine turning over made him twitch slightly in his seat. No one would be suspicious of a car starting up but there was something about the way it rippled into the night that disturbed him. He rolled the vehicle forward one hundred metres and swung around the corner. That was better, he had a clear view of his face now. He checked the photograph on his lap and looked up. It was definitely him.

Sharif flicked through his file. Twenty-seven years old, unmarried, works with his father in a studio in the souq carving wooden boxes. Smoker. He skimmed the rest of the notes, his family ties had been left blank. Sharif scratched his head. Why hadn't they collated any of the information on his parents or his siblings? He eventually landed on two words at the bottom. Yusuf Tibi.

Yu-suf. Ti-bi.

When their eldest daughter was born Sharif's wife had explained that when choosing a name people often focused on its meaning, but to do this was to forget about everything else. A common oversight was the syllables and how they went together. So if the first name had two syllables the second had to have three and vice versa. It rolled off the tongue better.

Holding the binoculars up again Sharif closed his right eye and observed how much less he could see with the left. He didn't like the idea that there was a part of his body that was so weak and made a mental note to train it over the coming months. It wouldn't take long before he could observe subjects using just this eye alone.

He had first noticed this seven years ago in the hazy days after bringing Rahaf back from the hospital. No matter what they did to try and encourage her to sleep, she would only close her eyes at night after one of them rocked her from side to side, sometimes for up to twenty minutes at a time. Sharif had had such problems with his shoulder that he switched and tried to hold her in his left. After three months he was as comfortable holding her here as he was on the other side. By the time his second daughter was born Sharif had learnt that if he stayed at work long enough, or took a phone call at the right time, he could avoid having to take part in any of these rituals.

Rabia and Sharif had met for the first time at a cousin's wedding. It wasn't the first time they had seen each other, but it was the first time they had talked. Sharif was not a huge fan of such social occasions, which ate up precious amounts of his time that could be spent working, neither did he like the vast crowds of people, but he had made an exception this time because it was a cousin who had been kind to his mother when she developed rheumatism.

There was nothing outstanding about Rabia that drew

him to her but as his brother had once advised him to look for in a woman, she ticked the majority of boxes. Rabia had a plain face in that none of her features particularly stood out as striking. If he had to choose one it would be her eyelashes, which were so long Sharif suspected they might be fake.

At the wedding, Sharif grew impatient with Rabia. She had a tendency to say each word slowly and he became distracted by other things in the room – the cake, the music, the bride – whilst he waited for her to finish her sentences. He usually showed his face at these events for an hour at most then made his excuses but she had hooked him into a long conversation on the outskirts of the dance floor.

When his cousin came to greet them both he made his excuses and left by the back door. Then at home that night, he found himself thinking about her and he became convinced his mind was playing tricks on him. He met Rabia a further two times after that, once at a shopping mall close to his mother's flat and another at his favourite fish restaurant. Each time he picked up something else that frustrated him – her tendency to talk rather too loudly or her interest in soap operas – but every time he was away from her, he could think of nothing but Rabia.

A week later he proposed, offering her a comfortable, stable life and a three-bedroom flat close to the centre of town but conveniently located on a backstreet. He hinted he wanted two children, not more, and she agreed before he finished listing his offers. Twelve months later they were navigating the pressures of family life, bills and a screaming child.

Sharif glanced down as his phone lit up with a text message from Rabia. These days, when they did communicate, she wrote as though she were one of their two daughters, which infuriated him. So as they went through the major milestones he would receive messages, "I rolled over today" or "I took my first steps today." These days they said "I miss my Daddy and I want to see him." He would like, just for once, to have a conversation again with his wife.

Sharif narrowed his eyes, turned so he was leaning against the window and looked again through the binoculars. So Yusuf has good taste in women. Was that the one he saw looking down at him from the studio that day? He didn't think so. She was younger, around twenty-three, and her face was rounder. He lifted his camera, zoomed in, and tried to get an accurate snap of her face. He would do some research on her when he got home.

Home. Sharif thought of his nine brothers and sisters and felt a moment of nostalgia sweep over him. Had he had a happy childhood? Yes, he considered himself lucky in that regard. His father had died in a car crash when he was four and there had never been any photos of him at home. He had no memory of his father and his mother never spoke of him so there was never anything to miss. It was his eldest brother who simultaneously brought him up and made sure the family always had enough money.

Sharif had struggled at school. He got bored quickly and was easily led by the other boys in the classroom who preferred to play tricks on their teachers and talk to the girls. When he started working for the government, that's when it all changed. That's when he felt alive, he had found his calling. He had a cause and he intended to fulfil it to the very best of his ability.

He looked up as he heard the car door click and saw the female subject leave the car. It wouldn't do to be getting all emotional about his family life, not when he was trying to work. He needed to keep a clear head, he had nearly missed her leaving.

Sharif pulled up at the traffic lights. He could see her straight in front of him, staring just above his windscreen, waiting to see if it was safe to cross. She looked up as the green man appeared on the pedestrian crossing, then put her foot onto the road and her weight followed behind. He waited until she had left the curb a safe distance behind, then pressed onto the accelerator. He kept his arms straight, his eyes on the road. He watched her turn, register him, then sprint to the other side. He threw his head back and laughed, his shoulders bouncing up and down, air snorting through his nose. Everyone registered fear differently. Hers was subtle, but unmistakable. A flailing of the limbs, the white face, the panicked look left and right.

He pulled over and released the seat belt then slammed the door behind him, locking it with the automatic control over his shoulder. He weaved through the traffic, raising a hand in the air to indicate the drivers should stop. He climbed the bank onto the other side of the road. There she was, checking over her shoulder, her pace increasing when she registered he was behind her. He made large strides, enjoying watching her scurry up the hill like a rabbit. Then as she slinked into one of the alleyways he stopped, waited to see if she reappeared, and then made his way back to the car.

Thirty minutes later, outside his flat, as Sharif searched his bag for his keys, he heard a high-pitched moan coming from behind the rubbish bin. He placed his satchel down on the ground and moved towards it. He could see a grey and black striped tail on the left corner and he crouched, reached out his hand in one movement, gripped the end of the tail and pulled the cat towards him. He looked at it for several seconds then opened the lid of the bin, placed it inside and checked the seal to see if there was any way it could get out.

Against the wall was a pile of wooden slats, the remnants of an old bed he and Rabia had kept meaning to throw away, but had never got around to doing. He piled them up in a criss cross shape, scrunched up some paper and inserted it in between the wood.

Inside the flat Sharif went to Rahaf's bedroom and pulled back the covers.

"Get up."

"Is it morning?" She tried to roll over, away from him, but he took her by the shoulders and turned her back to face him.

"Almost. I have to show you something."

"Ok Daddy."

He turned the torch on on his phone and shone the light in front of them so she could see as they walked down the stairs and when she tried to twist away from him he pushed her towards the front door.

"Outside? Daddy, I want to go back to bed. Where's Mummy?"

"Open the door."

She reached up, pulled at the catch and stood on the step, her embroidered nightgown swaying at the bottom from the breeze. He left her standing there, bent towards the pile of wood and set light to it.

"Come." He scooped the air, indicating she should join him. "There's something in the bin, I put it there for you."

"The bin?"

"Yes. Open the lid."

She moved until she was standing directly beside him and then pulled the lid. It was heavy, he could see her struggling. He stood until eventually she slid it so the back end was hanging off. She peered inside.

"Oh, a cat. How cute, can we keep it?"

"Take it out."

She bent over, undeterred by the rancid smell, and retrieved it, holding it up to her face and pressing her nose into the fur on its neck.

"Daddy I love it thank you."

"Throw it onto the fire."

"What?" He watched her body tense as she looked at the flames and back to her father. She was shaking now, unsure whether she was hearing correctly. He saw a line of urine roll down her leg and form a puddle around her right foot.

"I said throw it onto the fire."

She turned and tried to head for the front door, letting her arms go loose. The cat jumped and stood in between them and Sharif bent, picked it up by its tail and pulled his daughter by her hair. He spun her around and gave her the cat again.

"Do it."

She looked up at her father, then back at the flames, closed her eyes and threw the cat. She tried to turn away, lifted her arms up and over her ears so that she could block out the sound but he gripped her wrists and pulled her arms down and locked them by her side, forcing her to face the fire as the screams twisted into the darkness, burrowing into her ears.

CHAPTER FIVE

"She was a lovely girl, Yara. But she took it too far, didn't listen."

"I'm sorry, do I know you?" Shams looked to the right, he had slowed right down, she could hear the squeak from where the tyres were too close to the curb. They were on a side street, not far from the studio, she didn't even realise cars were allowed down here. She looked over her shoulder, there was no one around. She looked back at him.

"Sharif. I'm a friend of your brother's."

She turned to face him, he was far older than her brother. "You're a friend of Yusuf?"

"You could say that." He had stopped now and so had she, they were parallel, looking at each other through the wound down window. "Did you get the little present I sent you?"

"Present?"

He turned the engine off and she could hear him more clearly. "I sent it with a young man into the studio that day."

She took a deep breath in. The picture. She turned to run, but he was out of the car and was clamping her elbow. Slender, bony fingers wrapped around her arms.

"Why the rush." He pulled her an inch closer, the jolting movement pulled the muscle in her neck. "Don't you want to hear more about the photograph? And what happened to the lovely Yara?"

He locked the car over his shoulder with a click of a button, without breaking eye contact.

"She was a young terrorist, working for the enemy. She was sending articles to Europe." He threw his head back and laughed. "Well you could hardly call them articles, they were propaganda really and terribly written I might add." He looked genuinely upset. "No sense at all for the finesse of our language."

He got lost in a personal thought and she wriggled and tried to free her arm but he pulled her to him again.

"Sowing the seeds of discord in the community. Creating enemies, pitting people against each other. We tried first to warn her about what would happen, about the consequences if she failed to listen. That's when the arms went." He paused, took a step back and tried to gauge her reaction. "Those gorgeous slender arms of hers, broken in just three seconds. Snap. Snap. Snap. You wouldn't believe how easy it is to break someone's arms, really Shams it's actually a lot easier than you think. That should stop her writing for a while. Shams, do you know any other journalists, or should I say foreign enemies, who are involved in such work?"

"Of course not, how should I know that."

"Because we all have a duty to our country, whether they are family or not."

Shams took a step back, tried to free her arm again.

"Move closer." He pulled her so she was almost touching his neck. "I can't let a beautiful young girl like you run away." He stroked her hair, then burrowed his nose into it and breathed in. "Yara was also beautiful."

He stepped back and held her this time at arm's length. "So, what's Yusuf up to these days?"

"I told you I don't know."

He put his head to one side. "Come, there's something I want to show you in the car."

He pulled her arm until she was touching the wing mirror, then reached into the back seat and produced a small round pot, turned and smiled at her, then lifted it and tipped it over her head. She took a step back and as she gasped, she tasted bitter chemicals. Red paint poured down her hair, the sides of her face and filled her shoes.

He threw his head back and laughed. "Don't you look good in red." He put his head to one side and used two fingers to trace the outline of her face, in the air. "Tell Yusuf from me, next time it's his turn."

CHAPTER SIX

"Shams what the hell? Shams what happened?"

"It was that idiot that was outside the studio that day. He threw paint on me."

"Why?"

"Amin don't just stand there, get something to clean me with."

"Right."

"The supermarket. Quick, get some water."

Shams used her fingers to claw a space so she could see. The paint was everywhere, her dress was ruined. Every time she cleared it from her face, more would come from her hair, dripping past her ears and over her chin.

She looked up as a couple walked past and she squared her shoulders to face them. The woman stepped towards her, but her husband pulled her away by her elbow. "Don't get involved it has nothing to do with us," she heard as they turned left off the main street. She looked directly at the road as a car rolled past her, a child's nose pressed to the window on the back seat.

"Oh my goodness Shams, what happened to you?'

She spun around, Rasha was in front of her holding the water, Amin two steps behind. Rasha was wearing a black suit with a grey flannel shirt underneath it, the corners of the collar pinned down with brass buttons. Shams noticed that there was no colour left in Rasha's face which drew out the dark freckles that looked like they'd been thrown across her nose and forehead.

"Rasha. How did you know I was here?"

"I didn't, I just bumped into Amin in the supermarket."

"I see."

"Shall we do it in the studio?" Rasha turned and addressed Amin.

"No, we don't want paint on the boxes." Shams leant forward for the bottles then changed her mind. "Quickly, just do it here, pour it on my head."

Rasha gave the bottle to Amin and he hovered it above her hair. "Ready?"

"Yep."

The paint made swirling patterns on its way to the drain, rising up and over Rasha's polished boots. She drew it back quickly.

"Shams we have to tell someone." Rasha turned to Amin for support.

"Tell who?"

"The police."

She laughed and opened her eyes then shut them again as the water continued to cascade over her.

"Rasha, are you out of your mind? This was the police."

"Did they ask about Yusuf again?"

Rasha turned to Amin. "What do you mean: ask about Yusuf?"

"Amin, concentrate. More water please." She shuddered as the cool liquid found its way under her dress and rolled down her back.

"A man came to the studio on Saturday. Well actually he was waiting outside. He gave Shams a picture of a bandage, it was..."

"Wait a second, a bandage?" Rasha looked at Amin then back to her friend. "Shams how can you let something like that happen to you and not tell me? What does it mean, whose was it?"

"We don't know, that's the problem." Shams always knew when Amin was getting angry because his voice started to shake. The effort he took to disguise it only made it worse. "How can we know what to do when we don't even know what the problem is?"

"We do know." Shams stood up straight. Most of the paint was gone but she was soaking wet and her dress was clinging to her. "Her name was Yara, she was a journalist writing for some publications abroad. About the protests. They broke her arms to try and warn her off but she didn't stop so they killed her."

"Shams how do you know this?"

"He told me. The policeman, or *mukhabarat*. I don't know who he was but I'm certain he works for the government. He told me about Yara, before he threw this on me."

"A warning." Rasha said it softly.

"See Shams, this is exactly why you have to stop." Amin was looking at Rasha for support. "This is why you need to talk to Yusuf." He puffed out his chest. "I can talk to him if you like."

"Sorry you didn't tell me about Yusuf," Rasha turned to look at Shams again. "What's your brother got to do with all this?"

Shams stared at Amin. "Nothing. I have no idea. Does he even need to be involved? None of this makes any sense so how should I know what they're talking about."

Amin threw his hands up to his face, and kicked at the stream of red. "This has got to stop."

Shams took a step towards him. "No Amin, this is exactly why this can't stop, this is exactly why we have to continue. So *this* doesn't continue."

CHAPTER SEVEN

Xr pulled into the lay-by and turned off the engine, leaned onto the back seat and retrieved his bag. It wasn't really the best place to park, his car was too exposed, but if he drove to the end of the road until he reached the designated parking, he would have to double back on himself and the journey would take an extra forty minutes.

He swung back the small gate at the entrance to the pathway, stepped through and firmly clicked it back into place. Had he locked the car? He looked at it over the low wooden fence. He really should go back to check, pull the handles to see if it was safe, but at the last minute turned to face the top of the hill. If he went back once he would go back again and again, it was a nasty habit and he had been trying to shake it off for a while.

It had only been several days since he was last here but the brambles that cut across the path seemed to have doubled in length. He gripped them with his fist and parted them, hearing the thorns scrape at the canvas of his backpack as he navigated himself across the uneven cobbles. Just twenty more steps and he would be there.

As the cream corner of the building came into sight Xr began to feel the pace of his heart intensify. What if he arrived and there was nothing here? He really ought to tell someone what he was doing, in case something happened to him and he wasn't able to make it one day.

He held onto the corner of the wall to catch his breath, then called out.

"Antar."

He stood and waited for a few minutes. There was a light breeze and when it whipped between the gap in the concrete it whistled, rising and falling, with the intensity of the air. He tried again.

"Tutu. Tutuuuu." He drew out her name, listening as it echoed around the ancient walls, and turned and said them again, together this time.

"Antaaaaarrrr. Tutu."

That was odd. No response from either of them. He lifted his backpack off his shoulders, it was getting heavy and he heard the thud as it hit the ground. He walked around the corner and the courtyard opened up before him. He smiled. There they were, snuggled together fast asleep at the far end, where the branches of the trees boughed to form a roof above them. He bent over and ran his fingers across their ears but withdrew before he got carried away. He didn't want to wake them, they needed to sleep.

Xr retraced his steps and stopped where he was sure he had left his bag. It wasn't there. That was odd. He turned and looked towards the top of the path, then back again, then swung all the way around so he was facing the entrance to the courtyard. Yes, this was definitely where he had left it. Was that it there on the corner? Hadn't he just walked past here?

He stooped to pick it up and carried it back around the corner of the wall. He unzipped it and pulled out two plates and set them down on the ground, the left one spinning where it hit a loose stone. Next to that he placed a bundle of greaseproof paper, pulled the elastic band off and folded the corners down. Using his hands, he divided the meat between the plates, standing back to check he had made the portions equal, then pulled at the edges of one and transferred it to the other.

"Hello."

Xr fell forwards onto the plate and felt it crack beneath the weight of his body. He turned around to see a man in his mid-twenties in front of him, his sleeves rolled up so Xr could see the red tips of his elbows. He was wearing green shorts and a matching green t-shirt, which he noted gave the impression it was one outfit.

"Hi." He looked down at his hand, it was covered with meat, then considered the two enamel plates and tried to work out if the one he had fallen onto had been destroyed forever.

"What are you doing?"

Xr thought that was a stupid question given that from where he was standing whoever this was could surely see the two cats.

"What's that?"

He followed the man's finger and saw him pointing towards the top of the plates.

"It's their names."

"You gave the cats names?"

"Yes."

He looked at the plates then back to Xr again. He extended his hand. "Nice to meet you properly Xr, my name's Basel."

Xr stood up quickly and looked him directly in the eyes. "Who are you? How do you know my name? Have you followed me here?"

"Relax," Basel put his two hands up until they were level with Xr's chest. "I work in the morgue with you. Cleaning."

He dipped his hand into his pocket and held up his ID card so Xr could see it.

"I was cycling past and I recognised your car so I stopped to say hi. I thought you'd broken down, but when I locked my bike up I saw there was no one in the car and I was about to leave then I saw this small wooden gate and I guessed you had gone through it. I saw all the brambles had been snapped so I followed you up."

Basel lowered himself onto the ground.

"Do you smoke?"

"No."

"Are you alone?"

"I was."

"It's nice up here." Basel stretched out his legs and leant back on his hands, then tapped the ground next to him to indicate Xr should sit next to him.

"Makes a change from being in that hole all day. It's the smell in there. Can't stand it."

Xr looked across at the cats and saw that they were still sleeping. He came up here to have time to himself, to not talk to anyone, and certainly not someone from work about work. He would have turned around and walked back down the path as soon as he had seen Basel, but until Tutu and Antar woke up, until he could see they were ok and that they'd eaten, he couldn't leave them.

"How did you find this place?"

"I like walking. I found it on a walk one day." He gave in and kneeled next to Xr. He had nothing else to do.

"Carry on. You like walking, you were saying."

"Yes. I used to come here to read my book then one day I heard faint screams. I saw Tutu and Antar with huge red marks across their backs. I came back the next day and applied cream, bandaged them, and tried to make them as comfortable as I could on the grass. Then I came back and brought back some old bedding, some meat and some milk and slowly I managed to nurse them back to health."

He looked across to try and gauge Basel's reaction. He was staring at the cats. They both sat for several moments enjoying the silence.

"Antar seems to have recovered well but Tutu is still limping. I think she has something seriously wrong with her leg but I don't know what to do about it."

They both looked up as they heard squeals coming from the corner of the courtyard. Xr reached out his hands for Tutu and Antar but they climbed onto Basel's lap. He watched as Basel tickled Tutu behind the ears and then flipped her over so that he could see her feet. He ran his thumbs over her front two paws.

"Which foot did you say was the problem?"

"Back right."

He turned her so her face was resting on his knees and her striped tail came up across his stomach, then he ran his thumb again across her padded feet. He bent down to look more closely, felt again with his fingers, then in one swift motion pulled upwards. She let out a yelp and he comforted her with his right hand, then lent across with his left and showed Xr his palm. In the centre was a piece of broken glass, the edges tinted red from the blood.

"Did you bring your first aid kit with you?"

Xr delved into his bag and pulled out a tub of cream and a length of material then held it out to Basel.

He examined the label. "Nappy cream?"

"It's the only thing I could find. The woman in the pharmacy told me it's good for everything."

Basel shrugged, reached his hand in and took out a glob on the end of his finger, then massaged it into Tutu's feet. He took the bandage and wrapped it round until he reached the end.

Xr held out a safety pin.

"We can't use that, if it undoes itself it will dig into her foot."

He took the end of the bandage, pulled it out and tucked it into the edges. "Should be alright for a couple of days. Next time we come back we can take it off and it should have healed."

Xr nodded.

"Look there's another two."

They looked up as two younger cats slinked around the corner and positioned themselves next to Tutu and Antar.

"How come you're so good with cats?"

Basel laughed. He had a gap in between his front teeth and one of his eyes would sometimes slip and look in the wrong direction. His hair was shaved into perfect semi-circles around the ears with a flop of dark curls on the top that rested above his right eye.

"My mum used to collect cats."

"Collect cats?"

He smiled again. "She used to take all the strays into the flat, keep them in the living room, and feed them. It used to drive my dad mad, he'd ask, how many more cats this week? We can barely feed our own children. But they were her project, especially since me and my brother got older and we were out of the flat more. She loved them like they were her own children."

"What happened to them?"

"Nothing happened to them. She died and they no longer had a mother. My father couldn't stand it anymore, couldn't stand to keep looking at them, because they reminded him of her. So he let them all out of the back door and stopped feeding them until they found a new home."

"I'm sorry to hear about your mother."

Basel stared for a long time at the cats. Xr looked at his unshaven chin, the dark rings around his eyes, the shaky fingers. "How did it feel?"

"How did what feel?"

"Losing your mother."

Basel's face crumpled and all Xr could see were tears. He used the backs of his wrists to wipe them away and looked up.

"It's indescribable."

Xr unzipped the front pocket of his bag and retrieved a napkin. Basel blew his nose.

"So what is it you do exactly in the hole?" His voice was clouded with the extra phlegm, he was trying to keep it level.

There was the sound of scraping as Xr stretched out his legs.

"Take photographs."

"Of all those dead bodies?"

"Yep."

"They used to ask me to clean in there but they don't let me in anymore." Basel picked at a weed growing between the cracks of the concrete but it was stubborn and he had to wrap it between his fingers before he could loosen it from the earth.

"Anyway, the last few times I tried to do it there was no room. Too many piling up."

Xr nodded his head. "They're bringing them in from the other cities. I heard one of them say it was overspill."

"It's not right you know."

"What's not right?"

"What they're doing in there. They think we're stupid, like we have no idea what's going on. But we know."

Xr bit his lip.

"We have to do something. We have to do our bit."

"Do our bit." Xr snorted. "How can anyone do their bit. You've seen what's happening in the rest of the country, this is total madness."

Basel lay down on his back and rested his head on Xr's bag.

"You have access to the bodies. You take the photographs. Then together we get them out of there."

"The bodies?"

"No. The photos. They're evidence."

Xr pulled at a piece of loose skin next to his nail. "Get them out and then what? Give them to you?"

"Yes. But there has to be a third party who doesn't work in the hole because if they catch you the first place they'll look to is the other people working there. Is there anyone else you can trust?"

Xr thought for several moments.

"Don't tell me who it is. Just make copies for me and for them, then keep some yourself. Between the three of us one of us will get them out."

"Out?"

"Out of the country."

Xr put his thumb nail in between his two front teeth and ran it up and down the gap.

"We'll do it together Xr. We don't have a choice, we have to."

CHAPTER EIGHT

Abdullah walked two streets further, until the road opened out and he could see the five smaller domes of the mosque directly in his line of sight, the sixth and largest rising behind them. With his shoulders in line with the second he turned, crossed the road and there in front of him was the pharmacy.

The wooden interior gave it an old-fashioned feel and Abdullah hesitated before he stepped towards the counter. He had heard of pharmacists selling out of date medicine and though he was desperate, he knew it could be dangerous.

He checked back over his shoulder, there was no one behind him. "I need insulin."

The young woman turned her head and looked in Abdullah's direction. Her white overall had a yellow stain below the silver popper and he felt his eyes move towards it. He imagined her spilling her breakfast on it this morning, then finding she didn't have a clean one. She should have scrubbed it harder, it gave a bad impression.

"Ustaaz?"

He looked up, she had rested two hands on the counter and was waiting for his answer.

"Your prescription. I need to see it."

"Of course." He pulled out his leather wallet from his pocket then flicked it so it opened up on his palm. There was a zip along the back which was concealed with notes and he pulled them forward to get access, and as he did he revealed a photo of Shams and Yusuf together, their arms wound around each other. He looked up and saw the pharmacist staring at him. She busied herself tidying some papers next to the till.

As he placed the prescription on the counter, he smoothed the corners with his knuckles and then pushed it forwards using his four fingers. She looked down at it and then up again, then nodded and slid it back towards him. She disappeared into the back room then reappeared with a small package. Abdullah liked the sound the paper bag made as it crumpled in his hand.

"Would you like a plastic bag?"

"No." Abdullah turned the package upside down then pushed it into his pocket so that it didn't slip out as he walked. It looked stupid, bulging out like that, but he couldn't be walking around the street with a branded plastic bag from the pharmacy. He would have to leave it where it was, and hoped no one would notice it.

"Abdullah?" He looked up and considered the man standing in front of him. He was young, perhaps late thirties, and well dressed. He had a checked cotton shirt and had fastened the top button which made his neck appear longer than it was and his head smaller than it should have been. His black jeans were fastened around his waist with a brown leather belt, the excess pointing out to the side, the holes that held it in place fraying at the edges.

"Yes." He stood perfectly still and resisted the urge to touch the package in his pocket.

"Ali Miro."

Abdullah looked at his hand before he took it. "Ali Miro?"

"Yes. I'm your neighbour. Remember, we moved in last year, your wife brought us food and we brought the kids round to see you a week later."

Abdullah swallowed.

"You don't remember me, do you?"

"No. Forgive me, I have a terrible memory."

"No problem." He scratched his head and smiled. "So how have you been?"

"Fine."

"Are you going home?"

"Yes." Abdullah was getting impatient with all these questions. He had a task, he'd completed it and now he wanted to leave.

"How did you get here?"

"I took a taxi."

"Great. Well my car's just around the corner, I can give you a lift."

Abdullah watched the five domes disappear in the distance and felt the irritation swell inside him as Ali Miro almost immediately pulled up behind a queue of cars. He shifted to the right and tried to look around the line of traffic – how far ahead did it stretch and how long would they be in this car together for?

"What were you getting in the pharmacy?"

Abdullah flinched, he was taken aback at the directness of the question. He often thought things but was of the belief that if the other person wanted to tell him something they would, whether they were prompted or not. This annoyed his family, who constantly criticised him for being out of touch with his feelings, but he had no interest in spending time talking through what he felt and what he didn't, not to them anyway. Feelings were a solid fact, they were what he felt, they were not an idea to be interpreted.

He looked down at his pocket, then back up at Ali Miro, who was waiting for an answer.

"Insulin."

"Insulin?"

"It's used to treat diabetes."

"I know what it's for, but how did you manage to get hold of it? It's in short supply these days."

Abdullah felt the cheap material of the car seat squeak as he changed position. This is exactly the kind of conversation he had wanted to avoid.

Ali Miro put a cigarette in between his teeth and lit it. "Do you smoke?"

"I do."

"Feel free." He pointed at the packet which he had tucked under the hand brake.

"So how long have you been diabetic?"

Abdullah winced as he lit the end. It tasted cheap. He looked up at the line of cars again, which had moved two inches in the last ten minutes. He blew a stream of smoke towards the crack in the top of the window and lent back into the chair.

"It's my wife." He held up the cigarette to the steam of air and watched the ash as it blew behind them. "She was diagnosed last year."

"That must have been hard."

"It was." He took another drag. "It is."

"She's a schoolteacher at Nablus primary school, the one just near our flat. I mean, she was."

"I know the one, my nieces and nephews are there."

Abdullah shifted his shoulders back, he didn't like the interruption. Did that mean Ali wasn't listening, didn't want him to continue? Still he was enjoying this. What did Shaimaa call it when she was trying to encourage him to talk? *Offloading.*

"Sorry Abdullah, please continue. You were saying your wife taught at the school nearby."

"Right." He felt his shoulders relax. "It's a great school and she really is a great teacher, put everything into her work and loved the students. And they loved her also. But she came home one day complaining about her eyesight. She couldn't see the board, couldn't see their work. I took her downtown to get her eyes tested but the new glasses didn't make any difference."

Abdullah threw his cigarette end out of the window then lifted the pack again. Ali Miro nodded and he lit another.

"The following week she was in the classroom complaining of nausea. We thought it was all related to the problems she was having with her sight so I took her to another optometrist, one recommended by a colleague. He told me to take her to the doctor instead and they tested her blood sugar level and discovered she had diabetes."

"You had no idea before?"

"Yes and no. When she was pregnant with Yusuf, our first child, we were told she had gestational diabetes and that this might make it more likely she would develop it in later life, but she never really had any serious symptoms, we didn't know it would affect her in this way. What we really weren't expecting was for the way the school reacted."

"What do you mean?"

"They asked her to take extended leave until she felt better. Then three days after she was at home, we received a letter in the post saying they had given the job to someone else. Shaimaa was devastated, she put a lot of hard work into that job and the students really loved her."

Abdullah felt his throat catch and his eyes burn. He paused to let it pass, what would Ali think of him if he started crying? He had already said too much, he knew he shouldn't have got in the car. He breathed in sharply and turned his shoulders so that they faced the steering wheel.

"We actually think that it wasn't because of her illness."

"What do you mean?"

"I mean there must have been another reason why she was struck off her job. It was like someone had a personal grudge against us. It doesn't make sense just to be sacked because you are ill. Hundreds of people work every day with diabetes."

The traffic ahead started to move and Ali released the handbrake and rolled the car forward. The sun was directly in front of them and the windscreen was amplifying the heat. Abdullah retrieved a piece of square material Shaimaa had brought for him and used it to soak up some of the sweat from his temples. A beggar with one leg knocked on the window and rubbed his fingers together, then pointed at the loose change by the radio. Ali leaned forward, took a single coin and slid it through the window.

"You never told me what you do," he said, turning back to face the steering wheel and rolling the window back up. "You're always out and about at odd times, sometimes in the middle of the night. I mean I know about your business but if you're just making wooden boxes, why are you always so busy in the evenings?"

"Just making wooden boxes?"

"Oh, come on I didn't mean it like that."

"Don't worry I understand." Abdullah lifted his arm in the air. "You can drop me here."

"Here? But we're still four streets away."

"I promised I'd get some tomatoes for the dinner tonight. Must have slipped my mind earlier and this guy on the corner has the freshest ones in the area."

"Ok." Ali pulled in, the cars behind beeped. It was a main road.

"Perfect." Abdullah climbed out and turned to face Ali. "Thanks for the lift. Really appreciate that." He turned to leave then at the last minute ducked his head into the window. "Oh, and Ali. What I told you about Shaimaa and the diabetes. That's just between me and you ok?"

CHAPTER NINE

Yusuf reached the ancient gates of the citadel and paused for half a minute to scan the road. The streets were empty at this time so if anyone had followed him it was likely he would hear them. His arms went down instinctively to his pockets. Lighter in the right, cigarettes in the left. Through the denim he traced his thumb around the edge; it comforted him to think of his reward when the night's work was over.

Yusuf began to make his way around the wall. One, two, three cars and then he saw the fourth, a red, three-door banger which in his opinion was ready to be trashed. I guess that's the point, he thought, pulling at the handle on the front door. It didn't open and instead let out a low piercing sound and he quickly retreated into the shadows and tried to control his breathing.

With his back against the bricks Yusuf could see the benefits of the outfit he had chosen for himself. Black trainers, black trousers and a black jacket zipped right up to his chin. Black was a colour he rarely wore, but he could see how difficult it would be for others to spot him. He reached his hand under the waistband and felt between his thumb and forefinger the white cotton t-shirt underneath.

Earlier that evening Yusuf had role played to himself what he would do if he was stopped by anyone. Unzipping the jacket, the white t-shirt would be the first aspect of his clothing they would focus on, rather than the more suspicious black. Once they approached, he would ask for help because he was locked out of his car. In his bedroom he had felt confident about the plan but here on the streets he wasn't holding it together very well.

After five minutes trying to encourage himself to move Yusuf decided it would be safer to crawl towards the car, that way if anyone was watching from a distance, they would miss him. He dropped to his hands and knees and crept forwards feeling the cold concrete press into his knees. As he got closer, from his position on the pavement, he was able to slip his fingers between the door and the body of the car and prise it open.

Inside he opened the glove box and pulled out a sunglasses case, opened it and removed the shades. He ran his thumb nail round the edge and popped out the bottom to reveal several folded pieces of paper. He took them between his fingers and rolled them as tightly as he could then inserted half of them into the hem of his jacket.

He thought of Shams and how much he had wanted to ask her to come with him. Actually, he could have used some help preparing his jacket. With her thin fingers she would have found it far easier to pick out the stitches of his jacket and make room for the paper to be forced in. At the last minute he had changed his mind. He knew he could ask Shams to do anything for him but he had to set limits for this very reason.

And what about that idiot Amin who had been hanging around for years now. He was no good, Yusuf had decided not long after their first meeting. Yusuf thought of that day he had fallen asleep on the chair in the studio only to wake up to Amin's voice, interrogating her about the protests. He had pretended to stay asleep until he left just to avoid having a conversation with him, or with her for that matter.

Yusuf closed his eyes, relaxed into the seat and thought of his sister. There had been talk from the other women on the team of recruiting Shams for operations like this one. It was safer for women to collect the articles at night and bring them to be uploaded as they were less likely to be stopped by *mukhabarat*. Over the past few weeks they had started to receive documents that looked like they had been smuggled from the secret police headquarters, military correspondence that contained evidence of human rights violations carried out under official orders from the government.

What was holding her back? She was in denial, that much he could see. Then there was Amin. When he had tried to bring up their relationship with her the other day, she had avoided it. He considered the fact that he was growing apart from his sister. Their lives had taken such separate directions in the past few months and anyway, how could anyone be happy with such a boring partner.

If Yusuf was honest, when Sara had mentioned starting the newspaper, he wasn't too keen on the idea. He liked words but felt that images, like the ones he designed for his father's boxes, had a more subtle way of relaying information. He agreed because it was an excuse to spend more time with her. By realising the project their relationship would leave behind a legacy.

Over the twenty-seven years he had been alive Yusuf had experimented with a number of career paths without finding exactly what made him happy. His father had always refused to give him all the money he wanted in an attempt to force him into working for himself which made the young Yusuf resentful.

The first time he sat next to his best friend in a maths class at school, a portly boy with the weathered face of an adult who has already seen too much, he taught him that in order to make money you had to have money. This had seemed perfectly logical to Yusuf, who watched as Ghaith ripped open boxes of cigarettes he had coerced his older brother into buying for him, and sold them all individually to their classmates. He worked out that after forking out for the packets and paying his brother to purchase them he was making a three hundred percent profit on his small business.

Yusuf helped in whatever way he could, he even managed to recruit their history teacher into distributing them among teachers. He understood maths more than the majority of his classmates, so the numbers side of being an entrepreneur didn't faze him, but as hard as he tried, he could not think of any ideas of his own. Yusuf could see the benefits of becoming his own boss appealing but couldn't bridge the contradiction that he couldn't envisage the creative course of action that was paramount to him getting there.

Though he had always imagined an epiphany to come to him when he was doing something outstanding, it was when he was moving the sofa away from the wall at the request of his mother who wanted to clean behind it on a rainy Wednesday afternoon that he had his moment of clarity. All he wanted to do was draw and if he couldn't find a way to make money from it then so be it. He was happy to sacrifice that in exchange for doing something he loved every day and once he made the decision, he felt an overwhelming sense of peace.

The car smelt of old cigarettes and the seat felt damp beneath him. Yusuf shifted, trying to find a more comfortable position, but it was getting cold. He looked at the dashboard and fiddled with the knobs, imagining the comfort he would take in a heater and soft music in the background.

He was just starting to drift off when he heard a soft tapping on the window. He leant across the gear stick and opened the driver door from the inside. As Sara lowered herself into the seat next to him her perfume cut through the musty smell in the car. He cupped her chin in his hand and then stroked her cheek.

"Did anyone stop you?" He withdrew his hand and rested it on his lap. Her jeans had rips across the knees and through the gap he could see she was wearing black nylon tights. He smiled when he realised she was wearing his waterproof jacket, which rustled as she spoke.

"There are two soldiers directly on the other side of the citadel." She gestured backwards over her shoulder. "They're talking and they didn't see me but we can't leave the same way. More were arriving as I came here. We have to go now."

Yusuf opened his hand to reveal four pieces of paper and Sara took them one by one, inserting them into the hem of her jumper. Yusuf watched her thin fingers push them into the gap, admiring how her knuckles became white when she had to force the paper in. He wanted to reach out and stroke them.

One of the things that most attracted Yusuf to Sara was that she was kind. It seemed too simple, but it was one of those characteristics which didn't burn out, it kept you in love with someone. His mother had told him that. He wrinkled his nose. He didn't like to think too much about the intimate details of his father and mother's relationship.

Yusuf became distracted by the beam of headlights in the wing mirror. He watched as a car swung around the corner then parked one hundred metres behind them on the opposite side of the road. He bent his head so he could get a better view of the vehicle but he couldn't make out how many people were inside. He shifted his head to the right so he could get a final look at Sara. They should really get going.

Next to him she had almost finished secreting her articles. He knew it was too dangerous to stay but he wanted to savour this time he had alone with her.

"Let's read a couple of them now."

Sara zipped her jacket up. "Come on Yusuf, that would be suicidal." He noticed she had drawn her lips tightly together. He liked the idea of her being angry so he could be the one to calm her down.

"Just one," pleaded Yusuf. He sat up straight. "Do you ever miss me?"

Sara laid her hand out over his, which was resting on the handbrake. Yusuf felt his anger subside.

She reached out and lifted his chin up so she could see his eyes. "Let's meet on Thursday evening instead, in Point Café. At 6pm."

Yusuf made the calculation quickly in his head. Today was Monday, that was three days away. Of course, he would see her tomorrow at the protest, but they wouldn't be alone. He exhaled deeply.

"Ok." He shrugged his shoulders and looked down at his knees.

Sara nodded and then slid out of the car.

"See you soon," she whispered, closing the door behind her. He heard it click. He exited quickly on his side to catch a glimpse of her back as she walked away but she had already disappeared into the shadows.

In the distance he could see lights and hear the rise and fall of laughter. Yusuf dropped to his knees again, crossed the open space and stood up in the darkness, reaching down to brush the small stones that had become embedded in the knees of his trousers. He held out his right hand until his fingertips brushed the wall then used it as a guide and followed it all the way around, slipping through the alleyway where the road levelled out and upwards towards his family's flat.

When he reached the end of his road he finally reached for the cigarettes and pulled one out, sucking so hard on each drag he finished it in the space of a few minutes. As he crushed the butt under his heel red sparks littered the ground.

Object permanence. That was the expression he was looking for. His cousin had said it once about his niece, about why she always cried when anyone left the room when she hit roughly five months.

"In the beginning the baby thinks that when something has gone that it's disappeared, but as it gets older it realises that it hasn't actually disappeared, it continues to exist even if she can't see it."

"That's a good thing, right?" He had been genuinely interested.

"Kind of. That's why she cries when I leave, because she knows I exist, I haven't disappeared and she wants me back."

"I see."

Yusuf thought a lot about his cousin's explanation, about the pain he felt at being separated from Sara, and about how at heart we are all still children, with the same needs and wants, but with the extra filters that tell us it's not acceptable to show it.

CHAPTER TEN

"Last night I heard a story from a friend. It's not particularly pleasant but it's important for me to tell you, for you to tell your friends, for them to tell their friends and for us never to forget."

Yusuf and Shams were sitting across from each other at the narrow wooden workbench in the studio, their mother's red curtains drawn wide open which was causing Shams to squint as she lifted her chin upwards to listen to her brother. Yusuf had plugged his phone into a portable speaker and the lyrics of Umm Kalthoum were unfolding gently in the corner. Shams found this distracting but didn't want to say so and instead shuffled her chair closer to hear what he was saying.

In between them was a rectangle of white paper with a single horizontal line in pencil across the middle. Through the centre three circles were interweaved – it was the beginning of a geometric formation, the start of a lesson and the reason Yusuf had brought her here today. On the right of the paper was that old leather pouch he used to store his instruments and carried with him every day. Shams saw it as more of a burden since it was bulky and wouldn't fit inside his pocket, but in the last six months or so she had never seen him without it.

Yusuf reclined in his chair and used the points of the metal compass to tend to an itch on his forearm. Shams stared at her brother over the top of her coffee cup. She was relieved that the geometry lesson was over for now. It always started off so simply, just a few lines and circles here and there, but as the layers built up and up the lines started to bend in her vision Shams lost sight of where they should converge and how to measure the exact diameter of the shapes.

Shams thought back to their first ever lesson, downstairs, just fifty metres from where they were now sitting. At the corner of one of the passageways that led off the main thoroughfare was a tiny opening in the wall with a coffee machine placed inside it. Just in front Abu Said, the owner, had placed several plastic barrels with silver trays on top and Shams and Yusuf inserted themselves in here to drink their coffees. As the young men wheeled through sweets, piled high on their wooden carts, they had to lift the tables to the side to make room for them to turn the corner.

Above them the pointed arches that supported the roof of the market loomed. Her brother had taken a pencil and paper and sketched different shapes to explain the geometrical principle behind their design. But Shams had never really excelled in maths like he had and as he outlined the structure then drew more and more lines on top Shams struggled to keep up with his explanation.

"One of the most important activists in our revolution died yesterday." She looked up and brought herself back into the present. Yusuf had paused to gauge his sister's reaction. He interlaced his fingers and pushed them downwards and his knuckles cracked, one by one.

"Yusuf," said Shams, crinkling her nose. "Don't do that, it's so bad for you."

"Sorry. Anyway. This young boy attended all the protests and he would give the soldiers there bottles of water and flowers. He was a true leader before he learnt he was a wanted man and went into hiding with a friend. But then he got a phone call from a cousin of his friend to say he had been shot and he needed help. They both went and were ambushed by *mukhabarat*."

Yusuf paused again and drew both his lips inwards. "His body was delivered to his parents four days later. Bruise marks everywhere, a bullet wound in his abdomen, electric shock marks on his back."

With the compass he scratched two lines in the shape of a cross across the table. "Electric shock marks," he repeated, digging the point into the table. "They used electricity to torture him."

Shams could see the coffee in his cup shaking and she reached out her hand and placed it over her brother's. "Where was he from?" she asked.

"Just outside of Damascus."

"Did he have children?"

"His wife was about to give birth."

"How old was he?"

"Same age as you," said Yusuf. "Twenty-three."

They sat in silence for several minutes, Yusuf drinking his coffee, Shams looking at the paper on the table.

"Look Shams there's something I need to tell you," said Yusuf eventually. "Actually, I need to ask your advice."

Shams sat upright and felt herself go tense for the second time that morning. She gripped her hands together under the table.

"I..."

Shams swivelled in her chair as she heard the low creak of the door and stared at the young woman propping it open with one foot so that the door obscured half her face and her body.

Her olive-green jumper was too long at the sleeves and

partly obscured her hands and she was wearing jeans at least two sizes too big. Her casual appearance appeared to be a statement against her beauty, a kind of arrogance Shams observed.

Her hair looked as though she had run her fingers through it that morning then piled it on top of her head with as many plastic pins as possible and at various points you could see them protruding from the mass. Shams was tempted to stand up and press them in for her.

Yusuf rose from his seat and gestured towards his chair.

"I'm not staying." The words fluttered out too quickly and Shams turned to her brother for an explanation. She saw the disappointment on Yusuf's face and was surprised when she felt a twang of jealousy in the depths of her stomach. Huge pink spots appeared below his cheekbones.

"Just five minutes. Or have a coffee at least," he pressed.

Shams looked at the floor.

"This is my sister Shams." His voice was rising and the words were coming out too fast. Shams smiled, her upper body still twisted towards the door.

She was tall, perhaps even the same size as Yusuf though until they were side by side it was impossible to tell. She had an air of authority about her, as though she was used to getting her own way but without upsetting anyone.

"Sara," offered the woman, lifting the visible hand into a semi-wave. "I've heard a lot about you."

Shams smiled and nodded again. I haven't heard anything about *you*, she thought.

Sara held out three books to Yusuf and Shams tried to see what they were but Sara's fingers were clamped around the spine obscuring the titles.

Yusuf took hold of the door handle and pulled it towards him, finally revealing the whole of Sara's body and face.

"I'm going to get some cigarettes, back in five" he called without turning back.

"Bye Shams," she heard the low, plodding voice disappear behind the wood.

"*Bye Shams,*" mocked Shams under her breath, turning the corners of her mouth downwards and shaking her head from side to side. As she twisted back round to the table her lower back ached from her position. She stood, stretched, and made her way to the window following the outside of the room so that no one would see her. She pulled the curtain back from where it obscured her view and looked down onto the street.

They were standing less than one hundred metres from the front door, Yusuf looked animated, Sara was looking at the ground. They were arguing. She felt the corners of her mouth turn up into a grin.

Shams glanced up at the window and considered whether she would be able to hear their conversation if she opened it. She looked down again at the two figures below her then made her way to the staircase. As she peered out of the doorframe, she could see Yusuf had left the front door open.

Gripping the banister so that it took her weight, Shams made her way down the stairs and stood behind the oak frame. She could see them both between the crack.

"Why not?"

"Because it's too complicated. Another time."

"When?"

"I don't know Yusuf. Another time."

Yusuf's raised voice was drawing attention to them. He tried again.

"What are you doing tonight?"

"I have to stay at home and look after my younger sister. She's not well."

"You have a younger sister?"

"Yes Yusuf." Sara rolled her eyes. "I've told you that a hundred times."

"Ok I'll walk you home."

"I'm not going home… not straight away. I'm going to pick her up from school first and I don't think it's a good idea if you come with me. Another time Yusuf, ok?"

"Fine. I'll see you tomorrow?"

"Goodbye Yusuf."

Shams took the stairs two at a time and collapsed into a chair near the window. She used her toe to pull her sandals off her heel and hitched her legs up onto the one Yusuf had sat on. It was still warm. She watched as the sky turned from sea-blue, to orange, to black and listened as the daytime chatter of the market fizzled into shouts as the workers made their way home. She twisted the geometric pattern round and round with her hand before lifting it in a pincer grasp, crumpling it into a ball and throwing it in the bin.

When it missed, she stood again and scooped it off the floor and dropped it in the metal waste basket. She realised the album they were listening to had played on a loop at least four times and she reached out to press stop on Yusuf's phone. As she held the metal object in her hand she paused, looked over her shoulder towards the door, then tried to enter the phone but the screen was locked. She punched in Yusuf's date of birth but it shook and a red cross appeared. She typed in her own and the screen opened out before her.

Shams pressed the green phone symbol and the list of callers came up. The only name she could see was Sara, there were dozens of calls between them. She navigated to the messages and found her name again. "I miss you." Shams heard a thud on the stairs, closed the phone and returned to her chair.

"Are you ready?" said Yusuf entering the room. Shams

watched to see if he would approach the table to retrieve the sketch but he scooped his phone into his pocket, turned and propped the door open with his foot.

"Where's Sara?"

"Gone to pick her sister up from school."

"Oh, is that how you know Sara? Did we go to the same school as her?"

"I'm not sure which school she went to. Her sister is somewhere different. Al-Nour I think… the one near the citadel. Why?"

"Just wondering."

"Do you know her?"

"Sara's sister?"

"Not Sara's sister. Sara. Have you ever met her before?"

"No. Why should I have?"

"Not sure. Just asking." He stared at her for thirty seconds, and turned something over in his head. "Tomorrow we're going to a protest. We'll leave after lunch."

"A protest?" An eyelash fell onto the hollow just below his eye and she reached out, caught it under her nail, then blew it away.

"Shams stop it. Are you listening to me?"

"A protest. Great."

"What?"

"I'd love to come."

"Really?"

"I just said so didn't I?"

"We'll go together but if we get split up there's somewhere specific I want us to meet. It's called the Neon Cafe, it will be on the far corner, the opposite side from where we enter. You won't miss it, there's a picture of a coffee cup with steam rising out of it in red, but it won't be turned on because the café inside is closed down. Try not to let anyone see you enter."

"Right. The Neon Cafe, a neon coffee shop. Seems quite straightforward."

"Yes. And look Shams, if I don't get there…"

"Why wouldn't you get there?"

"I don't know, imagine I'm delayed, or I can't get through the crowds."

"Ok."

"Wait until it's quiet outside and then ask one of the people inside to walk you home. Give them my full name, they'll look after you. But of course I'll arrive, why wouldn't I?"

Yusuf lifted his hand up to the side of his face and let out a low groan.

"What's happened?"

"My tooth. It's been killing me for days now. At first it was just when I ate something hot or cold, now it comes and goes at any time of the day."

"Yusuf, you have to do something about that, you can't just leave it. It will get worse."

"I know, I just haven't had the time. Plus you know how much I hate going to the dentist."

"Go to Rasha. She'll be gentle and she won't rush you."

"Rasha? Has she qualified as a dentist now?"

"Kind of. She didn't make it all the way to the end of her studies. Became a nurse instead in a practice downtown."

"Really?"

"She's happy, that's what matters. I think she enjoys talking to the patients and she likes her boss."

"Who's happy?"

They both turned to see their father standing at the bottom of the stairs. He was thinner, thought Shams, and his baseball cap was pulled down low over his eyes. The light was shining off the peak, where it was worn from his fingers adjusting it. She stood for several seconds, as she always did, to see if he would hug her first.

"Why are you standing on the stairs?" He stayed on the square strip just inside the door, gripping onto his briefcase as though it would protect him from his children.

"We were just talking. We're leaving now." Yusuf pointed at the door.

"Why are you here so late?" Shams took a step towards her father and he took a step backwards.

"Some bits and bobs to tidy up."

"I'll stay and wait for you. We can walk home together. Yusuf has some other things to do."

"No, no." Her father looked flustered. "I don't know how long I'll be. Best you get home and I'll join you later."

CHAPTER ELEVEN

Xr leant in to get a close up of the lower back. It wasn't a part of the body he usually photographed, usually they had been placed face up by the time he got in here, but this one had particularly bad purple bruises that stretched from the points of the shoulder blades, across the length of his back and then curled around the waist, in the shape of a paint splatter. He pulled himself upright.

Click. Click. Click. He loved the sound the shutter made when he pressed the button, it reminded him of watching celebrities on TV with his sister and mother, when the paparazzi crouched as they walked down the red carpet and took photos of the famous people. That had been the kind of thing he had in mind when he first learnt how to use a camera. Not taking these kinds of photographs.

He listed several disciplines in his head – architecture, art, music – and thought about how each could be used as a force for good, but at the same time how they could equally be manipulated to create a force for evil.

Xr thought of the short, bulky outline of his mother and how the corners of her eyes smiled when she found something funny, though her mouth never seemed to move. She was the one who had nurtured his gift for photography when he was young, despite his father's protestations. What would she think if she knew what he spent his time doing here, in this hole as Basel called it? If he could ask her, she would know what to do, but it was safer not to tell anyone.

No one really keeps a secret, he knew that. You think you've told just one person but there is always the unbearable urge to pass it on. Then they tell just one other person, and then they tell another person, and before you know it the whole neighbourhood knows your business. No, the only way to keep a secret safe is not to tell anyone, ever. Basel was an exception, because he hadn't told him. He was here, he had seen it all for himself.

He thought of his new friend and his heart tightened. He didn't have the best relationship with his mum, or his sister for that matter, but he couldn't imagine living without her. He tried to conjure up how it would feel to be at home and receive the news that his mother had been taken away. He often worried that the volume of bodies in here was making him desensitised to the scale of the problem and had been glad when the story of Basel's mother had particularly struck him.

Xr didn't have many friends, he found it easier to be alone with his books or his films. Women, yes, he was interested in them, but he found it easier to confide in the cats than in the people he loved. It was an escape, that courtyard, all the fur, being away from people and not having to talk or to answer to anyone. He wasn't very good at accepting criticism and was unable to think sideways, out of the rigid ideas he had for what was right and wrong.

He heard the door whine on the hinges and he looked up to see the pathologist.

"You need to finish, we've got a new load coming in."

He nodded and walked to the far corner. There were ten

bodies, all piled on top of each other. "I have finished. Only these ones left."

"I'll help you. Put the camera down."

Xr looped the strap up and over his head and placed it on the corner of one of the metal tables. The pathologist was holding the arms of the body on top and he nodded to him. Xr stretched his hands round the ankles, they felt so cold beneath his hands. He held his breath so he wouldn't have to smell the decay. They kept going until each one had been laid with their shoulders touching, spread across the white tiles.

"Quickly, quickly," the pathologist pointed to Xr's camera and Xr side stepped around the row of bodies then positioned the lens in front of his eyes. He wanted to get them all in the same shot if possible. He moved the camera away from his face and pointed.

"You're stepping on his hand."

The pathologist looked down and then up again at Xr. "What does that matter now? It's not as if they can feel it."

He heard a crunch as the finger snapped.

Click. Click. Click. Xr swept the lens up and down the row of bodies. "Sorry the angle is awkward. Two minutes." He stepped backwards and pulled the camera up at the last minute. Click. He looked up. "Done."

"Good." The pathologist moved towards the corner of the room. "I need all these bodies out the back door now. Quickly. We can do it together."

"All of them?"

"Yes, all of them. I told you before, we have more coming in."

Xr and the pathologist started in the far corner and picked up one of the bodies, carried it through the door of the morgue and down the corridor. At the end was a large metal door and the pathologist dropped it. Xr flinched as he heard the skull smack into the floor.

He held the door open and laid the body in front of it. "We'll use this one as a doorstop." He dropped the arms then pointed back in the direction of the morgue. "Go. I'll send someone to help you."

Xr walked back down the corridor until he was out of sight around the corner. His throat was tight and his head felt light. There was the toilet just there on the left, if he could just make it a few more steps. Inside he closed the door and slid the lock across. He took some tissue out of the holder, used it to open the toilet seat and heaved out everything in his stomach. He turned and slid down the wall, enjoying the relief the cool concrete wall gave him.

He lifted the camera up from where it was hanging on his hip and opened the gallery. He clicked on the last photo he took and enlarged it. He had cut the top of his head off but had caught everything on the pathologist's face from his hairline downwards. He zoomed out again. You could clearly see the grey outline of the morgue and at least two bodies in the background.

He heard a banging on the door and pressed the power button off.

"Xr are you in there?"

He reached up to the sink and turned the tap on without opening his eyes.

"Almost done."

He waited several minutes then stood, holding onto the side of the basin to steady himself. He lowered his whole head and let the cold water run onto his eyes, then he scooped it up in his hands and splashed it around his neck.

There was another bang on the door. "Get a move on, I told you before."

Xr rolled his eyes. He thought he had got rid of him. He opened his mouth, let the water run inside, then swilled it around his teeth, hoping to remove the smell of sick. His stomach felt empty but full of acid at the same time, acid that was eating away at his stomach lining. His hands and feet felt light. He opened the door, water still dripping from his face.

"Everything ok?"

"Yep." He rubbed his stomach. "Bad chicken shawarma last night."

"You're not supposed to take the camera in there." He held out his hand for Xr to pass it over.

"Sorry I couldn't wait." Xr rubbed his stomach again. "I didn't manage to clean the strap properly, I was sick and it caught the edges."

That pathologist withdrew his hand. "Go and clean it now."

He nodded.

The pathologist set off down the corridor then turned and shouted over his shoulder. "The cleaner's waiting for you, he's going to help you with the rest of the bodies. You have one hour before the next delivery comes."

Xr nodded and stepped inside the cool morgue.

"Hey man."

He smiled. It was Basel. It was strange to see him here, in a different setting to the courtyard.

"So let's get this done as quickly as possible." Basel looked up. "I still have the whole of the upstairs to clean."

When they had finished there were around fifty bodies all piled up at the back entrance and they stood in the corner of the courtyard staring at them. Basel pulled a cigarette out of his pocket and lit it.

"I didn't know you smoked."

"I don't. But now seems like a good time to start."

Xr nodded, pulled it out of his fingers and took a couple of drags. "This is inhuman." He was mumbling, his back towards the door.

"Inhuman? There is no word to describe this." Basel snatched the cigarette back. "Have you had a chance to think about what I asked you? My proposition?"

"I thought about it."

"And?"

"I want to do it. The problem I have is that the pathologist is always in the room with me when I'm at the computer. Yes, he leaves me alone in the morgue but…"

"Why?"

"I think he's scared of the bodies. Doesn't like them. Maybe he's worried they'll finally wake his conscience up."

Basel snorted. "I doubt it."

"Anyway, when I'm in the office, when I'm at the computer, even when I'm on the toilet, he never leaves me alone."

"Who never leaves you alone?"

They turned. There he was, standing behind them. How long had he been there for? Xr wasn't sure.

"I didn't say never leaves me alone. I said always leaves me alone." Xr took another drag on the cigarette. "My fiancée. She's always too busy for me, always out with her friends, involved in some project or other."

"I see." Basel held out his packet of cigarettes for the pathologist.

"This is basic psychology." He stretched out his yellow fingers and slid one out. "In fact, I actively encourage it. Psychology that is."

He sucked on the yellow tip, turned slightly to the left and blew a stream of smoke out. "There was an employee who used to work here filing in the archives. What was his name again?"

He placed his fingers on his temples and rubbed them in circular motions.

"Anyway. It will come back to me. So, I found out his wife was going to have a baby and I knew he would need to take time off, want to leave work early, be tired when he came in, all of that. In fact, before he even told me I noticed he was cutting corners, arriving fifteen minutes late, making excuses to come outside and use the phone all the time. So I stopped paying him for a month here and there. He would come to me, ask me where his salary was, and I would tell him every time, it's coming, it's coming, there are problems with the finances, be patient, it will come to you."

He took another pull. "He would always remind me that he had a family to feed, his daughter needed some new shoes for school, his son wanted to buy a football kit."

He waved his hand around in the air to signify that he found all of this irrelevant, or boring.

"I would pay him, he would work harder for a few months, then he would slack off again and I would withhold his pay. I decided one day, why should I pay him at all. He just kept coming back and back and back to work, sometimes working hard, sometimes not, and the months ticked by and eventually he had enough and never came back to work."

He looked towards the cigarette, dropped it and kicked at it with his heel. "I also had a woman working here last year. One day she came in late, apologised, and later on confided in me on her lunch break that she had overslept because she was on medication. That evening I sent her a text message and told her not to come back. What's the point? She won't be able to do her job properly and I'm not a charity."

He looked first at Basel, then at Xr. "What I'm trying to say is that if you want something from someone you have to manipulate them until you get it."

He turned around to inspect the bottom of his shoe, the cigarette had got caught there. He scraped it off on the corner of the step.

"And if you think you can never manipulate them into giving you what you want, just get rid of them and don't even bother. Life is too short, move onto the next one."

He looked up at them. "Come on, the new delivery has arrived."

CHAPTER TWELVE

Sharif kept his feet together, leaned backwards and then looked up. This was the pharmacy they had been talking about at work.

He knocked on the door then took a step back, looked at the windows above. He saw a light flicker on and then off. So someone was definitely at home. He knocked again, but nothing.

He stooped, picked up a rock that had lodged itself in the corner then shouted upwards. "If you don't open this door now, I'll throw the rock through it." He tapped the jagged edge onto the glass three times and saw the hairline cracks appear. That would serve them right for cutting corners on the décor.

Three minutes later a young woman appeared at the door. Her clothes were bulky, perhaps she had just put her uniform on over her pyjamas. Sharif moved his head to one side. She had washed all her make up off, he could see the white remnants of toothpaste in the corner of her mouth.

"May I come in?"

"I'm sorry we're closed until the morning. We don't have a licence to sell medicine after 8pm."

"I didn't ask if you were open and I didn't ask about any particular licence." He looked around, the street was empty.

"I am from branch 290. Open the door or I'll fuck your mother and your whole family."

She nodded and moved to the side. He pushed the door behind him.

"I need to see the books."

She walked towards the shelves at the back. He heard a knob twisting, probably a safe, then the jangle of keys. He ran his hands around the counter, then knocked firmly on it. "Is this real wood?"

"Yes." She looked up. "It's walnut."

"Walnut. Unusual. Expensive."

"It was my father's favourite. In his spare time he was a carpenter, he did the interior for me and my husband as a wedding gift."

"How thoughtful."

"This pharmacy's been in our family for four generations now, my dad passed it on just before he died."

Sharif ran two fingers down the outside of his mouth. There was nothing he loved more than nervous chatter, that's when he could smell the fear.

"The wood wasn't there before. Before he died, I mean. He just added it to make it feel as though it was ours. To give it a new edge, make it individual. Everyone who comes inside comments on it, asks if my father would be willing to do theirs for them. Then I have to go through it every time, tell them he's dead, how he's died. I'm even thinking of just getting it removed just so I can stop having to…"

Sharif slammed his palm down onto the side and watched her jump backwards. "The books. Now."

The till was in front of her and she opened it and pulled out the plastic tray, the coins rattling together from where her hands were shaking. Below it was a red exercise book, it reminded Sharif of the ones he had at school, the faint lines guiding where the letters should begin and end. He leant over, took it, and flicked through it. He stopped mid-way, then ran his fingers down the lists.

"Names, illness, number of times they took a prescription. Something's missing." He looked up. "I didn't catch your name."

"Khadija."

"Khadija, there's something missing from here. Can you help me with that?"

She bent down, opened a drawer close to the floor. He could see her pink checked pyjama bottoms poking out of the bottom of the white overalls. She straightened herself out and handed him a bundle of papers that had been fastened together with a paperclip.

She leaned forward and pointed a red, manicured nail. "These are the addresses. Every prescription has to have the address on. Those are the names along the top. If you cross-check it with the name in the book, you have all the information you need."

"Thank you, Khadija. You've been most helpful."

CHAPTER THIRTEEN

As Xr pulled back the wooden gate that led onto the pathway he found himself hoping he would find Basel at the top of it. He hadn't seen his bike as he pulled in, but it was just possible he had walked or caught a lift with someone today.

As the courtyard opened up Antar and Tutu came immediately to greet him. Haroun and Nina were behind them and he held out his hand to them to encourage them to come over. As he bent, his bag went over his head and he tumbled forwards, then regained his balance and released the straps from his arms.

At the bottom of his bag he had wrapped the two plates in bubble wrap and he pulled at the tape binding them together. He laid them out on the floor next to Antar and Tutu's and retrieved the food parcel from his bag.

This morning, when he had sorted through the fridge, he couldn't find any meat so instead he had taken two cans of tuna from the cupboard, emptied them into a plastic container, and mixed them with some peas and carrots he found to bulk it up. He scooped the mixture onto the plates, being careful not to obscure the names, and guided Haroun and Nina to theirs.

"Hey."

He saw Basel appear from around the corner just as the cats leaned in towards the fish and he waved, then reached into his bag again and found the thermos flask full of coffee. He held it up. "There was something missing last time." He arranged two plastic cups between them. Had he remembered the sugar?

Basel wandered over to the cats and bent so that he could read the names Xr had painted on the top of the plates. He smiled.

Xr bent down to pick up pieces of stray food from where they had fallen onto the floor. He moved his body so that his shadow wasn't obscuring the sun and examined the scraps of food in the light. They looked clean enough.

"Whenever I'm up here I always think of Black Mirror."

Xr brushed his hands together so the food went back onto the plates. He stood and turned to face Basel, who was wearing the same outfit as last time, the green shorts and t-shirt together.

"What's Black Mirror?"

"It's that TV programme in which a blue bear runs for government."

"A bear? What?"

"Yeah. He says he's running for government and no one takes him seriously, in fact everyone sees it all as a big joke, shares all the news on social media, constantly covers the story until he's so famous everyone knows who he is."

Xr laughed. "I've never even heard of it. What happened?" He was sitting now, admiring how easily Haroun and Nina had taken to their new plates.

"Do you think you're going to watch it or shall I tell you what happens?" Basel sat beside him. He was excited.

"Not sure." Xr leaned forward and adjusted the tongue of his trainers. He couldn't remember the last time he had watched TV. "No just tell me, I want to know."

"So election day comes around and he wins with a clear majority of the vote and becomes president. Everyone's so shocked, they thought he was just a big joke." He stopped to see if Xr would make a comment.

"They were so stupid they didn't realise they were promoting him?"

"Exactly. But it's more than that. Look at these people we have in power across the world, whether they're elected or not elected, the sad reality is that a giant bear could probably do better."

"How?"

"Well perhaps because anything would be better than what we've got now."

Xr stared into the distance then focused again. "Maybe they'd be just the same. Maybe they're just all giant bears. I mean you look at a bear and what do you think. You think cute, cuddly. If you went on holiday you'd quite like to see a bear, or if you saw it in an enclosure you'd think of it as something nice to look at and you'd probably try to get a photo of it, or even a selfie with yourself in it."

"I guess so."

"But then if you corner it, challenge it, or face it by yourself, it's likely to get aggressive. So really you don't know what you're dealing with, ever, until a certain situation happens and you're forced to confront it. Everything – or everyone – has a cute exterior, or an exterior they show the world – but no one is like that really in private. Or forever."

"It's true." Basel was animated now. "It's like that idea that you never really know your own potential until you're forced into certain situations that make you experience them. For example, we may never know how evil or brave we can be until we live through war, or how we cope with extreme pain until we live through it. Women can have twenty children if they want to but many choose to restrict themselves to three or four. We never really know the full limits of our power as human beings, we die never really knowing what heights we could achieve if we are not forced to live through them. It's something I think about a lot."

"Right."

"Anyway, it's called the Waldo Moment."

"What is?"

"The episode. When the bear wins."

"Oh I see."

"So maybe Syria is close to missing its waldo moment."

Xr shrugged, poured the coffee and stared into the distance. "Were you in today?"

"No Monday is my day off. How was it? That last time was crazy, that pile by the door, that man telling his stories as though nothing happened."

"It was ok. It was the same as it always is. Worse probably. Every time it gets worse."

"Do you think about it a lot at night?"

"I used to. In the beginning it was hard, I hated the smell, I couldn't get it out of my clothes and especially my hair. I had a problem with blood, couldn't stand the thought of taking someone else's blood home with me because I felt like it was cursing me, like it would come back to haunt me, or I would be punished somehow."

Xr threw his head back and swallowed the coffee in one mouthful. "But I was surprised how much easier it became. How seeing the bodies no longer shocked me, how I could look at them, photograph them, even touch them without feeling disgusted. But then they started to pile in again and there was no room for them. And we were losing the identity of the people, there wasn't enough space, enough room in the files to record every single death. And I felt like I was losing control of the situation again."

"What do they tell you about what happened to the people?"

Xr shrugged and looked down. "All sorts of things. Respiratory problems, heart attack, natural but unspecified causes." He swallowed but his throat was getting tighter. "There are just piles of them everywhere, I don't know where to look, where to start."

"We can start with getting those photos out. They're evidence. Everything in that room is evidence of what's going on here. You, and to a certain extent me, are in a unique position to smuggle that evidence out. I mean, why are they recording everything, why is it all on paper? It's madness."

"I'm in. But how?"

"What do you do with the photos after you take them?"

"I have to upload them on a computer and save them in two files."

"What on that tiny ancient machine in the corner of the office?"

"Yes."

Basel stopped for a while, picked up a small pebble that was lying next to him and began to scratch at the floor with it.

"Email them to yourself."

"Impossible. There are too many and it would be easy to trace it back to me. Anyone could just hack into my account or demand that I open it. Anyway, we're not supposed to check personal accounts in work time."

Basel laid the pebble down again and lent back on his hands.

"So next time you save the photos on the computer make an extra copy and then put it on a usb key."

"And then do what with it?"

"I don't know, use your imagination." He started laughing. "Anything, swallow it. Forget that it's too big. Put it under your belt or in your shoe."

"What if they search me when I leave the building?"

"They don't do that every time, do they? They know you so well, why would they search you? Just make sure it's securely tucked away, the last thing they will suspect is that you're smuggling photographs out of the building. Come on, if they're stupid enough to record all the war crimes they're committing, they're too stupid to realise that someone might be smuggling them out. When you get home, make several copies, keep one for yourself, give one to a third person. We'll find a way somehow to get them out."

"And getting the pathologist out of the room?"

"Let me take care of that."

Xr bit the inside of the corners of his lips, he could feel ulcers beginning to form. He couldn't get the image of the girl out of his head, he was having recurring nightmares about it, the sensation of her hair coming away in his hands.

"Do you think they're thirsty?"

"Thirsty?" He looked across at Basel.

"The cats. Do you think they're thirsty?"

Xr nodded and stood up to go to his bag. He had put a carton of milk in the bottom and he twisted the top and then pulled at the foil seal underneath. As he poured it over the remains of their food, he thought about how he really ought to get them some new plates, that it wasn't right that they had to use the same plate for their food and for their drink.

CHAPTER FOURTEEN

Abdullah stood in front of the fridge and cast his eyes down the bottles of fruit juice, then up to the bananas that had been suspended from the front of the stall and finally to the left at the oranges that had been grouped into net bags. He nodded at the man behind the counter, took a step back, then eventually decided to take one of each.

He placed the notes on the counter, and gathered the plastic bags in each hand. He couldn't quite see why they had given him two but he didn't like to say anything. Once he was around the corner, he pulled the bottle of juice out of the bag, checked the lid was secure, then continued up the path and knocked solidly on the door three times.

"Abdullah."

It was strange to look at Ali from this angle, since the whole of the last journey he had been looking at the side of his head.

"I'm glad you could make it." He stepped back and gestured into the flat. "Come in."

Once he was inside the hallway Abdullah reached out and offered the two plastic bags. Ali took them as though he was expecting them and walked into the hallway, which opened out into a small, square kitchen.

"Where are the kids?"

"Haya took them out to my mother-in-law, she lives just around the corner."

Relieved he raised his eyebrows and pointed at the chair.

"Of course, of course." Ali swept away some papers he had laid out over the surface. "Feel free." He turned towards the cupboard, pulled out two tumblers and set them on the table.

"Sorry, I hope you don't mind the message I sent." Abdullah cleared his throat. He felt awkward here in the kitchen, like he needed to justify his presence.

"It's not a problem, I told you to call any time and I meant it. We're neighbours after all, that's what I'm here for."

"It's just everything I told you about my wife. I'm worried I said too much. You know my family, we don't really like people knowing our business." Abdullah thought of Shams and Yusuf. "Well it's me really, you know. You don't really know who anyone is these days, and I'd hate to think that everyone in the neighbourhood knew what had happened to Shaimaa. Knew that she was ill."

Ali poured them both a glass from the juice Abdullah had bought and looked up at him waiting for him to continue.

"You see my wife, she's a very sensitive person. I worry about her sometimes." He twisted the glass round in his hand and pulled a cigarette out of his pocket.

"You see the way she dresses, the jewellery she has. Her manner. A lot of people think she's stuck up, I certainly did the first time I met her. But really, she struggles a lot in certain situations. She's shy, she doesn't always know how to relate to people."

"I see. I wouldn't have known that day we came for dinner."

"She told me the other day about a remark one of her colleagues made to her at work, when she was still there. They asked her why she was so competitive, why she was always trying to be the director's favourite. At the time, and I can just imagine it now, she waved her hand in their direction as if to say she didn't care what she thought, and then twenty minutes later her boss found her in the toilet crying."

"What did you do?"

"That's the problem. I didn't know what to do. When I came home late that night, she was in the living room waiting for me, her eyes were all red, I knew she'd been crying, but I was annoyed."

"Annoyed?" Ali spun to face him.

"Yes. I wanted to go to bed, I was tired and I had to get up early the next day. When I saw her and then when I heard the story I thought, why couldn't she have just found a way to cope with it by herself. Why was she so weak she had to cry and why couldn't she deal with such issues by herself?"

"Abdullah. That's a little harsh."

"I know. It is harsh. But it's what I feel when I see her, a part of me recoils at her weakness and I can't talk to her about how I feel or about how she feels. But when I'm away from her I understand her pain and I feel sorry for her. But it's too difficult for me to say this to her."

Abdullah looked at Ali's face. He had said too much again, but he couldn't help it.

"For a while I wondered if I even loved my wife anymore. There were times when I loved her and times when I hated her, though I started to notice that the times I loved her were becoming less and less. I recalled something my mother used to say, when I questioned her on how she had stayed together with my father for so long."

He reached for the tumbler and downed the juice, then set it back on the table. "She said that a relationship with a spouse is not that different to a relationship with a child. You don't love them all the time, in fact they sometimes do things that drive you wild, but those that choose to stay and live together learn to live with the love and the hate."

He picked up the glass again and swilled the dregs around. "The problem is, I never accepted the hate part of the relationship with my kids."

"What do you mean?"

"I mean, Shaimaa always used to say, these two terrors fill my heart with joy and make my blood boil in equal measure. Only I never got the whole joy part of it, I only felt my blood boil."

"I see."

The glass made a dull thud as he set it down on the table. He lifted his hands and ran them over the sides of his head.

"Have you ever hated your wife?"

"Hated my wife?"

Abdullah nodded; he could see the question running through Ali's mind as he sat there opposite him at the table. How honest are people during these conversations? He didn't know, because he never had them.

"I've never hated my wife." Ali paused; he was thinking it over. "But she infuriates me. The little things she does, like the stray hairs in the sink after she's been in the bathroom and the fact that she never wipes the food off the kitchen surface until at least two hours after she's cooked." His voice softened. "But I like the fact that she infuriates me, what fun would it be if you were happy with someone all the time. You would never enjoy the good times."

Abdullah closed his eyes momentarily, then stretched them wide open to prevent himself from sleeping. He cleared his throat. "I used to hate my wife. Not all the time, but a few days a week. But somehow since she's been ill, we're closer together again. It's nice, I'm enjoying it. It's not even a case of, we're staying together because of the illness. I'm just starting to enjoy her company again. Maybe again is not the right word. I'm just starting to enjoy her company."

He stood up and stretched out his hand. "Ali it's been a pleasure to see you again, I best get home, Shaimaa will be wondering where I am."

"But I thought we were having dinner together?" Ali pointed behind him, he had chopped all the vegetables and laid them on the side.

"I must run. I've said too much. And I've taken up too much of your time."

"Not really. We are neighbours after all, you are most welcome any time. Why don't you come around for dinner one night next week? It would be great to catch up all together."

"You mean with Shaimaa?"

"Yes. The four of us."

"I'm not sure, let me have a think about it."

"You're welcome anytime."

CHAPTER FIFTEEN

As Yusuf set off for his round that evening, he pulled down the zip of his hoodie and enjoyed the warm air on the skin around his neck. This was his favourite part of the descent into summer – when the heat remained long after the sun had gone down.

The football scores that morning had lifted his mood and he caught passers-by staring at him as he smiled to himself. His team was doing well, he was in love and he and his sister were reconnecting. Why shouldn't he be happy? Let them watch.

Yusuf took a left into the Judaydah district and inhaled as the smell of jasmine hit him. He had been here every night for the last week but had only completed half of the deliveries, it was a huge area to cover. A mezzanine ran around the interior walls of the courtyard enclosed by an iron handrail that was curved like a pregnant belly and partially obscured with green flowers. There were stairways which ran up the side of the yellow brick. Getting to the flats at the top had slowed him down considerably.

In the centre of the courtyard stood a square fountain and Yusuf used this to gather his bearings. To the left of his vision double doors had been framed by black and white brick.

To the right of it were three large windows and, just below, square vents. Yusuf crouched to get a better look. He loved the swirling iron pattern that covered the gaps in the wall.

He stood again and surveyed the flats around him. Really, what would be sensible, would be to start with the upper floors first, get those out of the way so that he didn't have to exert his knees going up and down the steps. But the heat was making Yusuf lazy and he walked towards the double doors instead. He studied the wood for several seconds, there was no obvious post box. He couldn't tell if this was an outer door or if there was a separate place for leaving mail.

Stretching out his hand Yusuf pushed down on the handle and leaned his weight into the door. It gave way easily and he heard his footsteps echo in the square concrete porch. He could smell onions frying. Just ahead of him was an arched entrance with a beaded curtain separating him and whoever was behind it. He heard the sound of a knife hitting a bread board and a spoon chiming against a mixing bowl.

Yusuf looked around. He had come too far, he should never have entered the courtyard. His palms were sweating as he looked around for a suitable place to leave his delivery. Retrieving a paper from his bag as slowly as he could to avoid making noise, he placed it in the corner.

The beads above his head clinked together and he looked up to see a man of fifty. His beard had turned completely grey but his hair was black – he has almost certainly dyed that, thought Yusuf, noticing silver strands protruding from his ears and out of his nostrils. His eyes fell to the man's hands. He was holding a kitchen knife, the tomato seeds dripping onto the floor between them.

"My apologies for intruding, I was looking for a friend's place and I got lost." Yusuf looked at the paper out of the corner of his eye. Unless the man turned to his left, he wouldn't be able to see it.

"Which number does your friend live at?"

"Fifty-seven."

"We are fifty-five. They are our neighbours. What is his name?"

Yusuf swallowed. "Aziz."

"Aziz what."

"Aziz Ibrahim."

"Aziz Ibrahim. I see." He rubbed his beard and the hairs crackled from the friction. They stood for a minute staring at each other. "Actually, we were expecting you."

"Expecting me?" Yusuf was taken aback. He didn't think they had met before.

"Come," he said, pulling back the curtain and pointing inside with the knife. "My wife is just about to serve dinner."

"That is a very kind offer." Yusuf began to walk backwards. "But my family will be waiting for me for dinner."

"I thought you were on your way to see a friend?"

Yusuf felt his neck go red and he scratched behind his ear. "I am. I have to see him first and then get home."

He held out his hand to feel for the door – he was sure he had left it open – but as he turned the man leant into it and slammed it shut. Yusuf pulled his fingers away just in time.

"It would be rude to turn down an invitation to eat, don't you think?"

Yusuf twisted his hands together behind his back and followed him into the kitchen. The interior was far simpler than the outside of the building. The floor was covered in dark red tiles, most of which were hidden by the wooden, rectangular table which ran the length of the room.

In the centre was a plate of stuffed vine leaves and the beginning of a tabbouleh salad. He noted that they had used whole tomatoes, quartered, rather than chopping them up into small pieces.

"Sit." The man pointed to the table. He was still holding the knife. "People in this area have been making complaints about you," he continued, sitting squarely in front of Yusuf. "They say you're bothering them with leaflets or papers or something. They don't want it." He leaned in closer and drove the point of the knife into the table. "We don't want it around here."

The room was silent. Yusuf could not see his wife anywhere.

"I have been watching you all week, posting your rubbish through people's letterboxes, sliding them under doors. People have brought them to me, asked what they should do with them. I knew it was only a matter of time before you passed my door. What is your name?"

"Ahmed."

The man rolled his eyes. "What is your name?"

"Ahmed."

"Yusuf. Let's try another question. Are you working for foreign powers?"

"Excuse me?"

"You heard what I said. Are. You. Working. For. Foreign. Powers? Who is controlling you, who are you reporting back to? Who are you spying for?" He leaned in closer and lowered his voice. "Who owns Yusuf Tibi?"

"No one. That's ridiculous. No one owns me, no one has ever owned me."

"For who are you distributing these papers?"

"For myself."

"And who else?"

"Nobody."

"Who else?"

"It's just me."

"I see." The man picked up a toothpick and began poking at a strand of meat between his bottom front teeth. On his wedding finger he wore a ring that was solid around the base, but where it came over the top the gold had been twisted together to form the shape of a tiger.

"Take a look at this." He produced a brown envelope, placed his fingers at the bottom of one corner and slid it across the table towards Yusuf. "It's time to choose. Take a look," he nodded at the envelope.

Yusuf swallowed and pulled back the flap. It still had the strip of paper concealing the sticky adhesive and he ran his finger across it. It felt smooth in his hands. He pulled back the opening with his thumb and forefinger and let the contents fall out onto the table. His mouth felt dry and his throat was sticky.

Yusuf flipped the photographs over and stared down at them side by side. He held his breath and pulled his lips together so that tears wouldn't come out of his eyes. One was a picture of Shams and the other was of Sara.

CHAPTER SIXTEEN

The overpowering assault on Shams' nostrils came from the tyres that were being burnt on the fringes of the protest. It came from the depths of the sewers, empty food packets on the ground and the sweat that rolled down backs. The chanting was getting louder and louder, the chorus so strong it was making her legs vibrate – "The people want the fall of the regime" echoed in waves across the crowds.

A whistle went off in her ear, followed by a thousand others; flags soared above heads. Shams didn't think she had ever seen so many people in one space in her life. The woman next to her held out a bottle of water before lifting a megaphone to her mouth: "Leave" she bellowed, scooping the air towards herself, motioning for Shams to join her.

Shams turned instead to the crowd in front of her. Hundreds of bodies were packed together, she had to push them forcefully to move past. After twenty minutes sidestepping through shoulders and crouching under elbows she looked to the left and saw the coffee shop on the corner with the luminous red sign outside. That was the one Yusuf had told her to meet him at, if she could just get close to the entrance, she was sure he would appear. She closed her eyes and tried to remember his instructions.

Shams wanted a cigarette so badly she could feel the blood in her arms throb. Later, she told herself, looking up as the crowd in front of her parted to reveal a makeshift stage that someone had built out of planks of wood. The men on top of it draped their arms across one another's shoulders and slowly started to jump around in a circle. In the centre a boy of around nineteen sat on the shoulders of his friend shouting into a microphone. They laughed and sang, lifting their faces upwards to catch the last of the evening heat. Shams watched the sky turn orange and then red as the sun began to set.

Then suddenly gunshots. They sounded like a whip cracking, only louder. Shams had heard about the *shabbiha*, the thugs the government sent to break up the protests. The men lost grip of each other, their eyes searching for the source of the sound. There are thousands of people here Shams thought, scanning the crowd as they began to run.

The sound of the whistles, the voices and the stamping of feet merged into one dull noise that drilled into her ears. Shams felt her whole body convulse and her heart pound against her ribcage. Her knees felt dull and she let the weight of her upper body begin to push against them. Crowds of people rushed towards her knocking her shoulders as they tried to exit the street.

Shams turned her back towards the people and tried to regain control. She tensed the muscles in her legs to keep her body upright to stop herself getting swept under their feet. A man to her right pulled on her arm and screamed at her to jump onto his back, but she didn't want to lose sight of the cafe. Why hadn't Yusuf arrived yet? She took out her phone, tried to call him, but she couldn't even hear the ringtone.

Shams pushed herself against the sea of people but she wasn't moving anywhere. She turned to check she could still see the cafe but there was just a line of grey buildings. She moved to the right and took in the black and gold sign of a restaurant. She narrowed her eyes as her vision blurred. Her hands felt clammy and she let her knees buckle beneath her, placed her arms over her face and kneeled on the ground.

CHAPTER SEVENTEEN

Shams remembered feeling two hands underneath each armpit and the sensation of being dragged backwards. She remembered cold hands on her cheeks and water being dripped between her lips.

When she woke up enough to process what was in front of her, she registered four people staring at her, one of them with her finger pressed against her lips. She looks like a cartoon character, Shams thought, taking in her oversized clothes and messy hair in her half-conscious state. She stood up, tried to locate her bag and gazed around her. Her head felt like it was full of bricks.

The windows and the door of the building she had been pulled into had been sealed with wood so it was difficult to see in the dim light. The four people had lost interest in her and were peering outside through the cracks. Still feeling weak Shams stepped forward and followed their gaze.

At the end of the alleyway two men in green uniforms stood poised, their guns strapped around their waists. One of them was singling out protesters and the other was pushing their heads down, forcing them into the back of a vehicle. A woman on the far side of the road turned to run away before she tripped. Her arms went into the air, her body raised off the ground and then she fell, blood seeping from the back of her head.

Shams took her phone out of her bag, lined up the screen and captured the image.

"When was the last time you saw Yusuf?"

She jumped and the phone fell out of her hands. "Sara?" Shams had not recognised her at first. She felt nausea rise up in her stomach and she bent over and vomited on the concrete floor. "Yesterday," she squeaked. "Same as you, in the studio." She found a napkin in her bag and wiped her mouth then lowered herself onto the floor and picked up her phone.

"I thought you were supposed to be coming together? That's what he told me."

Sara looked concerned. Or was she angry? "We were. But he got held up this morning."

"Got held up? Doing what?"

"He didn't say, just sent a message to say I should go on without him."

"That's weird."

"Weird?" Shams rolled the napkin into a ball and pushed it into her pocket. "Why is that weird?"

"It's probably nothing."

"Tell me."

"Well we were also supposed to come together but he called to say that you were delayed and he was waiting for you. He didn't say anything about being delayed himself. Have you tried to call him?"

"Yes, about an hour ago. I think the phone lines are down."

"They're not. My sister just got through. Let's try again." Sara produced her phone from her back pocket, pressed the green call button and put it on speaker. It rang once and then went dead. "We'll try again later."

One of the men produced a gas stove and was boiling coffee on top. Sara placed five plastic cups in a line and poured the black liquid, half filling each before distributing them evenly among the group. She picked up a plastic box filled with sugar, took four heaped teaspoons and emptied them one by one into her portion then stirred the coffee below, tapped the spoon on the side of the cup before resting it on a napkin.

"How do you know my brother?"

"I met your brother here. Well we did not exactly meet here for the first time but not long after we met, we started coming here regularly."

"I see."

"So, what do you think of our offices?" Sara drained her cup and placed it on the ground in front of her. From where she was sitting Shams could see the granules of sugar glistening in the dregs.

"Not bad," she looked around her. "How did you find it?"

"It belongs to the father of one of our contributors. Not long after we started advertising for writers inside the university one of them left a note to say this was empty and invited us to use it. His father is a businessman but since the revolution started there aren't enough customers to keep it open. He offered it to us."

"And what's Yusuf's role in all of this?"

"Yusuf and I came up with the idea together. We wanted to do something to help;" she paused, then corrected herself. "To contribute. And we thought one of the easiest ways to do this was to start up a newspaper."

Sara poured herself another coffee before holding the pot up in Shams' direction. She shook her head.

"After we first discussed the idea, we were unsure how much interest the project would attract. The notice we left in the university was tiny," Sara laughed. "I suppose we thought that if it wasn't big it wouldn't attract the wrong kind of attention."

"Back then, we asked people to leave their articles among the pages of books in the library. This was signified by just drawing an open book in the bottom right-hand corner of the advert. Every student has to read books and if they were caught picking up or dropping off a letter at least they would have some kind of cover story."

"After one week almost every book in the library was filled with some kind of article. One week." She held her forefinger in the air, then leant back on her hands.

"Over time, as our list of contributors grew, we widened the number of drop off points and encouraged some regulars to pick up for us. That is everyone who you see in here," she waved around the room. "We kept adding drawings to the bottom of the notice so people could choose where was most convenient. The contributors were growing so rapidly we had to find other drop off points – we found an abandoned car next to the citadel and an empty post box in an apartment in the centre of town."

"Sorry I didn't catch your names," said Shams turning to face the other four in the room. She wanted to hear someone else's voice other than Sara's.

"No, no, we don't use names," said Sara quickly. "I mean, the people in this room know mine and Yusuf's but we don't ask anyone else working for us to tell us who they are and we ask for anyone who does know us not to tell anybody else."

Shams raised her eyebrows.

"In case one of us is captured. They can't reveal who we are."

"I see. So how do you know who to let inside the cafe?"

Sara looked at Shams for several minutes, pulled up her sleeve and motioned for her to come closer. On the underside of her wrist, far enough down so it could be covered by her clothes, was a small sketch of a diamond.

"Is that real?"

"It is. Well kind of. We use a permanent makeup machine to do it, you know the kind you can do your eyebrows or eyeliner with."

Shams nodded. Her mother had one of those.

"In the beginning Yusuf and I wanted to design a logo for the paper together. We went through all sorts of designs, ones that were on the boxes, more modern images." She paused and looked into the distance. "Yusuf is teaching me geometry. He's a very good teacher."

Shams looked at the floor and drew the shape of a flower into the dust with her finger.

"In the end we went for something simple," Sara continued. "The diamond which forms the centre of many of these patterns. Then, when it was established as a logo, we wanted to get it inked on our bodies as a way of saying, or proving, that we had decided to be together. And to celebrate the project we had created. It was only later we had the idea of expanding it to anyone who was working for the paper."

"One member of our inner circle was arrested recently." Sara paused. "We thought it might be a good way for their family to identify them. Hopefully in the future that can happen. Neither we nor their family has any idea what happened to her and the government has refused to divulge any information."

"If they were arrested, the *mukhabarat* must know about this cafe then?"

"The cafe has never been compromised. Not yet anyway. I mean, we use it as a drop-off point because it's so conveniently located, but people just think it's empty, they don't know we use it as a headquarters."

"You see people admit to working for the newspaper, they admit it exists, but they don't know we have a base. They don't know that this has become the main drop-off point for articles. Most people only really use one or maximum two of the drop-off points and we know they will probably give up that information, but we're trying to keep the main headquarters protected. All these symbols we left at the bottom of the notice. They're far too stupid to work that kind of thing out by themselves."

Shams waved the palm of her hand through her sand flower then drew an eye where the fresh dust lay. She sketched out the lines of the iris, encircled them with an oval shape then drew a curved line just above it. She framed this with thick vertical lines to represent the eyelashes then arched the eyebrow over the top. Shams relaxed back onto her hands and considered how sinister this single eye looked in the middle of the floor. She looked up. Sara was still talking.

"We never had to worry about this until recently anyway. In the beginning we enjoyed relative freedom. Well, I say relative freedom, I mean there didn't seem to be so much" – Sara looked around the room for the right word – "pressure. You saw what happened today," she pointed towards the window. "It wasn't like that in the beginning."

"So we learnt to use computer software to hide our IP addresses and started to track our readership. We started off online you see but as more and more people started reading us, we worried it would attract too much unwanted attention. We had become like a network; people were posting videos and pictures of protests on our website but sometimes we didn't even know who was doing what under our name. Then there was the problem with the internet. We're now mainly in print."

"Problem with the internet?"

"Not everybody has the internet. So we got a wider range of stories when we agreed they should be handwritten."

Shams felt her head begin to spin again and she looked

down at her coffee which was almost cold. She felt her scalp begin to itch.

"I want to go home." She had had enough of this dark, dusty cafe and she wanted to see something familiar. And more importantly, she wanted Sara to stop talking.

"I'll take you." Sara pulled on Shams' arm and led her to the back of the cafe where piles of unopened crates of bottled water and fizzy drinks stood. The back was boarded up as well but Sara parted two loose planks and squeezed through, turning to deliver more instructions: "If you ever need to come back, only use the back entrance."

They wound their way through the streets until they were standing outside Shams' apartment block. "Go and check if your brother is there and then turn the hall light on and off to let me know he's inside," Sara whispered. "If he's not there, turn it on and off twice." Shams hadn't even considered the possibility that her brother wasn't there, what did Sara mean, she thought, flicking the latch of the front door upwards and sliding inside.

Shams felt the floorboards creak below her feet as she stood outside Yusuf's door. It was ajar but she could see nothing from her position on the landing. She pushed it with one hand and it let out a low, long creak as it opened. Inside the room was so dark she had to put out both hands in front of her and guide herself towards his bed.

She reached the foot of it and stretched out her hands. Nothing. She worked her hands all the way up the blanket but there was nothing there. She sat down, her hands shaking.

"What are you doing?" She jumped as she heard Yusuf's low voice behind her. She could see his silhouette in the doorway, still wearing the white vest from earlier but on the bottom half a pair of red and white striped boxers.

"What are *you* doing," she replied. "Where have you been?"

"I arrived later and by that time the crowds were too dense, I couldn't make it to the cafe. Why are you so late?"

"I've been in the cafe. Sara's explained the whole operation to me."

"Everything?"

"Yep." Shams stood up and kissed her brother on the cheek. "Let's talk tomorrow." As she passed the hall light she reached out for the switch, standing in the bright line for thirty seconds before snapping it off, heading to her own bedroom and crawling underneath the covers.

She took out her phone and composed a message: "Can you talk?"

"Sure."

Shams pressed the green call button. "Rasha, I have to talk to you about Yusuf, I'm worried."

"What's happened?" Shams heard Rasha turn over in bed.

"Rasha he's involved in the protests. And he's using the studio…"

"Using the studio? What do you mean?"

"I mean I found cameras in the studio."

"What type of cameras? Where?"

"On the window ledge. In between the books. Pointing out of the window."

"That's so weird."

"I know. What shall I do?"

"Do nothing. Pretend you haven't seen them. Then you are not responsible for anything."

"Have you found anything else or just the cameras?"

Shams paused for a moment and thought about all the papers under Yusuf's bed, the café she'd been in today.

"Nothing else."

She heard Rasha breathe in and out through her nose.

"How's Amin?"

Shams paused. Why was Rasha asking about Amin when she was talking about the protests?

"He's good," she replied eventually. "Night night Rasha."

CHAPTER EIGHTEEN

Xr muttered a prayer that morning as he opened the door to his locker. There had been a protest last night, he had a busy day ahead of him.

"Ahmed. How are you?"

"I'm fine Xr, doing fine."

Xr looked up at Ahmed. He didn't look fine.

"Everything will be ok, you will see."

"Will it?"

Xr moved forwards, then lowered his voice.

"Don't worry Ahmed, ok."

Xr could smell the bodies before he turned the corner. He stepped over three, tapped the door softly and then entered the room. He hoped there would be no one inside the office.

"I thought you weren't coming." The pathologist was pacing the room, he must have been waiting for him. Xr checked his watch. Three minutes late.

"Sorry the traffic was bad."

"One to a hundred. You have an hour, we have more bodies coming in."

"One hundred in an hour?" Xr did the calculation in his head. That was less than two bodies a minute. "That's impossible."

"You had better stop talking and get started quickly then, hadn't you?"

Xr nodded and turned to leave.

"And get those corpses out of the hallway."

* * *

Exactly fifty-five minutes later Xr fired up the small computer in the corner of the office and watched the screen as it whirred into action. He kicked aside the copper rectangles the pathologist had placed under the chair. For Xr, the fact that the pathologist was worried about soaking up radiation from the computer but not about the families of the people tortured to death next door, encapsulated everything he needed to know about his personality.

He released the memory card of the camera and slotted it into the side. When the icon appeared, he dragged all the images into a folder on the desktop under today's date and sat back as they moved across.

After several minutes he heard a soft tapping on the office door. He watched the pathologist from the computer screen leaf through his notes. He was ignoring it. The tapping got louder.

Letting out a huge sigh the pathologist rose to his feet and swung the door open.

"Yes?"

"Ustaaz, you're needed upstairs." Xr heard the sound of Basel's voice.

"I'm busy."

"Ustaaz this is urgent."

"What's it about?"

"They wouldn't tell me. Just told me to come and get you and that you must come."

The pathologist looked at Basel, back to the room and then stepped outside. Amin heard his footsteps echo around the corridor, and then fade into the distance.

Xr closed his eyes, took a deep breath, and then focused on the computer. He created an extra folder and dragged across copies of the images. He leaned down towards his shoe, retrieved the usb key, and plugged it into the computer, using his left hand to steady his right. Sweat formed unwelcome beads on the end of his nose and ran down the length of his spine. His armpits burnt.

After the computer recognised the usb Xr dragged the entire contents of the first folder onto it then deleted it from the desktop and its duplicate in the trash bin. He cracked his knuckles – why was it taking so long for them to move across? He leant backwards, then forwards again as he heard the notification to say it had finished. As he leaned down to retrieve the key, he heard the door open and he jumped, hitting his head on the corner of the desk.

"Haven't you started printing yet?" He turned. The pathologist was only a foot away and he could smell his cologne. Was that rose petals? Up close, Xr realised what was so familiar about him. He had the same vacant look behind his eyes as the bodies laid out in the next room.

"There's something wrong with the computer," he replied, lifting his arm into the air, pointing at the screen and allowing the plastic to fall down his sleeve. "I was switching it on and off." Xr commanded the computer to print and the pathologist returned to his notes.

Inside the locker room Xr bent to pull his shoes on, letting the key slip out and into his foot. He fumbled around for his sock and slipped his shoes into position, pulling the laces as tightly as he could. He had never seen a camera in here, but that didn't mean that there wasn't one.

Once he was in his car Xr revved the engine, then

slowed down as he approached the checkpoint. The soldier knocked on the window and he rolled it down.

"Identification."

He nodded, reached his hand into his pocket and tried to pull his wallet out but there was nothing there. He felt around in the side of the door, then opened the glove box. Nothing. He looked at the soldier and shrugged his shoulders.

"Must have left it inside."

"Name?"

"Amin Rashid."

The soldier turned, said something into his radio, then moved further away. He could hear crackling. The soldier summoned someone else over and passed the receiver to him. Why was it taking so long?

In his head he tried to retrace his steps as he came out of the office and into the locker room. He had left his hoodie in the boot, he was sure it was in his pocket.

He opened the door and stepped out and the soldiers looked up at him, started moving towards him.

"Get back in the car." The one in front was shouting, his jawline flexed. "We need to search the vehicle, get back in the car until I tell you to move."

"It's in the boot. In my hoodie."

"I said get back in the vehicle."

"Have I done something wrong?"

"As of yesterday, we're doing random checks on all vehicles and people. Need to tighten security, things are getting tough out there, there are a lot of people against us."

Amin nodded and got back inside, exhaling slowly through his nose to try and calm his nerves. He heard a creak as the boot opened, felt the force as it shut again. One of them had his hand on the bonnet, was bouncing it up and down, then more crackling from the radio.

"Bring the dog." He ducked his head and checked the wing mirror, there were five of them now. Had he heard that right? A dog?

He heard scratching against the side of the door and checked his mirrors again. One of the soldiers was holding a metal chain. He could hear the dog barking.

Tap. Tap. Tap. It was a different officer this time, he looked older, more senior. He moved his hand in a circular motion to indicate Xr should roll the window down.

"Amin Rashid?"

"Yes."

"The dog can smell something he likes in your car. Can you think what it might be?"

Amin maintained eye contact and shrugged his shoulders. Then turned and pretended to rifle through the pockets on the back of the seats. He pulled out a paper burger wrapper and the dregs of a take-away coke.

"Does he like burgers?"

The soldier snatched the wrapper though the window and threw it at the dog who began to rip it apart with his claws.

"Guess so."

Amin breathed out, forced a smile.

The officer held his gaze for thirty seconds. "Don't bring your empty food packets here again. It's a waste of our time." He lifted his sunglasses onto his head. "Understand?"

Amin nodded. "Of course."

He held out his hand and flicked the plastic so it landed somewhere near Amin's feet. "Your ID. You left it inside the locker room."

"Thank you."

Back in his bedroom Xr retrieved his laptop from his drawer and sat with his back against the door. He had to twist his shoes from side to side to free his foot before he could peel off his sock, which was covered in blood from where the key had cut into his skin. He stared at the red pool for a while. The blood was concentrated in the centre then became lighter as it filtered through the material. He felt comfortable with his own blood, but would rather not bring anyone else's home with him.

The stick felt warm from where it had been nestled in between his toes and he plugged it in and waited for the files to bounce onto the screen. He copied them onto the first hard drive then labelled the folder 'family pictures.' On the second he labelled the photos 'finances.'

Amin stood and hovered beside his bed for a few minutes, thinking of a suitable hiding place before casually throwing the drives into his drawer as though he had nothing to hide.

Under the pounding shower water Xr thought again about the injuries he had seen on the bodies, how they had been piled on top of each other, their skin so badly damaged they were barely recognisable. He heaved and brought up thick yellow lumps. He watched the water swirl around them and poked them into the drain with his big toe.

CHAPTER NINETEEN

"Abdullah."

He could hear the voice behind him, hear the urgency in it, but he kept his eyes ahead of him. As long as he didn't flinch there was no reason for Ali to think that he was ignoring him.

"Abdullah."

He was closing the gap. There was a hand on his shoulder. He turned to see Ali's smiling face. He forced a greeting.

"I was shouting at you from back there, you've got quite a pace on you. It's lucky I caught you. I called your phone, thought that might make you stop, but you didn't answer." He reached out, placed a hand on Abdullah's shoulder.

"When you didn't get back to me I was worried something had happened."

He stood, waiting for the reply.

"Not at all." Abdullah cleared his throat and looked down at his briefcase, then up again at Ali.

"I've just been busy with work, trying to put in some extra hours since Shaimaa stopped at the school. The business has been doing badly recently. You know, since the protests started."

He did like talking to Ali but he was starting to find it quite frustrating that he seemed to see him everywhere he went. There was something comforting about talking to someone about your inner problems in the safety of their home, but it was something else to see them in the middle of the street. He felt exposed.

"There's a really nice coffee shop just around the corner, how about we go there and have a chat?"

"I'm not sure. I have hundreds of things to do and it's almost dinner time, Shaimaa will be expecting me."

"Ok I'll drop you home and we can talk on the way. My car's just up here."

Abdullah squeezed the corner of his lips into a smile and gestured with his hand to indicate Ali should lead the way. Ever since Yusuf had crashed their car four months ago, he had been taking taxis, and although he enjoyed the freedom having his hands off the wheel had given him, he missed playing his own music and more importantly the air conditioning which so many of them failed to have.

"I saw Yusuf last night."

"Oh." Abdullah looked up, he didn't realise Ali knew Yusuf's name. He pulled at the door handle and climbed inside.

"Where did you see him?"

"I was at a client's flat, went to fix his computer. That's what I do, I'm a computer technician."

Abdullah nodded. He probably should have known that by now.

"We were sitting in the front room when someone approached the flat. We heard something go through the letterbox, looked out and I was sure it was him."

"Yusuf? Are you sure?"

"Yes, I'm almost one hundred per cent certain it was him. I'm not sure if he saw us looking through the front window, but he ran away pretty quickly."

"What was it?"

"What was what?"

"What was it that he posted through the front door?"

"It seemed to be a newspaper. Or a resistance publication, something like that."

He tapped on the glove box with his nail and Abdullah could see he was wearing a leather bracelet, the strands had been plaited together and tied with a silver clasp.

"I put it in there for you to look at."

Abdullah reached forwards and pulled at the plastic catch and let the door fall against his knees. He could see piles of CDs, some out of their box, a packet of biscuits and a tin of mints.

"On the back of the door is a fabric pocket. It's in there."

Abdullah placed his hands into the material and immediately felt a piece of paper. He drew it out and placed it over his lap and carefully unfolded the corners. He scanned the page; something about political prisoners, someone who had been tortured, a small map detailing police checkpoints, some advice on how to get through them without being caught.

He closed his eyes and breathed out. "Are you absolutely sure it was him?"

"Yes. Have you seen it before?"

Abdullah shook his head and looked down at it again. He felt it between his fingers, the paper was good quality. It was his pad, he knew it was. He had actually bought it by accident, had meant to buy the standard paper but when he got it home realised it was actually thicker than he needed it. He slid it through a gap in his briefcase, then tapped the corner until it disappeared.

"I don't even know how he has time for something like that. I thought he was busy working." He shifted slightly in his seat. "That's what I always taught him anyway, to keep his mind on work and keep success as his highest achievement, the goal that he should always aim for. Everything else in life should be a side focus, or should complement this higher aim and everything that gets in the way of it has to go."

He turned to Ali. "This is the problem Shaimaa has with me, she thinks I take my work too seriously."

He paused.

"Well I do take my work seriously because work is the most important aspect in my life. You don't make money out of having a family or taking your children to football practice on a Friday morning. You make money by putting in long, solid hours in the office."

Ali stepped on the accelerator and tried to manoeuvre the car into a gap in front.

"I actually disagree Abdullah. Your family can help advance your career if you keep them stable. They're a solid base for you to come back to whilst you advance your career. If you don't nurture this, it's hard for you to concentrate on your work."

Abdullah leant his elbow on the window. "Perhaps."

"What's your relationship like with Yusuf?"

Abdullah closed his eyes again. That was a big question. "I struggle with Shams and Yusuf." He looked across at Ali. "I know what the problem is. When I had children – or when I thought about having children – I always had such a specific idea of what they would be like. The interests they would have, their mannerisms, the clothes they would wear. Even down to how I thought they should act in public and how they would talk to me. But I realised quite quickly that it was never going to be like that and I think I despised the loss of control. I despised the fact that they weren't the image of the children I had in my head."

He pulled at a bit of dry skin on the side of his lip.

"Yusuf is bright enough, but we don't agree on the small things, the little details – how to run the business, for example. He has all these grand ideas, says he wants to modernise it, but spends all of his Saturday afternoon in bed. And now this," he gestured towards the newspaper that was poking out of the bag.

Ali pressed the brake as they hit a traffic jam. "And Shams?"

"Shams is a sweet girl, much more forgiving than Yusuf. She actively pursues a relationship with me but there is not much for me to tell her, I find it hard to find common ground. To be honest I get on better with her fiancé, we have more in common. Probably more than they have between themselves, but it's easier somehow for me to communicate with him."

"Who is he?"

"His name's Amin, I've known him for a long time actually. I introduced them..." Abdullah trailed off and stared out of the window for a couple of minutes. "He's very sensible. With him you get the impression you know what he's doing, he's not liable to suddenly veer off on a tangent or follow his impulses quite so easily, which is what I worry about with Shams. Actually, I can see they're growing apart in many ways which was probably inevitable, but I am still trying to support the relationship. Perhaps because that's my only connection to her."

"How did you know him from before?"

"I knew his father; we were at college together. We lost touch but Amin and I formed a special bond. It's..."

They both stopped talking as a motorbike went past the window and clipped the wing mirror. Abdullah rolled down the window and readjusted it.

"You were saying. About Amin."

"Oh this is a long story, I'll tell you another time."

The traffic started to move again. Abdullah scanned the knobs on the car, he couldn't see air conditioning.

"And Yusuf, he must have a girlfriend or a fiancée?"

"Yusuf?" Abdullah laughed. "Not sure. He would never tell me anyway. I think he'd be too embarrassed to ever introduce someone to me. And I'm probably the last person he would ever confide in."

"Ask him one time. He may like it."

"I don't think he would. In fact, I've already tried that. I came to the studio one afternoon when I wasn't supposed to be there and saw him on the corner arguing with someone. She was in her late thirties, tall. It was obvious from her body language that there was something going on between them but when I asked him about her later, he told me she was a friend of Shams. I asked Shams separately about it and she told me she had never seen her before. It was quite odd."

Ali swung the car into their street, pulled up outside his flat and turned the engine off.

"Abdullah there's one last thing I wanted to ask you, I'd forgotten."

"Yes."

"Well I was telling my wife that I bumped into you in the pharmacy and she was interested to know where you get your insulin for your wife."

"What do you mean?" Abdullah felt the panic rise up inside him. "Ali, I told you not to tell anyone about that."

"I didn't. Well not specifically about Shaimaa. I said you were also getting it for a colleague."

Abdullah felt the fury unleash inside him. This was how it started. This is why he never told anyone anything, because they can never resist telling someone else. This is how rumours start, how people you don't know form impressions about you. Once this happens, you can't control the narrative. He gripped his knees to contain the anger.

"One of her colleagues also has diabetes and has been trying to get insulin from all over the city but there are severe shortages." Ali looked up in the mirror as he heard a car horn, stuck his hand out the window and motioned for the car to go around him.

"She's suffering now and finding it really hard. My wife recommended she go back to the pharmacy I bumped into you in and she did, but they told her they stopped supplying insulin months ago. Where are you going now? I mean, where is Shaimaa getting her supply from? And how did you manage to get it so recently?"

"Oh, I see." Abdullah reached down and pulled his briefcase up. "Well I'm not sure what happened with that. I got such a large batch last time, it's kept Shaimaa going until now. Maybe I took the last load? I hadn't really thought ahead about what I was going to do next, I didn't think that particular pharmacy was in danger of running out."

He pulled at the catch on the door.

"That must be it. Well if you hear anything, do let me know."

"I will."

Ali raised his voice after Abdullah who was already standing on the pavement. "We're still really keen to have you round for dinner sometime when Shaimaa is feeling up to it."

Abdullah pulled on his cap and swung the car door shut.

CHAPTER TWENTY

There was something about the absence of dusk in Aleppo that always fascinated and frustrated Shams in equal measure. As the day edged towards its close it was easy to get caught in the wrong place when darkness enclosed the green shutters and obscured the iron curls that held the streetlamps. Shams was sensitive towards the change in mood the disappearance of the sun inspired in her – ultimately, it was when the hot rays warmed her skin and lit the corners of the passageways that she felt alive.

The road began to incline gently and with the extra effort Shams could feel the cigarettes in her lungs. They were tighter, as though weights were pulling at them. She wondered if she could ever persuade Amin to come to a protest. She wondered if she could ever persuade Amin to do anything she liked. Perhaps she was being unfair, they liked eating out together. She would add that to the list. She considered how strange it was that she found her father so difficult but at the same time wanted to please him. He loved Amin and wanted the relationship to survive.

"Have you got a light?" Shams looked up to see a gaunt figure in front of her waving a cigarette in her direction. She reached into her bag, annoyed that her train of thought had been interrupted. She ground a match across the strip and held it in the box so that the wind wouldn't blow it out. As he reached out to light his cigarette Shams noticed a purple and white scarf around his neck, it was too hot to be wearing a scarf. Yusuf had one just like that.

She continued up the hill and tried to refocus. The irony of the fact that Shams' favourite restaurant was actually in the Old City of Damascus, one which she had never been to with Amin, did not escape her. The tables were decorated with intricate mother of pearl designs and there were backgammon sets and works of art on the wall with the same patterns. Her father had taken her there on her sixteenth birthday, just before she was due to start spending her weekends in the studio.

"This is what I want our boxes to look like," he said, running the palms of his hands across the table. He called for the waiter to change the coals of his sheesha then sat and smoked, watching Shams as she ate her way through half a roast chicken. Every birthday since she had begged to be taken back but he always refused.

Shams decided that her relationship with her father was defined more by his absence than his presence. She loved him for all the activities she imagined them doing together. The restaurants they would eat dinner in and the cafes they would drink coffee in. Even the days they spent in the studio together he wasn't really there. His mind always fixed on the task in front of him or the evening that would follow it.

Shams did love her father, she was just never quite sure why he seemed to love his solitary wooden boxes far more than he loved her and Yusuf.

Shams stumbled backwards as a car beeped its horn. Her keys fell from her pocket and hit the ground. "Shit," she muttered under her breath and stooped to pick them up.

Out of the corner of her eye she saw the purple tassels on the end of a scarf. Wasn't that the man who had stopped to light his cigarette?

Shams ducked into a side alley that cut through onto the parallel road, emerging on the other side closer to the market where it was wider and the extra space allowed her to breathe more easily.

As she weaved her way through the crowds, she took an alley that led her to the back of a restaurant from where the owner was dispensing buckets of sludge out onto the street. The smell of fish hit her nostrils and she pulled her sleeve over her hand and covered her nose. Shams tried to avoid the liquid on the floor but there was so much of it, she felt it creep inside the flimsy soles of her trainers and she had to grip the corner of the building as her feet slipped underneath her.

When she cleared the liquid, she was close to one of the entrances to the souq and she looked downwards to see she was leaving a trail of footprints on the dusty road. But there were other, thicker prints around the hollows she had left behind.

In danger of slipping, Shams lifted her head, confirmed her location and noted an underpass was coming up to the right. The building covering the tunnel was a grey, concrete affair and the passageway below it plunged into cold darkness, offering few lights to brighten her way. Shams changed direction as though she might descend into it before curving around the edge, pausing momentarily at the curb to assess the traffic then negotiating her way through the cars.

At the bus stop on the other side an elderly man held a cigar and the smoke curled around the collar of his jacket. She could hear the thump of music coming out of earphones. On the plastic benches behind were a couple, both staring downwards at their mobile phones, and Shams stood in between the three people as though their proximity might offer her some form of protection. She rummaged in her pocket and pulled out an orange; the acidic smell cut through her memory of the figure behind her.

Eventually, when her hands had stopped shaking, Shams started to loop around and head back in her original direction until she reached her juice bar. From her position on the corner she could see the whole road. Shams loved watching the families interact, try to haggle with the shopkeepers, and the young couples who spent their afternoons flirting with each other. She rubbed her eyes, she was feeling sleepy. She really should just get to work.

She drained the glass, spitting the pips out into the plastic cup then gathered her phone and her purse and walked into the centre of the souq. Shams reached the studio and pulled the heavy wooden door to find the stairs were in darkness. The electricity must have gone again. She balanced the door against her left foot and using the light that streamed through from the street searched for a lighter, spun the wheel, and a small flame appeared. Using her free hand, she bent down, picked up a candle from a plastic tub by the door and lit the wick, closing the door behind her.

Closer to the top Shams could hear raised voices and she blew the flame out, closed her eyes momentarily as the sharp smell of the smoke hit the back of her throat, and took the stairs two at a time. On the landing she turned to the left and saw two young men, not much older than Yusuf, standing over her father. His right eyebrow was heavy with congealed blood coming from a gash on his forehead. Behind her father, Yusuf was slumped on the floor.

"Hello Shams." His teeth were bright white, as though they had been bleached.

"You're the one I just saw outside. You asked me for a light."

"Correct."

"Did you follow me here?"

"I've been following you every day for the past month."

Shams moved to the left to try and reach her father and Yusuf but the man in uniform sidestepped to block her path.

"Make me a coffee?"

"What?"

"You heard what I said. I want a coffee."

"No."

He reached out a long arm and struck Shams on the jaw. She spun around and scrunched her eyes closed, then opened and closed her mouth to check if it was broken.

"Shams just do it. Please."

He flexed his hand then pulled his cigarettes out of the front pocket of his shirt, tapped the bottom of the box until one popped up and caught it with his mouth. "You heard your father. Be a good girl and do as you're told."

He produced a matchbox from his pocket, slid the pink bulb across the edge of it, lit the tip and then threw it into the room.

Her father's gaze followed the wooden stick as it landed an inch away from a pile of boxes. Shams pulled at her bottom lip as she watched the flame die down into a glow before a single line of smoke rose from the burnt end. She walked towards the stove.

"We'd like to know where you were yesterday," said the taller of the two men. He began to circle the room, flicking ash on top of the boxes, across the workbench and then onto Yusuf's face.

"And we'd like to know where Yusuf was." He turned so that he was in front of Shams. "I would ask him myself but he seems a little preoccupied right now." He leaned in closer. "We've been told that if there's anyone who knows what Yusuf is doing it's you." Shams flinched as his index finger hit the space between her chest and throat.

"I saw him for the last time two days ago." Shams' voice was loud but she was trembling.

"Have you been going to the protests?"

"Which protests?" Shams wiped her palms across her hips and as her clothes moved, she could smell the sweat.

The buttonholes on his shirt had formed an oval shape from where the fabric was stretched trying to fit across his chest. He stared at her, then straightened up, walked over to the window and gazed down at the street below.

"Your brother did quite well I have to say." His hands were clasped together behind his back, the cigarette still hanging from his fingers. The fact that he was talking into glass took the edge off his voice.

"You see everyone in branch 290 has been talking about a neat little website called Al-Thawra which has been growing in popularity over the last few months. I ordered my team to follow all the activists that are known to us to see if they led us anywhere but no one seemed to be working on an underground newspaper. Or should I say, no one had heard of this particular one."

He paused, then turned to the room. "We were under a lot of pressure from people higher up to put an end to this terrorist activity. But your brother hid his little project so well it was impossible to tell who was behind it."

He took a deep drag on his cigarette. "But then he became cocky." He paused to light another cigarette off the other which was now down to the butt, walked over to Yusuf and drove it into his arm. Yusuf screamed and Shams jumped backwards. "They always become cocky in the end, think they know better, think they can get around us."

He placed his fingers over his nostrils then took a deep breath in.

"You see they weren't content with just writing propaganda, Yusuf and his friends; they turned their focus towards films." He paused, smiled to himself. He was clearly proud of himself, pleased with what information he had uncovered.

"They gained quite some traction on the internet you see. Someone started filming the protests once or twice a week, sometimes for eight hours at a time, and uploading them. Where were these videos coming from, we wondered, and how could we stop them?"

"The one thing any fool could see is that they were recorded from high up." He went back towards the window.

"They always showed the same road yet the shops and restaurants around had been blurred out and we had great difficulty pinpointing the exact street." He used his index finger to circle the air.

"I watched the footage every day. It was always the same, no clues, until one day something changed." He turned to face the room as if to invite suggestions.

"One of the videos seemed to have a red border that was partly obscuring the view."

"Then the very next day I was at the corner of the souq watching yet another protest and I looked up here." He tapped the window with his black nail. "And I saw that someone had drawn some heavy, red, velvet curtains across your window." He poked a finger into his mouth and used his nail to free some trapped food. "I never liked red. My wife refuses to have it at home, says it makes people angry."

He lifted the books on the windowsill one by one and held each by its front and back cover, letting the pages hang from the spine. From each one cameras fell onto the floor beneath. Shams watched as he crushed each of them beneath the heel of his boot, then stopped.

"What do we have here?" Shams lurched forwards to pick it up, but he held his arm out to stop her. "A diary." He smiled and tucked it into his pocket. "I shall enjoy reading this."

He walked towards Shams and took her chin in his hand. "Let me tell you something." He stroked her cheek with his thumb, then pinched her with his fingers. She let out a gasp. "You two and your mother are never going to see Yusuf again. And if you continue to go to the protests, I'll put you behind the sun as well."

CHAPTER TWENTY-ONE

Shams' knees felt cold against the floor and there was a sharp pain in her right shoulder as if someone were poking the muscle with a hot knitting needle. The first twenty minutes were the hardest, she told herself. After that the pain just became a dull ache.

Shams worked methodically as a way to manage the mammoth task ahead of her. With both hands gripping the wooden scrubbing brush she started in the corner and made small circles in a horizontal line down the width of the room. When she felt the dull crack of the brush hitting the skirting board, she moved it towards her and came all the way back up. She watched the foam all the time, making sure there was never a dry patch between the two lines. It took longer this way but at least she knew the entire floor had been covered.

When she buckled her legs to get close to the floor, Shams could feel the bruises at the tips of her knees. Her palms were riddled with calluses and dry skin and her nails were ripped with a permanent layer of dirt underneath them.

"Wear these." Her mother held out the yellow gloves, and bent down next to Shams, adjusting her glasses as she landed awkwardly on the floor.

"I don't want the gloves. I want to *feel* what I'm cleaning."

Shaimaa rolled her eyes. "Shams it's bad for your skin, your hands will become tough."

"Stop fussing. I said I don't want them."

Her mother turned to face the centre of the room. "Where did Yusuf used to sit?" Her voice was cracked, she was about to cry.

Shams stood and pointed to a chair near the window. "Here. Sit here, it was his favourite seat."

Shams sat on the corner of one of the tables next to her, pressed her nose against the window and stared down at the road below then upwards, taking in the grey, polluted sky.

"What time's Dad coming?"

"He didn't say."

"The whole point was that we were supposed to be doing this together, as a family." She turned to face her mother. "To find closure. To find a way to come back to the studio."

"I know."

"He hasn't been here for months."

"I think it's hard for him to come back after what happened. I think he feels responsible."

"Why?"

"You know what your father's like, he doesn't talk much. Maybe he feels that if he'd been strong enough, he could have stopped them from taking Yusuf."

"I doubt it. You should have seen them; they weren't going to stop at anything." She leant back on her hands. "Why do parents always blame themselves for everything? The guilt you and Dad harbour, it's not healthy. Especially when you try to transfer it onto me."

"What do you mean?"

"I just mean there are healthier feelings than guilt. It eats you up from the inside out. It's corrosive. I would have thought now we are dealing with grief also it would be time to put that aside."

"Grief is for death Shams. Yusuf is still alive."

"Well that's the problem isn't it. That's why this situation is too difficult. Because we don't know whether he's dead or alive and so we don't know how to feel. We're in the twilight zone."

"Yes and no. The day I heard Yusuf was taken, the day you told me. That was the worst day of my life. It's hard to imagine any other piece of news being as bad, as destructive as that." Her mother reached out and smoothed her collar. "Shams you're a mess."

"I'm not a child, you can't talk to me like that anymore." Shams looked down. Her jeans were darkened at the bottom from where they had dragged against the pavement and her woollen jumper had loops of fabric poking out from where she had caught it on pieces of broken wood in the doorway as she retrieved the cleaning equipment from the cupboard.

"Let's put some music on, lighten the mood." Shams fiddled with the knobs of her father's radio until sound crackled out of the black speakers. "That's better. Now you sit and let me finish."

"I want to help."

"You know you can't. You can barely see. It will be quicker if I do it. Just sit there and wait for me."

Shams took in a deep breath and headed towards the back of the room – she always saved the toilet until last, her least favourite task. She reached into her back pocket and pulled out a square of red cloth, held it by the corner and shook it out. Next, she folded it into a triangle, placed it over her mouth, tied it at the back of her head and entered.

She threw the mop and sponges back into the cupboard and walked back into the main studio. There was a figure at the bottom of the stairs.

"Dad. You made it."

He nodded, started the ascent, then turned into the studio. Shams watched her mother stand and embrace him. "You did the right thing by coming." She was whispering, her back to Shams. "The longer you leave it the harder it is."

"Right." He stood back and looked up at the window. "I came for the curtains."

"The curtains?"

"Yes, we agreed we would take them down. After what happened."

"Right." Shams dragged the chair closer to the window and stood and unpicked the fabric from the rail. "It's going to drop, stand back." It made a thud on the floor.

"What shall we do with it?" Her mother was stroking the fabric. "I can't bear to part with it but I don't want it as a reminder every day."

"I think we should burn it. It will be symbolic."

"Shams that's a terrible idea." Her father walked around it and folded the corner over. "I'll take it."

"Take it where? Dad there's no space at home."

"I'll find space. I want to keep it."

"We'll take it together now." Her mother was looking at Shams. "Give you some space here by yourself to finish up."

Thirty minutes later, as she turned left towards home, Shams couldn't hear anything apart from the cars that raced past her and the motorbikes that revved their engines and beeped their horns. The white outline of the citadel rose against the skyline.

She pulled her phone out of her bag as it vibrated and flicked the button on the side to light up the screen. Five missed calls from Amin, seven messages from Rasha. She turned it onto silent, unzipped the side pocket and dropped it inside.

A bus stop loomed to the left but Shams buried her chin into her coat and carried on walking. Darkness had begun to obscure the outside of the buildings and turn the trees into shadows against the sky. Shams felt the prickle of tears as she finished the last stretch of road. Her boots rubbed into her left heel and she felt the beginning of a blister begin to form.

As she turned the key in the door, she felt a tight knot around her stomach. As it swung open Shams was met with a pile of shoes and patches of damp across the walls of the hallway. They were letting the flat go since Yusuf was taken.

Without stopping she turned immediately right into her room, dumped her bag and coat on the bed and flicked open the double doors. It was the best room in the apartment and Shams considered herself lucky to have a space from which she could overlook the city.

She sat on one of the two plastic chairs she had put outside, hitched her legs onto the railings, and gazed at the apartment blocks that rose before her, trying to imagine who was behind those tiny windows and what kind of evening they were preparing themselves for.

Around halfway up the one directly in her line of sight she could see a figure hanging out white washing onto a long railing that stretched the entire length of their balcony. Every five minutes or so they disappeared into the flat to replenish the basket and reappeared to begin again, reaching down, shaking the clothes off and filling the line until eventually they blocked the entire front of the flat.

The smell of cooking drifted up from the streets below, a strong, thick smell that meant whatever was on the stove had been bubbling away all day. Shams drew the smell of meat in through her nose and inhaled it right down into her lungs. Probably lamb, she thought, exhaling.

Shams had never really enjoyed cooking but she had certainly enjoyed eating with her family. Her brother, on the other hand, would spend hours in the kitchen preparing different dishes, marinating the meat and kneading the bread. Once she had spent three hours by Yusuf's side in the market as he squeezed the different vegetables and brought them to his nose, inhaling them as he tried to decide which were suitable for the dish ahead.

His favourite to prepare was tabbouleh; not so much because he liked it himself – he once confided in Shams that he found the parsley overpowering – but because he knew it was their mother's favourite. Once he had passed Shams a knife and asked her to chop the tomatoes but after inspecting them afterwards, declared she had cut them too big. She attempted again and again, eager to please him, until finally he agreed they were the right shape and folded them into the bulgur wheat.

Shams watched the room opposite until the light went off and it faded into the dark sky. Eventually she pulled herself off the chair and walked to the side of her balcony where a row of plants lined one of the walls. Shams swept her hand across the petals and watched them drop to the floor. She pushed one of the pots back with some force, so that it chimed against the wall, and retrieved a silver key that was sitting underneath it. It felt cold as she clenched it in her hand.

Back inside her room she reached under the bed and slid out a wooden trunk with leather straps on either side and undid the buckles. After she had unlocked it Shams pulled out six pictures, and fanned them out into a semicircle in front of her.

In the middle was a picture of Yusuf, his navy hoodie pulled up over his ears and his white teeth exposed as he smiled at the camera. Mum had tried so hard to get rid of that jumper, thought Shams, running her fingertips down his cheek and feeling the tears crowd her vision. Several drops fell and landed in the middle of the picture and she drew her sleeve over her wrist and tried to wipe it away.

To the left of his face she had placed a picture of Sara, her hair still pulled up into that messy bun, her eyes looking down at the ground. Shams had spent hours online trying to find a good one of her until eventually she had found one tucked into the back pocket of Yusuf's laptop bag.

Next to Sara was Amin's face, half his cheek missing from where Shams had ripped the picture in two to remove herself. That picture had been taken at Reem's wedding, the first time Shams had met Amin's family.

To the right of Yusuf was a picture of their dad and to the right of that a picture of her mum. Shams stretched her legs out into a V-shape around the images, leaned forward and added another one. Rasha. One of them must have given Yusuf up.

CHAPTER TWENTY-TWO

Rasha buttoned her coat all the way to the top. It wasn't cold but there was something about the way the collar stood up around her neck which made her feel safe and protected. Of course, in an environment like this she was not protected at all, but when the world as we know it starts to crumble around us human nature forces us to look for security in the smallest of details. Amin had taught her that.

Last month, as she had listened to Shams' concerns about Amin she had felt, not for the first time, that her friend was selfish. There, she had said it. Shams was her best friend and she loved her, but she was the most selfish person she knew.

Often, Rasha had asked herself what the role of a best friend was. Shams was fun to be around and they never stopped talking, but was that enough? Why is it we only think of relationships with lovers as instances that come and go, but when it comes to a friendship, we always presume it will last forever and rarely consider breaking it off?

Everyone has a moral line, Rasha had decided, and the more someone's actions upset us, the more it makes us feel differently about them. At some point they cease to be just a flawed human being and move into the realm of bad people. Rasha didn't like to admit there was anyone bad in the world, just those that we didn't align with, but Shams was forcing her to re-evaluate this.

Amin was so kind to Shams, buying her beautiful presents and spending time with her in the studio when it was not what he really wanted to do. Amin was like Rasha, he had far more interest in goings-on in the real world. Carving boxes, this was a hobby not a career. Shams should appreciate what she had rather than inviting Rasha to sit in a café and reeling off a long list of complaints about her fiancé. If it hadn't been for what happened with Yusuf, she would have just accepted that their friendship had run its course.

She thought back to the time in the university canteen when Amin had first introduced himself to her, offering to carry her tray of food back to where they were sitting, he could see she was struggling. But Shams was already at the table, and he had spent twenty minutes talking to her instead. If Shams had just spent ten minutes longer in the toilets, answered her phone when it was ringing, it would have been Rasha that Amin had invited out, not Shams. Since then, she had stayed away from men at least, she promised herself, until she was happy and secure in her career.

Rasha breezed past the front desk and hung her coat on the back of the door. She looked around the treatment room, everything appeared to be in order. She picked at the plastic that covered the chair and made a note to tell Doctor Suheir when she arrived that they needed to order a replacement.

She took the small key that was kept in a bowl by the window and bent down to retrieve the instruments from the cupboard, running each through a cloth before lining them up on a wheeling table next to the chair. Mirror, pliers, probes. She reached across and pulled the black swivel stool so that it was in line with the head of the chair, pushed the light upwards and then filled the kettle.

When she was at school Rasha had always wanted to be a dentist. Her parents had never really understood why she had chosen to spend her day looking at people's teeth when she could have pushed herself a bit further and become a general practitioner, which was more prestigious. But Rasha did not like blood, and neither did she like the idea of having to spread her knowledge over many different parts of the body. The thought of mastering the mouth and all the complexities within it seemed far more realistic.

Not long after she started studying Rasha found the long hours and the intensity of knowledge she was expected to retain, tiresome. She had been impatient to get started on her career and believed that in the future, if she wanted to resume dentistry, it would be easy to pick up where she left off. So instead she became a dental nurse. Her parents had objected a second time, but short of physically stopping her changing the course there was really nothing they could do. She told them so and they didn't ask again.

Rasha sat down on the chair in front of the computer and slurped the skin of her boiling hot tea. She was happy with where she was in her life – a steady job and an income that arrived into her bank account at the same time each month. If things had worked out how she had wanted them to between her and Amin they would be married by now, with two children and a nice apartment to go home to each night.

She pushed the button and waited for the screen to light up. The problem with Shams was that she had no real direction in her life. Working in her father's studio was not a career, it was a compromise, and it was not sustainable for the future if she wanted to provide a stable home for a family. Shams should have pursued her own dreams not her father's.

"Good morning."

Rasha rose as Doctor Suheir entered the room.

"How was your evening?"

In the beginning, when she was new in the job and she heard this question, Rasha had listed everything she had done the night before, whether it was dinner with a friend or watching TV at home with her parents. It hadn't taken her long to realise that Doctor Suheir was less interested in what she was doing and simply saw the question as part of a formality which had to be adhered to in the morning.

"I'm great," replied Rasha, piling coffee granules into a mug, pouring water over them then placing the cup next to the computer as Doctor Suheir checked her morning emails.

Rasha had noticed long ago that the doctor never wore any part of the same outfit twice in one week. Her tops always had a collar, whether it was a silk blouse or a suit jacket, and her shoes were never without heels. Rasha suspected that if she were ever to get a glimpse of her feet, the arches would look like a looped bridge where they had moulded to fit her shoes.

She considered her own clothes beneath the blue overalls. A black pencil skirt and a white blouse. She had got caught in a rut and put on the same boring outfits every day, partly because she knew they would be obscured by her uniform. When there was a man in her life, then she would start to make more of an effort but in the meantime, she preferred to wear grey or black because to do so was easy. She had once tried to wear brighter colours but they had the same effect of somebody talking too much to you in the morning when all you wanted was peace.

Rasha always felt calm around Doctor Suheir because she talked little, preferring instead to focus on the treatment she was administering to her patients. The effect this had on the people that attended the clinic was a comfortable atmosphere into which they offloaded their concerns, worries, or just their day-to-day happenings. They seemed to be happy with this arrangement and Rasha suspected that at least forty-five per cent of them came to the dentist just to have a chat.

The bell rang at the entrance to the clinic and Rasha ran her finger down the list of appointments which had been laid out in the room that morning. Case in point – it was Maryam Ashraf, a seventy-something retired music teacher who came to get her teeth cleaned every far too regularly.

"Maryam, how are you?" inquired Doctor Suheir as she shuffled into the room. "Please. Put your coat in the corner. Feel free."

Maryam hooked a thin navy jacket onto the peg and sat down sideways on the chair, before swinging her legs around and lying back. "A bit higher," she instructed and Rasha pressed the button at the side to elevate her, then pulled the light down so that the doctor could fully inspect her mouth.

"I have a pain in one of my molars at the back," she began, rubbing the side of her cheek. "I'm worried."

"Any other symptoms?"

"No. Just quite a few mouth ulcers recently," she replied, closing her eyes and waiting. "As soon as I get rid of one another appears."

As Doctor Suheir prepared her tools and tied her face mask behind her head, Maryam took her opportunity.

"Yesterday we got news from a cousin in Homs," she began, her eyes fully open now. "Her son has three daughters who me and my husband have heard little about until today."

The doctor moved closer to her mouth, instrument in hand, but it was clear Maryam wasn't going to stop so easily.

"Three nights ago, their mother walked past their room and overheard them playing inside. One was pretending to be a regime soldier and the other two opposition members."

"My goodness," said Rasha.

"Exactly," said, Maryam, sitting up now she was confident she had an audience.

"Then, that evening they had family round to dinner and fighting started up not far from their flat. Each were able to distinguish between what was a sniper and what was an anti-aircraft gun. Can you believe that?"

She looked around for confirmation from Rasha and the doctor, then laid her head back on the chair and opened her mouth. Rasha took in the hair, which had been blow-dried into a bouffant. She was wearing round white earrings, possibly pearl, which matched a beaded white necklace. Her red lipstick was perfectly within her lip line, though there was a streak on her front right tooth.

"Everything looks fine in here." Doctor Suheir rolled backwards and began to type the notes onto the computer. "The ulcers are likely to be lack of iron, try to eat more green vegetables or buy liquid iron from the chemist. You can also try vitamin B."

She pulled her mask down and offered her hand to Maryam to help her off the chair. "We'll see you back here in six months. Please take care of yourself."

Maryam took her time standing, walked to her coat and pulled it over her shoulders. She was wearing a dress cut high at the top, with blue and white flowers printed across it. It made Rasha's eyes go blurry so she looked away.

"Children are our future," she said, one hand on the door handle. "We must look after them."

CHAPTER TWENTY-THREE

That night Shams struggled to find a comfortable position to sleep in. On her back she found it hard to breathe and she coughed and wheezed. She turned onto her side and looked at the wall. Were they tiny black bugs crawling up, or were they specks that contrasted with the light?

"Shams. Shams." She flinched. Her mother was hovering over her, holding a warm flannel against her forehead. She felt a drip roll behind her ear and she lifted her shoulder up to catch it.

"Mum it's Yusuf. He can't breathe."

"I know darling."

"He can't breathe. It's that same dream over and over, he's underwater, he's tied up and he can't get out. He can't get to the surface. I'm trying to get to him, trying to reach him so I can help him but I can't, I'm just two millimetres away from his hand but I can't reach him." She rolled onto her back, it felt as though someone had tied weights to her arms and legs and there was a boulder underneath her ribcage. "Is it morning?"

"No Shams, it's three o'clock. Close your eyes, I'll stay with you until you fall asleep."

Her mother pulled the blanket up and over her shoulders

then tucked it underneath her body so that she couldn't move her arms. "When you were a baby, swaddling was the only way your father and I could get you to sleep."

CHAPTER TWENTY-FOUR

Shams opened her eyes before she understood what had woken her. The buzz of her alarm clock sounded like it was submerged in water on the other side of a giant room. She rubbed her eyes, threw back the blanket and lifted her toes up against the cold floor before pressing them down and lifting herself into an upright position.

Can you keep someone alive in your imagination? Is it healthy to do so? Does it compensate for the real thing, the warmth, the smell, the interactions? It occurred to Shams that often you appreciate people more in their absence as when they are there they are just there. You take them for granted, stop listening, stop interacting. In absence the mind has a wonderful ability to forget all the bad things and just focus on what is so special about a person, even creating an entirely new person altogether.

But then if someone in your life represents only absence, inevitably you will forget about them completely. Which means you need both, absence and presence, to build up a complete picture or have the full experience with someone. She rubbed her eyes. This was becoming complicated. What if you just couldn't have both? She supposed that then it's up to you to keep them alive. So that's exactly what she would do today and for the first time since she could remember, she had a project. She had a purpose. She would keep Yusuf alive, in the way she wanted to remember him.

Shams pulled off her nightclothes and found a green dress in the back of the cupboard and pulled up a pair of grey leggings underneath it. There were some wet wipes on her bedside table and she took one and held it against her forehead for a few moments before running it under each eye and then around her mouth. As she pulled it away from her face, she could see the black smudges of make-up from where it had run yesterday and merged with all the tears.

Shams picked up her sponge bag and fished out a brown pencil which she used to fill in the gaps in her eyebrows and accentuate the points, then distributed the colour more evenly with a soft brush. She looked downwards into her pocket mirror and brought the mascara wand upwards to lengthen her lashes. She picked up a water spray from near the bed and tried to tame the frizz that had built up on the sides of her hair from where she had slept.

Today she would go through the material she found underneath Yusuf's bed and finish what he started with the newspaper.

Shams began to sort the papers by subject. First-hand accounts, news reports, interviews, human interest features which were piled and labelled with red, blue, orange, and green.

She took a deep drag of her cigarette and flicked the butt over the edge of her balcony then pulled out one of the articles and squinted to read it:

Myself and four friends from the university are helping to deliver aid to the rural areas north of Aleppo. As we carry the boxes of clothes, food and medicine we feel under pressure to work quickly because we can hear the fighter jets ripping through the skies above us; the ground shakes every twenty minutes from the sound of bombs.

Yesterday we visited a hospital, there is no soap in any of the bathrooms or operating theatres and the shelves are completely bare from the lack of basic medicine.

The cries of children fill the hallways and pregnant women lie wounded in the beds. A young woman in her mid-twenties tugged on my sleeve and begged me for help. Her son has diarrhoea because there is no clean drinking water and she believes he will die any day.

There is a severe shortage of doctors yet more wounded pour into the hospital every day. We watched a student who was studying medicine before the fighting broke out perform an operation with a surgeon in Europe directing him over Skype.

As we rode in the truck back to Aleppo, we passed towns that have been emptied of people, only their ghosts reside there now. AF

Shams closed her eyes and tried to imagine who AF was – were they male or female and how had they met Yusuf? Did their family know they were writing articles and were they still alive? Had they been interested in politics before the revolution or had the protests piqued their interest?

She stood up and shot her arms in the air to stretch then stepped through the doors and into her room. She wiggled a second one out from under a blue paper clip in a pile at the foot of her bed and laid it next to the first, then changed her mind and put it back into her pocket. It was time to eat.

In the kitchen she retrieved a tin of beans from the cupboard and pulled back the metal cover just enough so she could drain the liquid. The splashes of hot water in the pan caught her wrist as she emptied the contents into it and left it to boil. She drew out a wooden chopping board from behind the microwave and sliced tomatoes and garlic and pulled the green parsley off its stalk by running her nails up the length of it. She added it to the mixture with a squeeze of lemon, cumin, salt and a huge glug of oil.

She laid out the article against the wall, took the beans off the stove, and read it as she pressed the back of her fork into the mixture.

> *Today there have been reports that activists belonging to the 'Syria Freedom' movement have placed a new round of stickers on street signs around the city.*
>
> *According to sources close to the movement, the names of 10 activists forcibly disappeared by mukhabarat have been printed onto plastic road signs and fixed on the top of existing names.*
>
> *One of them bears the name of Ibrahim Qashoush, the famous Syrian artist who sung for freedom at one of the protests and was later found dumped in the square with his vocal chords cut out.*
>
> *Others include the footballer Abdullah Baset al-Sarout, and living icons of the revolution like cartoonist Ali Farzat.*
>
> *Syria Freedom made their name first in Damascus when they added red dye to the fountains to represent all the people who have died in the Syrian war. SF*

She left it there and kept going back to it, reading it four times over the course of the day. In between she mixed bulgur, ground meat and deep-fried pine nuts. She piled the kibbeh into a plastic tub, placed it in the centre of the table then placed a post it note on top and smoothed down the adhesive. 'EAT ME' she scrawled over it, then headed back to her room.

From her balcony she could see her neighbour across the street hanging out the washing again. Shams found the regular rhythm with which she dived into her washing basket and hung the clothes over the wire therapeutic. She was intrigued to know why all her clothes were the same colour.

She checked her watch. 10pm, she wasn't tired yet. She had meant to save the final editing until the morning but she may as well get it all done now if she could. She slid the box out from under the bed and threw open the buckles. One by one she pulled out piles of paper fastened together and laid them out along the floor. One final read through and she was ready to go.

As she ran her finger through the pile, she picked out one of the papers which were bigger than the rest. It was the only one written half in Arabic, half in English. She held it up towards the balcony. She didn't think she had seen it before, that was odd.

"9.30am leaves for work;" "12.30 visits the neon cafe;" "8pm arrives home," read the scrawling handwritten script.

Shams narrowed her eyes and stared at the piece of paper. It was Yusuf's handwriting, there was no doubt about that. She turned it over – some more time entries, a doodle of a flower. Her eyes fell downwards and got caught on a word in the bottom right-hand corner. She squinted and brought it closer but it was impossible to make out the letters which had become obscured behind a brown ring from a hot drink.

Shams climbed beneath her duvet cover and produced the note. She read each side three times then flipped onto her stomach and looked at the words from her new position propped up onto her elbows. With her right finger she traced the letters Yusuf had produced then lifted the paper to her nose to see if she could smell him behind the words. Shams rolled onto her back again and screwed her eyes shut. She thought of Sara, she might know what the notes meant. Where was she anyway? She hadn't seen her for days.

CHAPTER TWENTY-FIVE

Before he left for work Sharif kissed his two daughters on the head, laid his hands on their backs one by one and watched them breathe in and out. It wasn't often these days he saw them awake, which caused a certain level of friction between him and his wife, but if he was honest, he found his children easier to deal with when they were sleeping. There was a lot of noise in the daytime, and he found it hard to concentrate.

In the beginning he had found it relatively easy to maintain a healthy work life balance but as he had been put up for more and more promotions this became harder to manage. His home life suffered but when he looked back on the path he had taken to get to where he was today he felt an overwhelming sense of pride. At first he had joined the infantry, then found out that the State Security Branch in Aleppo 290 was recruiting from within the army so he submitted his request to join and was accepted. Sharif noticed with satisfaction how his own relations with the people around him had changed. They stood up for him when he entered the room, offered him their chairs and gave him extra large portions of food. They were keen to be respected by him. They were scared of him.

Sharif enjoyed the privileges that came with the job but he often told himself that what came first was the system. So he was serving the system and enjoying the rewards of that, rather than serving the system as a means to get straight to the reward.

That said Sharif believed there was no such thing as blind faith, whether that concerned religion, politics or work. A case in point is the way terrorists are dealt with. There needed to be a more personal way of getting to them, a more calculated way to make them suffer than the physical torture favoured by most of his colleagues. In fact, he thought the ease with which other officers roughed up the prisoners was proof to him that they were no good at their job. It wasn't that he was against it. It's just that he thought psychological torture was harder to bear in the long term.

One of the biggest crises of self-doubt for Sharif was when a prisoner dragged their heels on divulging information. He liked to think of himself as a well-oiled machine, able at any time to extract accurate information from the people who cheated the system. When it didn't go well it made him angry.

When Yusuf had failed to live up to the standards he set for him Sharif had sent him to the black room. He had come back bruised. Perhaps bruised isn't the right word, he was barely breathing. He hadn't asked for that, what if he couldn't speak. That was what he had been trying to explain, torture is not always the best way to get information out of people. So he had admitted that the car was one of the drop off points, but he already knew that, had already seen him cosying up to his girlfriend inside. He needed more.

Since observing him in the car Sharif had thought over and over about how best to deal with Yusuf. During these brainstorming sessions he recalled something his mother told him when he was young. If you don't know what to do, do nothing until it comes to you. He had followed this advice for exactly eleven days until one morning he rolled over in his narrow bed beside his wife and it came to him.

As he had done for the past three months, Sharif tapped his fingernails against the corner of the table and tried to put himself inside Yusuf's head. Everyone knows that a suspect will say something during an interrogation, but nobody considers what goes through their minds in the ten minutes before it begins. He rubbed his finger across the plastic and then shuddered as the friction let out a high-pitched squeak. Family and friends, he supposed. And the future – whether or not they would see it.

The door opened and Yusuf stood in the doorway. He gestured towards the seat.

"Have you thought about my proposal?"

"Your proposal?"

Sharif laid his hands flat on the table in front of him and thought of his daughters. They often asked him to spread his fingers in exactly that position so that they could draw round them. He always refused, there was never any time and anyway, what would people in the office think of him if he came to work with felt tip pen across his hands.

"Several months ago, you were caught in Judaydah handing out contraband material."

He produced three photographs of him and laid them out an inch from the edge of the table. He made a note to show his manager the one on the furthest left. He had managed to capture Yusuf posting the paper through the front door and his face. Sharif had exceeded himself with that piece of investigative work.

"I believe you went into the home of one of my colleagues who asked you to make a decision on who to give up."

He saw the incident register on Yusuf's face.

"So my colleague asked you to choose between your sister or your girlfriend, I kept to my side of the deal, but I can't hang on forever. Now that you're here with us I want to ask you again about the third option. I want to see how loyal you are to Syria. Don't forget your mother in all this. What is best for her?"

CHAPTER TWENTY-SIX

Rasha wasn't sure exactly which of her patients had inspired her to write but she knew that Maryam had become the source of most of her content. She worried often whether this put Maryam's life at risk so when she did record her stories, she tried to obscure any identifying details. There were never any names and the number of children or cousins often went up or down.

Yesterday's story had been short, it wouldn't take her long to get everything down on paper. Two weeks in she had studied other people's handwriting online and changed a few of the letters so that her articles could not be traced back to her. She couldn't tell whether carrying out such a measure was an exaggeration but it comforted her to do so.

Once the story had been composed, Rasha folded the paper and slid it into an envelope which she then sealed. On the front she wrote "electricity bill," then forced it between the pages of her book. She flicked her wrist towards her and checked the time. 5am. She would be able to make it to the café before going to the clinic but she would have to wait until she arrived at work before she had her morning tea.

There was something about being up and out on the streets so early that Rasha always enjoyed. She liked to call it the pre-bustle because there weren't too many people and the roads were relatively calm. Whilst this meant it was less likely someone would spot her, it also meant there were fewer people for her to blend in with, to obscure her movements. She tried to look casual as she looked back over her shoulder to check it was safe to cross the road. All she was doing was going to pay an electricity bill.

There were just two intersections left before she reached her destination. Rasha was making good time so she slowed to a more reasonable pace. She rounded the corner, panted slightly up the hill and as the street opened out before her, she saw the familiar red neon coffee cup glowing against the grey, polluted sky.

For the last several weeks her tactic had always been the same. As she approached the café she would barely stop, just stoop down as though to lace up her shoe and in the same action slide the envelope under the front door. But today, as she tried to push the paper through it got stuck and she stumbled forward. She fell onto her hand and checked it – small stones on the pavement had drawn blood and she squeezed it with her other hand. When she looked down, she saw half of the envelope was still sticking out onto the street.

Rasha glanced behind her. She couldn't see anyone, but rush hour was approaching and the crowds would arrive soon. She needed to move off the street quickly. She bent down, pushed again but the envelope still didn't move. "Shit," she muttered under her breath, sweeping it out and folding it twice. She tried once more and managed to push it through at the corner. Rasha pulled herself upright, wiped the sweat from her forehead with the sleeve of her jacket, then turned to face the street and hailed a taxi.

She had to be honest, when she had first seen the call for writers being advertised in the hallway of the university, she had wondered who had been brave enough to pin up the advertisement. Then afterwards, at home, she had wondered whether it had in fact been reckless. She was lucky to have seen it, she had only been there for one day to talk to recent graduates about dentistry.

Rasha had been delivering her stories to the Neon Cafe for around three months now, but always on the day she made the delivery she found it hard to make eye contact with Aida at reception, and with Doctor Suheir. The feeling evoked something within her that her mother had told her when she was young – when you've done something you shouldn't have, people can see it.

"Hey love."

Rasha nodded at Aida, walked into the treatment room, closed the door and then leaned against it. Had she been rude? She hoped not.

When Rasha had first met Aida, she had thought it was her who was stuck up. Perhaps stuck up wasn't the right word to use – it was more that she just didn't seem interested in small talk. Neither was Rasha really, but she had always been taught this was the polite way to behave in the workplace.

The second thing Rasha noticed was that her teeth were browning slightly at the edges and her nails were ripped, never filed. It just wouldn't do to have a receptionist greeting customers who cared so little about her appearance, but at the same time Rasha was too embarrassed to tell her.

Several weeks after she started Rasha noticed Aida was always watching something on her phone which she propped up against the files that were laid out on her desk. "Is that a game?" she asked, gesturing towards the mobile. Aida's face cracked into a smile and she giggled. "I'm addicted." She brought her finger to her lips to indicate Rasha shouldn't tell anyone. "Can't stop watching. Give me your number and I'll send it to you, you'll see what I mean."

That evening at home Rasha received a link to play Heroes against Aida. She ignored the invitation but replied to the messages when they came through. "How's your day? You seemed busy," she received. "Everything is fine?" Aida had a penchant for cooking and would send Rasha updates on what she had created that evening. Rasha looked forward to her brief exchanges with Aida.

She sat down on the edge of the chair, unpeeled her boiled egg and laid it beside the flat bread she had prepared the night before. As the kettle whirred behind her, she heard the handle of the door flick down then up again. It was Aida. "Someone here to see you."

Rasha's heart rate increased and she looked down at her shaking hands, then curled them around the warm mug to steady them. No one ever came to visit her here, not even Shams, though she had hinted on more than one occasion that she would love to show her friend around her workplace.

"Tell them I'm busy," she said, without turning around.

"They said it's urgent." Rasha looked out of the window but it was too high to jump.

The door swung open and Rasha swivelled.

"Amin?" They stood staring at one another from opposite ends of the room.

"Rasha," he said, then turned to Aida. "I'll only be two minutes, I promise." She nodded and reversed out of the room though Rasha noticed she left the door open.

She stood, pulled her uniform straight from where it had ruffled around her hips, and wiped the corners of her mouth to discard the crumbs.

"Amin," she said again, softly this time.

"Can we talk?" His voice was soft and deep. "What time do you finish?"

Rasha bit her lip. She was owed so much annual leave, surely Doctor Suheir wouldn't mind if she took it.

"5pm," she said eventually, then immediately regretted it. What if he had other plans for later and changed his mind?

"I'll be outside waiting for you at 5pm."

Rasha nodded, breathed out and returned to her seat. She pinched some salt onto the opening of her egg. Her stomach was fluttering, there was no way she could finish it. She wrapped it in the napkin and pushed it into the bin.

* * *

"Mirror." Doctor Suheir looked up over her mask at Rasha. "Rasha they're the pliers." She sounded irritated. "Rasha quickly."

Rasha looked around her but she couldn't see the mirror anywhere. She was sure she had put it on the table. She pulled out the drawer, retrieved it and took the opportunity to look up at the clock. It was already 4.50pm.

"Rasha, are you alright?"

"Yes I just didn't get much sleep last night, I keep having anxiety dreams then wake up all disorientated." She looked down at Amira and up again at the doctor. She shouldn't have said that in front of a patient, that was very unprofessional. "Sorry," she mouthed.

Rasha knew Amira from her days as a student, her father was a well-respected businessman who lived in Damascus. She had attended some of Rasha's lectures at university before dropping out and studying marketing abroad. As far as Rasha could gather she had become used to the cash her father sent her every year and was yet to decide the exact path her career would take. She wondered what Amira thought of her in her role as a dental nurse. Was she impressed?

Doctor Suheir cleared her throat. "Amira, you were saying."

"It only hurts when I press it. I wouldn't have even noticed but the gum has started bleeding a lot recently."

"Do you floss every night?"

"Every other night."

That probably means once a week if that, thought Rasha.

"My old dentist told me that eventually the teeth on either side might die off. He recommended I wear a gum shield when I do sport. What do you think?"

"It does seem a bit extreme."

Rasha checked the clock again. It was 5pm. She considered how strange it was that time was a constant yet sometimes we wanted it to slow down so that we could savour every minute and at others we were desperate for it to pass. On certain occasions it seemed to go so quickly, at others it would drag past. She would have to intervene.

"Amira the same thing happened to my sister last year after she fell off her bike. Why don't you come back next week, we can book you another appointment and take a longer look? We will have time to do all the x-rays then."

"Well I was hoping to get it finished today…"

"Rasha's right." Doctor Suheir rolled back on her chair. "Make an appointment with Aida on your way out. I need to pick my daughter up."

At 5.34pm Amira eventually stood up to leave. Rasha ripped her scrubs away from her body, discarded her mask in the corner of the room and flew down the stairs.

Outside on the street she searched for Amin but there was no sign of him besides the familiar line of taxis and the kiosks selling cigarettes. Rasha felt her body begin to shake as the anger rose up inside her and hit her throat. Surely, he wasn't that impatient.

"Rasha," she turned to see Amin standing behind her. She relaxed her shoulders. He stretched out his hand and offered her a plastic cup filled with coffee. "Given you're doing overtime, I thought you could use this."

Rasha smelled the cardamom and wanted to heave. She smiled. "Thank you."

Inside the cafe Rasha cringed as Amin ordered two more coffees. What would that do to her teeth? She leaned forwards to show she was ready for what Amin had to say to her.

"Look Rasha, I know this is awkward, Shams is your best friend." Amin nodded to thank the waiter as he placed the cups in between them. "But I need your help."

Rasha felt the corners of her mouth turn upwards into a smile. She picked up the cup and took a slow sip to disguise it. She couldn't appear too keen. As she did, she felt the liquid scald her lips and she spluttered over the surface. She felt her cheeks go red.

"I feel like I'm losing Shams," started Amin, looking down at the table. "She has withdrawn from our relationship, she's no longer interested in seeing me. In fact, ever since her brother died..."

"Disappeared."

"Yes disappeared. Ever since her brother disappeared, she's been acting very strangely. I was wondering if we could do something together. You and I."

Rasha nodded.

"I want her back Rasha, I want the old Shams back. And I want you to help me."

Rasha looked up sharply then felt her nose burn in the familiar way it did just before she was about to cry. He didn't appear to notice.

"As a woman, if you wanted a man, if you wanted them to sit up and take notice of you, what would you like him to do?"

Rasha stared back at Amin. "I would want to know that I was being appreciated and not taken for granted," she snapped. "I would want a break from the routine, to not feel like I was being treated as I am on every other day of our lives together. I would want someone to listen to me, not talk at me."

"I see." Amin, took a sip of his drink.

"I have to go Amin." Rasha stood up to leave.

"But we haven't finished… and you still have your full coffee left."

She shrugged his arm off and turned towards the door. "I hate coffee. Especially when it has cardamom in it."

CHAPTER TWENTY-SEVEN

To Sharif, a meeting with his bosses was an opportunity to impress, to prove his worth and of course there was always the chance of a promotion, to climb further up the career ladder. Sharif didn't feel he had an extra special talent for his job, but he did work harder at it than anyone else he knew. That's all success was at the end of the day. Hard work.

He could see colleagues' faces when he got promoted, got picked out for special tasks. He knew they thought he was the chosen one, but no one is favoured without reason, are they? If they spent less time complaining and more time putting in the hours like he had, they would be where he was now.

"What do we have so far?"

He nodded, rose from his seat, and looked at the papers in front of him. They had sent two of them today, this must be an important case. He turned and pinned a photo of Yusuf to the wall then made eye contact for twenty seconds.

"As you know I was following suspect x, aka Yusuf Tibi in the weeks leading up to his arrest. One of the most notable discoveries from his capture is this." He turned and pinned another photo on the wall. It was a close up of his wrist.

"This is the diamond tattoo. It is a symbol adorned by members of this particular activist group, one that identifies them to each other. I don't know if you remember but several weeks ago a suspect by the name of Aisha Halim died here in custody. I can't remember what happened to her."

He paused and leafed through his notes until he found a photograph of her. He scanned the words below it.

"Ah yes. Asthma attack followed by asphyxiation."

He looked up again.

"Aisha had the same sketch, also on her wrist. It was through her that we first became aware of Yusuf. She gave us his name when she was interrogated."

"What else do we know about the group?"

Sharif hesitated. He found it disconcerting that they had not offered their names. Should he ask them? In his head he labelled them officer A and officer B.

"We know they are running an illegal newspaper called Al-Thawra. Activity used to be mainly online but recently they switched to a paper version. Yusuf was caught making films from his father's studio, that's how we got him in the end. We're now working on other members of his group, a priority is his girlfriend Sara Fouad."

"Why is she a priority?"

"I think she was instrumental in creating the project so if we can get her, we potentially have access to a number of other contacts. I also think she would be great leverage."

"To get more information out of Yusuf?"

"Exactly."

"Is he not cooperating?"

"Not entirely. But the good news is that we've managed to close in on another one of the contributors also."

Sharif turned around and pinned a paper to the wall. "This is one of the first articles she wrote, I think she has a contact in Homs, the city comes up again and again in her work." He watched officer A and B squint to read the headline. "If I may?"

They both nodded and he cleared his throat. "Regime torture artists in Homs."

He took a step back, let it sink in for thirty seconds. "We know that this person is a dentist or works with a dentist."

"That's very specific, how did you work that out?"

Sharif unpinned the article and handed it to the two officers in front of him.

"Smell it."

"Sharif, have you gone mad?"

"I have not. Smell it."

Officer B lifted it tentatively to his nose and drew a deep breath in.

"What can you smell?"

"Something chemical. Like cleaner."

He passed it to officer A.

"Mouthwash."

"Almost. It's actually teeth cleaner. The type they use to polish your teeth at the dentist."

"I see."

They exchanged glances. Sharif could see that they were impressed. At times like this it was hard not to look smug so he turned away momentarily to obscure his face.

"So the next task is to search all dentists for contraband material."

The two officers exchanged a glance. "That will take a long time."

"Correct. But it's highly necessary. It will be a worthwhile use of our resources."

"Right. Do you think they are using the dental clinic as a base to meet?"

"It's possible. Could be one of many. One of the places

I followed Yusuf to is an old car up by the citadel though searches of the interior have come back with nothing. Perhaps they were on to us and they cleared it out or perhaps it was a false lead."

Sharif paused to take a sip of his water.

"We've also got people inside the library at the university, I was tipped off that people were dropping articles there."

"So you've found the drop off points but no central meeting point?" Officer A let out a long, exaggerated sigh. "Sharif, you know that until we find a central meeting point it's likely that this newspaper will continue to be published."

Sharif bristled. He had worked hard on this case, presented a lot of information, brought a lot of people to them. He didn't like the implied criticism in his voice. He turned to the board. One, two, three, four, five… he had learnt that when he was angry counting to ten before replying often made the answer less aggressive.

"Everyone we've interrogated so far says there is no central meeting point and that everyone works alone from home. But of course, we are looking into that."

"And what about the family?" Officer B was having a turn now, he had the feeling they were doing it on purpose. They were testing him, despite everything he had done for them. "What have you found out about the family?"

"The father is claiming insulin at the pharmacy downtown."

"The father. I see." He straightened some papers into a pile on the table, then slid it along so that it sat in the corner of the table.

"Let's leave the father out of it for now. What about his sister? Is she involved in any way?"

"We need to keep the sister in play for now, she's a bargaining chip, and has more potential as an asset if we keep her going. Scare her a bit, and ultimately she will lead us to the others."

CHAPTER TWENTY-EIGHT

When she arrived at work early one of the ways Rasha liked to pass the time before Doctor Suheir came was to polish the tools before she laid them out for the day. It was part of her job to clean them at night but in her view, when it came to cleanliness, you can never be too careful. She pulled two blue latex gloves out from under the sink, stretched them over her hands, then reached to the back to pull out a white bottle which contained disinfectant.

She sprayed the surface, washed it down, then squeezed more of the product on, before placing the white instrument tray on top of it. She put the tools one by one into the sink and covered them in disinfectant also. It was the sound of the scrubbing that most satisfied Rasha because she imagined with the grating sound all the bacteria coming away.

The brush reminded Rasha of her nieces and nephews because she had once watched her sister using the same instrument to clean inside their milk bottles, around the rim and inside the teat. She had seen Fatima miss so many spots on the plastic she had wanted to take the brush from her hands and scrub it herself.

Rasha held the tools under the tap for some time. She

was starting to feel hot and the cool water running through her fingers lowered her body temperature. She shook them dry, filled the steriliser, lent across to close the tap, then sat in her usual place by the window and began to peel her egg.

She had almost finished when the telephone next to the computer began to ring. "Rasha, your first patient is here" came Aida's voice. "Miss Fouad."

Rasha glanced up at the clock. 8.50am. "It's too early. We don't open until nine and Doctor Suheir is not here yet. Keep her where she is." She heard the receiver click on the end of the phone, reached in her bag for her mobile and scrolled to Doctor Suheir's name. She tried to call but the phone went straight to answer phone.

Rasha heard the beep to tell her the steriliser had finished and she waved away the steam with one arm as she opened the door. Using a soft cloth, she took each instrument out, polished it, then placed it back on the table next to the chair. She turned back to where she had been eating and wiped the crumbs off the surface with one hand, letting them fall gently into the other, then emptied them in the bin and disinfected her hands. The telephone rang again.

"Rasha it's me," Doctor Suheir's voice came clearly through the receiver. "My daughter was feeling unwell this morning and I was late dropping her to school. I'm on my way, prepare the first patient for when I arrive."

"Of course." Rasha hung up with her finger, then dialled one for the reception. "Send her in."

The woman who came through the door was wearing acid wash jeans that had been ripped across the bottom and the frayed edges were just touching her white canvas shoes. On top she had a navy shirt with white polka dots and she had painted her nails a colour that was somewhere between red and pink. That smacks of indecision, thought Rasha, looking down at her own nails which were unpolished but perfectly filed to mirror her cuticles. Natural is always better. People take you more seriously if you are natural.

As Rasha moved away from the phone she noticed that the patient in front of her had lines around her mouth and eyes that made her look older than she was. She was clearly nervous but that was ok, Rasha was used to patients who were scared at the dentist. In fact, one of Doctor Suheir's biggest compliments during her last appraisal was Rasha's ability to settle people before their treatment.

Rasha smiled and pointed towards the chair. "Please sit down," she instructed, manoeuvring herself out from her position by the window. "Doctor Suheir is on her way. The chair looks nasty and plastic but actually when you lie back on it the memory foam moulds to your body shape. It's quite a nice experience."

Miss Fouad offered a tight smile and did as she was told. Rasha leant across her and tucked a large piece of blue kitchen towel into her neckline. "Let's try and save your beautiful shirt." She patted the paper with her right hand, reached for the plastic glasses then slid them over her temples.

"Rasha isn't it?" enquired the young woman when Rasha had straightened herself up.

Rasha cocked her head to one side. "Yes." She paused. "I'm sorry I don't recall how I know you."

"My name's Sara," said the woman quickly. "I'm a friend of Yusuf's, he told me about you."

She swallowed. "How do you know Yusuf?"

"We work – worked – together. At Al-Thawra."

Rasha swallowed. "What's Al-Thawra?"

She offered a patronising smile. "Rasha we saw you drop the articles off. You can't see in from the outside but if we're there in the right position we can see everything on the street outside. Yusuf recognised you one day."

Rasha shut her eyes and exhaled slowly through her nose.

Sara was sitting upright now, though she hadn't removed the glasses or the paper from around her collar. Her voice was so low Rasha had to strain to hear her.

"Rasha, first of all thank you for what you have done, your contribution has been invaluable. Really your work has been great."

Rasha looked at the floor.

"Listen, I'm not here about your articles specifically today," Sara continued. "I need to talk to you about something else."

Rasha nodded.

"I think someone is following me," said Sara quickly. "I think I'm in danger. I… I don't even know why I'm telling you this, but I figured that if I am in danger, perhaps you are too."

She flicked up the glasses so they were on the top of her head. "You're the only other person contributing to the paper who I've managed to track down. Look, we think the café has been compromised, that's never happened before. It's best you don't leave anything else there."

"Right" Rasha looked behind her. "Does Shams know?"

"Good morning," both women looked at the door as Doctor Suheir came through it, hung her bag and coat on the back of it and turned to face the room.

"I'm so sorry I'm late," she said, extending a hand to Sara, then touching the left side of her ribcage to ask for forgiveness. "I believe you're a new patient, is that right?"

Instead of waiting for the reply she walked towards the kettle and flicked the switch. "You are more than welcome here," she called over her shoulder. "I hope Rasha has made you feel quite at home."

"She has," replied Sara, lying back down.

Eight hours later, Rasha unravelled the crinkled piece of paper Sara had slipped into her hand after her treatment that day. She found her phone in her bag, punched in the numbers then held it up to her ear. Nothing. She walked closer to the window, sometimes the reception was bad in the clinic. She tried again but there was no sound coming through the other end.

Rasha waved goodbye to Aida, pulled on her coat and headed down the stairs. Outside on the pavement she tried the number again and heard a long beep and then silence. Rasha tucked her mobile into her jacket pocket. She would try again when she arrived at home.

CHAPTER TWENTY-NINE

It wasn't until the neon cup rose into view that Shams remembered Sara had instructed her to use the back entrance. She stood on the corner of the road and took in the black and white tiles which lined the pavement to the right of her vision. Beneath the open shutters the owner of this coffee shop had started to put out small circular tables and brown chairs, the kind that had a strip of wood in a semi-circle that served as a back rest.

Shams preferred the more traditional design of the café on her right, but she suspected that several months ago she would have felt more comfortable going into the Neon Cafe. For a start, the windows were smaller and she could drink her coffee inside relatively unseen without the worry of someone she didn't want to find her, finding her.

From the corner Shams decided it would be better to double back on herself, cross the road and take a right at what she presumed was the parallel street running behind the cafe. She crossed the road and turned to find a walkway lined with cobblestones.

At certain points she had to push herself right up against the wall to avoid the plastic bags of rubbish which were falling over each other where they had been piled so high.

One of them had been ripped open, probably by a rat, and the contents had spilled across the path including several soiled nappies, the tape still strapped at the corners but the smell deep and offensive.

About halfway down Shams was in a position to stop and take in the six doorways to her right. Each were the same size and had been painted black. The paint had seen fresher days and was peeling off the wood. She moved closer – hadn't she and Sara stepped through some wooden panelling last time they were here?

"Good morning," Shams spun around to see an elderly man standing behind her. From which direction had he come? She smiled.

"Good morning."

"What brings you here?" He waved his walking stick in the direction of the alleyway she had just walked. "This path is for the delivery of goods to these cafes."

"Oh, I see," said Shams, backing away from him. "Thank you for letting me know." She produced her mobile phone and fiddled with the keypad. "Have a lovely day."

She watched as the man turned and walked in the opposite direction. As he rounded the corner, Shams looked behind her, confirmed the alleyway was clear again, then bent down. In front of her was a small window covered in wooden planks and she brought her face level with the boards, reached out, found there was no glass covering them, and prodded three of them until one moved. She jumped backwards as it fell to the ground with a crash. Shams looked around her again, then bent her knees, slid one leg inside, pulled the rest of her body behind it, then stood upright. She gripped the edges of the slat and balanced it between the others.

As Shams groped her way around the boxes into the main area of the café, she had to cover her mouth with her sleeve to stop herself from retching. She stepped over to the window. No one had cleaned up after the last time she was so ill. On one of the tables, she found a box of tissues and she gathered a clump in each hand then used it to scoop up the vomit, placing it in a plastic bag, tying the handles together and throwing it into the back room.

Shams pushed the light switch up and down several times but it responded only with a low buzz. She produced her phone out of her back pocket, switched on the torch and used it to survey the room. Everything was exactly as they had left it that day, the disposable cups still containing coffee in the centre of the room and the white plastic tables and chairs pushed to the edges. In the corner, where she had been sitting the first time she had come, even the eye she had sketched into the dust was still there.

Shams circled the tables and chairs at the edge of the room. Some still had glass cups the shape of tulips resting on their saucers, a single teaspoon laid on the side. Along the back wall was an archway built of brick though it was just for decoration and didn't lead anywhere. Just below where the two sides connected into a point, a television hung on the white tiles. Shams rested her cheek against the wall and from behind it she could see the wires hanging down, the edges frayed as though they had been cut. On either side were red embroidered wall hangings with the words 'Aleppo' sewn into them. The corner of one of them had come away from its fastening and was hanging like a diamond, about to fall at any time. Just below was a pile of folded tablecloths, ready to be spread onto the tables for a day of service ahead. Shams lifted one and a spider ran across her hand.

A pile of white paper at the front entrance caught Shams' attention and she shone her torch at it, then approached to take a closer look. She crouched, picked up one of them, put the phone in her mouth and used her free hand to open it out. "Syria's children learn to distinguish between weaponry."

"Articles," whispered Shams under her breath. She eased herself onto the floor next to them, took a handful and opened them out, then placed them into a pile on top of each other, smoothing the surface across with the palm of her hand so they would stay in place. She pulled a hair grip out of her bun and used it to secure them together.

She scanned what was left and groaned. She had barely dented the pile, it would take her hours to go through all the material. Anyway, why hadn't Sara cleaned them all up already. It was Tuesday today, she was sure this was the day Sara told them they met – or was it Wednesday? – Shams couldn't remember. Either way, the articles here must have been piling up for at least a month.

Shams pulled out five pieces of red paper. These looked urgent, the rest could wait until next time and anyway, it would be impossible for her to secrete everything and take it home with her in one go. She scanned the first one: "Is everything fine? Let us know. FR." The second was more direct: "We are worried. Has something happened? Why has the paper stopped?" Shams rubbed her forehead and added them to the pile she had already made.

She stood to stretch her legs and held onto her knees as they cracked under the weight of her torso, then she twisted each ankle in circles and waited for the blood to return so she could feel her feet again. Sitting on the floor for so long had left cold patches on the back of her thighs and she rubbed them to try and bring back some heat.

Into the top of her leggings Shams tucked the pile of papers, feeling the edges of the hairgrip nick her skin. She stood for several seconds then reached beyond her waistline and pushed the papers further so that they landed somewhere between her hip and her knee, then pulled her dress over her legs so that it covered the bump. She circled the café three times to check she could walk without them falling.

As she reached the far corner Shams concluded the papers were safe. She turned to make her way out but then froze as she heard three sharp blows behind her. She squinted in the dim light. At the window she could make out two dark silhouettes, see the bulges of their uniform.

She glanced towards the back entrance. If she ran from here, she could make it but she would have to cross the room diagonally and risk them spotting her. The thumping started again, an instrument pushing against the glass. Shams bent her knees and walked like a crab towards the back room, keeping as low to the ground as possible.

At the wooden panels Shams tried to remember which one was loose but they had all blurred together. She scratched her scalp. The banging was getting louder behind her. She pushed at the edges of them with a finger, then withdrew as one of the front windows crashed to the ground. She heard boots crunching broken glass.

Shams looked up at the wooden slats. She had no time to remove them and even if she did, whoever was here would hear them fall to the ground. She scanned the room. In the corner behind the boxes Shams saw a grey blanket and she rolled over to it, covered herself, and pressed her stomach to the ground.

"What are these?" Shams heard a hand rifling through the papers on the floor.

"Pick them up, take everything," barked the other.

"Listen to this one." More rustling paper. "Children identify government weaponry."

"What's that?"

"Something about young children learning the difference between a bomb and a sniper."

She heard one of them laugh. It was too loud, too forced. "It will teach them to be good soldiers. Best to start them young."

"This is another great one..."

"We don't have time for this. Just get them in the bag and let's look around the place."

Shams listened as the tulip glasses crashed to the floor and the tables and chairs scraped across the room. She patted the lump of paper in her leggings, she hadn't left it behind. She twisted her torso gently, there was a light shining behind her. She had left her torch on. She brought it around to face her so she could slide the switch off.

"Is there anyone here?" Shams held her breath and held her phone as still as possible. Through a fold in the material she could see black boots.

"I can't see anyone."

"What's out there? The old man said someone was hanging around the back." The footsteps moved out of her line of vision. Rustling plastic.

"Just the rest of the stock."

"Is it worth taking?"

"No – just some soda, they're probably out of date now." Shams heard someone pulling at the plastic surrounding the cans. They were less than ten feet away from her.

"It stinks out here. Something really bad." She breathed out as the footsteps retreated. "There's a really bad smell out there," he repeated, his voice quieter this time.

"Take that, it could be worth something." Shams heard a chipping sound and the fall of plaster as they pulled the television off the wall.

"Check one more time out the back. Are you sure there's no one here?" Shams held her breath again. Shuffling footsteps, the smell of a cigarette.

"No one. It smells so bad out there, can't have been anyone here for weeks."

CHAPTER THIRTY

Shams pulled up the plastic mask so it sat on the bridge of her nose and adjusted the wings that came out of the centre so they made semi-circles beneath her eyes. She wriggled her nose up and down. There was a nerve just next to the bone where the frame sat that had always prevented her from wearing sunglasses. She had waited too long to hear from Sara, today she would deliver her own paper.

Yusuf's black hoodie smelt damp as she pulled it over her head, tucking the stray wisps of hair inside and pulling the strings to tighten it around her face. The plastic edges of the mask dug into her cheek bones. Shams had found a pair of her brother's gloves, extra-large to try and make herself look like a man. She patted the black canvas bag she had slung over her shoulder and ran her gloved fingers across the rolled-up pieces of paper. She was ready.

As she walked the narrow path which led to the front door Shams felt something between excitement and terror. She stood on the step and moved from one foot to the other for thirty seconds, then reached into the bag, threw down one of the papers and rapped loudly on the door. She turned and cleared the gate with a leap, crossed the street and stood in an alleyway opposite and watched as the door swung open and a triangle of light appeared on the garden. A figure bent down and gripped the paper, shut the door and the light was gone.

Shams had chosen four stories per side of A4. At the bottom, on both sides, she wrote a line of names of people she knew had gone missing and appealed for information. Shams had drawn a bright pink box around the names. Now it would be the first item people looked at.

She decided it was better not to wait to see if anyone collected the papers because then she would not think so much about the chain of events it knocked into motion. She moved onto the next apartment block and sized up the building. The obvious place was the letterbox and she pushed it through, wincing as the sound of the metal flapped against the door.

Immediately she heard a bolt slide through its metal case. She turned and scanned the front garden. Whoever it was must have been passing the door. Straight ahead of her was a fence but the only way to access it was a path directly in front of the door, there was no way she could get to it in time before whoever was inside saw her. Shams spun around and flattened her back against the wall. She could hear shoes scuffing against the concrete step and she breathed in.

What she noticed first about the young boy who approached her was his tiny ringlets, which bounced on top of his head as he moved. Around his ears they had flattened against the sides of his head from where they had become damp with sweat. His pyjamas were cut from towelling material and in his right hand he was dragging a blanket along the ground that was fraying at the edges.

"Go. Go."

She pointed back towards the front door but he didn't move.

"Your mother is calling you. Quick. Move. Get out of here."

His eyes filled with water and his mouth contorted, the moment before a scream. She pulled the hood down and flipped the mask upwards and the boy's face softened.

"Walid," the voice was getting louder. "Walid, where are you?"

Keeping as close to the wall as possible Shams crept around the corner. Here it was not so dark as the neighbours' lights illuminated the wall. She headed for the corner at the far side and crouched, her face turned inwards. Without the mask she felt vulnerable.

Shams felt his tiny hand on her shoulder. "Hello." He waved his hands. "What's your name?"

Shams dug around in her pockets and pulled out a sweet. The plastic wrapping crinkled as she held it out.

He shook his head.

She bit her lip, then drew one of the papers out of her bag and smoothed it over her knee so she could fold it down the centre. She unfolded it again, pulled the top two corners down and the edges in then brought the entire right side over the left.

Walid's eyes were following her fingers as she worked, his small head flicking up, down and across. She exaggerated her movements, pulling the tip of the paper down on either side, then threw the aeroplane some distance to demonstrate to Walid how it worked. He retrieved it and stuffed it into his pocket then squealed and disappeared from view. Shams eventually heard the front door close.

Shams pulled the mask down, readjusted the hoodie and kept her gaze to the ground as she walked down the path and headed home. She felt her cheeks tingle at the thought of Yusuf, knowing she had only managed to deliver two papers.

Once she could see the outline of her front door Shams stopped in the street and checked the road behind her. It didn't look as though she was being followed but just in case she walked right to the end of the road, then doubled immediately back. As she opened the door, she could hear the murmur of the TV and see a strip of light at the bottom of the living room door.

Shams pulled the latch back and closed it so it wouldn't make a sound and walked as softly as she could into her room. She pulled at the canvas bag and tipped her head to the side so it would easily slip over her head. As she bent down to unlace her trainers there was a banging on the door. The windows shook from the force.

Shams looked down at the canvas bag, there were at least thirty pieces of paper in there. She opened a pad on her desk, unrolled them, and slid them inside.

Bang. Bang. Bang.

She crossed the landing, and peered over the banister. Her mother was about to open the door.

"Mum don't answer it. Ignore it."

She craned her neck and looked upwards. "Shams I can't do that. You remember what happened last time."

Shams returned to Yusuf's room, hung his hoodie up in the middle of his clothes, placed each glove in the pockets. She poked her finger into a protruding nail to calm herself down.

"We need to search the place." She was at the opposite end of the flat but his voice was clear. For the neighbour's benefit she supposed, stepping out onto the hallway so she could see what was happening.

Shams' mother moved to block the officers, stretching out her arms and gripping either side of the door frame. "You've already taken my son. You're not taking anyone else."

"We have orders to search the flat, please move aside."

"You have no right to be here. Please leave my family alone." Her voice was low, but it was trembling. The officer leaned on the door frame, the corners of his mouth turned up into a smirk. She heard a crack and her mother retracted her hands.

"Move aside. Or we'll break down the door and anything in our way."

"Shaimaa. Shaimaa." She heard her father's voice from the living room. "We have nothing to hide, let them in."

Shams sidestepped into her room, got into her bed, picked up a book and began to read. She heard boots in the hallway.

"Everybody in the living room now."

She looked up, there were three officers in her bedroom.

"I said move, now. I know exactly what you've been doing, I know all about the protests you attend, I know all about your brother's little website." He raised his voice. "Get up."

As she twisted herself to get off the bed she felt something sharp under her right leg. The mask.

"I need some privacy."

"Privacy?"

"Yes I need to get changed before I come down."

The officer at the front turned to the group and whispered something.

"Five minutes." He shut the door.

Shams looked around the room for somewhere to hide the mask. Then there were the papers, there was always the chance they would look at the pad. She took them into the toilet, threw them in and then flushed it.

Bang. Bang. Bang. The bathroom door was shaking. "What are you doing in there? I said five minutes, it's been seven."

She looked down; the mask was still there.

"I'm coming now."

She pulled it out and slid it behind the bathroom cabinet.

The door flew open. "Get out of there now. Bring your mobile phone."

In the living room her mother and father were sitting on the sofa, her mother's glasses had cracks in one of the lenses.

"Mum, are your glasses..."

"Shut up. No talking."

As Shams sat down, she felt her phone in her back pocket. Had she deleted the photos from the Neon Cafe that day? She couldn't remember.

The light fitting above them shook. Shams heard muffled laughter, then the grind of wheels going backwards and forwards.

"All clear," it was the same officer that had been in her bedroom, she recognised his voice. "Let's get out of here."

Shams' mother ran into their room. "They've taken everything. My gold, my clothes."

CHAPTER THIRTY-ONE

Sharif spun the paper around three times on the table, picked it up using his fingers and scrunched it into a ball. He had let this go on for too long.

He stood and walked to the corner of his office, closing the cheap wooden door and leaning against it so that nobody could see into his office from the hallway. To be honest, he preferred to work like this, cut off from what was going on outside, but if he did it too often people would start to ask questions. Dealing with others in the workplace was such a waste of time. If he were alone every day, he would do what he had to do in half the time.

He picked up the telephone.

"How are you Sharif?"

"I need an address."

"What's the name and file number?"

"Yusuf Tibi, 22 November 1984, mother: Shaimaa."

"47 Green Street."

Sharif replaced the receiver and pulled his jacket over his shoulders. Twenty minutes later he reached out his fist and pounded three times on the door.

"Sharif Halabi, branch 290." Sharif removed his sunglasses and stared back at the man at the door. He counted to thirty in his head. This was the length of time it took for fear to appear on a person's face. He was about two inches taller than Sharif was and he was younger. Handsome.

"Mr. Ali Miro isn't it?"

"Has something happened?"

"It's about your neighbours."

There was a pause. Ali swallowed. Sharif heard the cry of a young child and the man turned towards the noise and then back again. He moved aside and indicated for Sharif to come inside. In the hallway he nodded and Sharif turned to see a wooden bench, the backrest carved into the shape of a feather. It creaked as he sat on it.

Sharif cleared his throat, bent down and produced a notepad from his bag. He could see that the man's right knee was trembling.

"Am I right in thinking that the residents of the flat in the block to your left are a married couple and their two children. One boy, one girl?"

"Yes. Unless they have moved out recently."

Sharif rolled his eyes and looked up. "Are you aware that they have left or that anyone else has moved in?"

"No."

"So the answer is simply yes or no." He cleared his throat. "Let's try again. Am I right in thinking that you live next door to a family of four?"

"Yes."

"Now I understand that Yusuf and Shams are both training to work in the souq carving wooden boxes, is that correct?"

"Yes."

"I presume the business belongs to their father, is that correct?"

"Yes."

Sharif looked up. "We don't appear to have any more information about Abdullah. What else do you know about him?"

Sharif watched Ali Miro's eyes as they looked at the floor and then up again. He scratched his nose.

"We don't know them that well. My wife offered a few times to cook for them but they always refused. The parents are quite private people."

"I see." Sharif was getting impatient. "What do you know about them? Tell me anything, no matter how trivial it may seem."

"I know he has another job."

"Abdullah? Another job? Are you sure?"

"Yes. Something to do with the government."

"The government?" Sharif put his pen down. He wasn't expecting that.

"Yes. Visa department. Or passport. I can't remember exactly."

"I see. And how do you know that? Did he tell you?"

"Yes. Or I heard it from someone. Can't remember."

Sharif leant back on the bench. It creaked again. He held his palm upwards to indicate that he should continue.

"I went around one evening to look for him and Yusuf told me he was out at work. I thought it was unusual that he was carving wooden boxes so late at night. I asked him about it another time and he told me he had a second job."

"What about the mother, Shaimaa..." Sharif flicked back through the pages of his notebook.

"Rahman."

He looked up. "Shaimaa Rahman. What do you know about her?"

"She used to teach my niece and nephew at the school."

"I see."

"Wonderful teacher. They loved her."

"Loved her? In the past? What happened?"

"She left. Or she was kicked out. Abdullah seems to think they had something against her."

"I see."

"She had a medical condition. Something to do with her heart, I think. Or diabetes, yes that was it. I first met Abdullah in the pharmacy, he was getting insulin for her. She was told she had to rest by the doctor and they agreed that she would go part time then after that she got sacked."

"They?"

"Her and Abdullah."

"I see." He placed his thumb on the knuckle of his left finger and pulled it down until it cracked. "For someone who doesn't know the family very well you seem to have an awful lot of information about them."

Sharif turned the page of his notebook and found a clear space. He smoothed the centre with his finger and looked up.

"What can you tell me about the two children?"

"Well as I'm sure you're aware Yusuf was arrested several months ago. Handing out illegal newspapers. As far as I know the family don't have any information about where he is."

"And the daughter?"

"I hardly know anything about Shams."

"Engaged?"

"Yes. For years now."

"To who?"

"Amin."

"Amin what?"

"Amin Rashid."

Amin Rashid. Sharif wrote it down on the paper then circled it. The name looked familiar.

Sharif heard the shriek of a child again. He felt a small hand on his knee and he looked up to see a girl the same age as his youngest daughter. He stood without acknowledging her and let the front door swing behind him as he left.

CHAPTER THIRTY-TWO

'Appeal.' Shams liked the squelching sound of the black marker pen, and if she was honest the smell also. She leant back and thought for thirty seconds then scored a line through the letters and rewrote them in capitals. She added: 'For any information on the whereabouts of these people.' Then she wrote down the number of the first mobile phone she had ever bought.

Shams turned it over in her hands, then bounced it up and down, it felt so heavy. She thought about a time before mobile phones existed, when people had to write down telephone numbers and memorise them. She had heard someone say on the radio once that if smartphones ceased to exist, we would all learn to memorise numbers once again, but she wasn't so sure. Surely this digital age was having some effect on our ability to retain information. She stopped herself and concentrated on the paper in front of her. She was starting to sound like her mother.

When she had written her message on each of the papers, she folded them into squares as small as she could. Around each of these she wrapped a ribbon so it made the shape of a cross and then secured it with a small bow before cutting the excess away. With the papers in this form she was able to fit more in the canvas bag and she piled so many in that several fell over the edge and landed on the carpet. She used her hand to pull back the main bulk, picked them up off the floor, and slid them down the side.

Outside on the street the mask seemed to fit easier and the gloves helped, rather than hindered, her movements. Shams was smiling as she turned out of her road and headed up the hill towards the residential area which would be the target of this evening. Once they saw the ribbon the people inside would not be able to resist picking them up. That was the logic.

Later that night Shams lay on her bed staring at the ceiling, thinking about Yusuf. She decided that the pain of not seeing her brother was like a hole burrowing into her organs. At first it had burnt every day, so strongly that she would have to lie down for hours and clasp her hands over her belly to ease the pain because the agony stopped her from doing anything. Today the pain was still there, only it was a dull ache. She was frightened of losing it and she poked the space beneath her ribs with her fingertips to try and elicit some feeling.

Shams rolled over, took some water off her bedside table and gulped it back. She had never seen Yusuf drinking water, only coffee or milk. Or was it milky coffee and coke? She put her head to one side and tried to remember. To be honest, the memories were escaping her and becoming blurred round the edges. She would ask Sara next time she saw her.

She placed the glass beside her old Nokia and noticed the screen was illuminated. She drew it close to her. Twenty messages. She used her free hand to pull herself up on the bed, clicked the central button and read the first one.

"Rami Saleh is in Sednayna Prison." The second one: "Khalid Bakry, Adra Prison." The third was less gentle: "Fuck off and leave us alone or I'll report you to state security branch 290."

Shams commanded the black bar to run through all the messages. Eighteen had information about missing people from the paper and two were abusive. She read the last one three times:

"I have some photographs I think you will be interested in. Where can I leave the usb key? Xr."

She took another sip of water, then looked around the room for inspiration. "Leave them in the female toilets at Point Café near the citadel," she typed using both thumbs. "There's a framed photograph of a cat on the back wall. Put it behind there."

Within thirty seconds the reply flashed on her screen.

"Ok. Tonight."

Shams flipped the phone over and laid it face down, pulled her legs over the side of the bed so they were squarely on the floor and tried to think. What kind of a name is that, Xr? Maybe initials, but she couldn't think of a name that began with X. She walked over to the window and searched her handbag for her other phone, scrolled through her contacts and pressed the green call button.

"Rasha, it's me, Shams," she paused when there was no reply. "It's been ages."

When was the last time Shams had seen Rasha? She couldn't remember. "I finally did as you advised... you know, with the lists... and wondered if we could meet to discuss it."

That was ages ago, she must have spoken to Rasha since then. There was thirty seconds of silence on the other side of the phone.

"Sure, I can come to your place."

Shams panicked and turned to face the interior of her room. "I haven't been out all day," she said quickly. "Can we meet at the cafe close to the citadel, the one we used to go to after college. Point Cafe?"

CHAPTER THIRTY-THREE

Shams watched the ripped mint leaves sink to the bottom of the vessel then dropped two cubes of sugar over the side and ground them down with her spoon before lifting it to her lips and drinking the grassy liquid.

She looked up at her friend. Rasha's cheeks were permanently blushed red whether she was running, embarrassed or just sitting. Her long nose, which protruded out to the left, contradicted her eyes and mouth which seemed to Shams to be almost entirely symmetrical. Once, Shams had reached out to touch her face with the back of fingers because it looked so smooth.

There was an atmosphere between them that Shams couldn't quite define. She sensed animosity from her friend and wanted to bridge the gap but felt indignant herself. Those few seconds of silence where you both have so much to say, but neither wants to say it.

"Where have you been, I haven't seen you for ages?" Rasha said eventually. She scooped up the mint leaves from her glass, tapped them into the ashtray and sucked the sugar off her spoon. "How is everything. You know, after Yusuf?"

"It's tough. It's the not knowing that's killing me. I want some closure, but I don't want to know at the same time."

"I'm so sorry Shams. How are your parents?"

"Grieving. Not talking about it." She took a sip of her tea. "No change there."

"And the *mukhabarat*? Are they still hassling you?"

"They won't leave us alone, it's like it's not enough for them that they have Yusuf, they want to destroy our lives, pull apart the entire family. They raided our flat the other night, and for what. Seems they were mostly interested in my mother's gold."

"They're punishing all of you. For Yusuf's work."

"Exactly. And what do they want to get out of it? It's not always that clear." She stared into the distance, trying to suppress a painful memory. "Anyway, let's change the subject, it's nice to take my mind off it occasionally."

"Right." Rasha stared at her friend. "So, which was longer?"

"Longer?"

"The list," said Rasha. "You said you had been working on your lists. You said you wanted to meet to discuss them."

"Ah yes the lists. Cons." She shrugged her shoulders and rolled her lips inwards. "Much longer."

"If you had to pinpoint what it is about Amin that annoys you the most what would it be?" Rasha ran her finger around the rim of the cup to catch the last of the sugar granules that had secured themselves to the edges. Shams looked down as she inserted her finger into her mouth. She heard it pop as she pulled it between her lips.

"He's too rigid," replied Shams, leaning towards Rasha. "He likes to play by the rules and when I try to encourage him to be impulsive it frustrates him. The predictability. It's boring."

"Do you think you could manage two of you? Two impulsive, non-straight down the line people?"

"I have thought about that also…" Shams nodded and

took another sip of her tea. It was getting cooler and the mint was getting stronger.

"There's a couple of other things," she said, slotting the glass mug back into the circle in the centre of the saucer. She watched Rasha lean towards her.

"He's too particular about his clothing, or his possessions in general. He goes mad if he gets food on his top if we're eating in a restaurant and he'll never put his bag on the floor in case it gets dirty." Shams wrinkled her nose. "And I don't like the way he eats."

"Shams. That's ridiculous." She looked thoughtful for several seconds. "Don't you like the idea of a lifetime of happiness with someone? To know someone will always be there, whatever good and bad you go through, you have someone who loves you for the rest of your life?"

"Rasha come on, life isn't like that. That's the whole problem, this idea that something should go on forever, that's why me and Amin – or I should say – that's why I'm in this whole mess in the first place. Life is made up of short bursts of happiness rather than the promise of something forever. That's what kills the passion, pledging to someone you will always be there, who can do that? Who knows how they will feel in five, ten, twenty years? We'd be better off just admitting that something lasts as long as it lasts and enjoying it while we have it."

She looked at her friend, she was considering it at least.

"Shams, what are you holding out for? This has gone on for too long now. Why don't you just let it go?"

"I want it to go back to how it was in the beginning. When it was new and exciting and everything Amin did was great. When we were happy."

"And how long did that initial stage even last for?"

Shams looked down. "About a year."

"So all of this, all of this pain and anger and uncertainty is all because you can't let go of a feeling you had for someone for one year, if that. When you've had years of frustration?"

"In a way, yes. But it's also my family. My father, specifically. He loves Amin and I don't want to disappoint him."

"Shams you're living in your head, you have to try and look outside the situation and do the right thing for both of you, your father will understand, if not now, he will in the future."

"Listen Rasha, I understand what you're saying, but there's one other thing I need to talk to you about."

Rasha raised her eyebrows.

"I've met someone who I can really connect with."

"What?" Rasha rolled her eyes and threw her arms in the air.

Shams looked over her shoulder to see if anyone was close enough to hear, then began to whisper.

"It was totally unexpected really. Just kind of happened."

"Where did you meet?"

"Well that's the strange thing about this whole situation. Actually, we haven't met at all. I think he can somehow connect me to Yusuf, as in, he reminds me of my brother. He..."

"Hello ladies."

Shams swivelled to see Amin standing behind her.

"Amin." In her hurry to stand up Shams' chair tipped on its back legs. He caught the back of it and her arm at the same time. "What are you doing here?"

"I was passing by and I saw you two inside so I thought I'd come in and say hi."

Shams felt a knot of anger tighten in her stomach. She would not be able to finish her conversation with Rasha, Amin must have followed her here.

"It's "8.30, it's getting late. Let's go. I'll drop you both at home."

Amin walked to the waiter, took some notes out of his pocket and thrust them in his hand.

Shams looked at Rasha and widened her eyes. "What shall we do?"

"We'll talk later."

Shams bent under the table to retrieve her bag and realised it was missing. She looked across at Amin who was already standing by the front door. He was gripping it tightly with his right hand.

"Have you got everything?" she looked up at Rasha.

"Yes, but I need to go to the toilet." The toilet, thought Shams. She had almost forgotten.

At the back of the cafe the toilet door flicked from red to green and Rasha appeared. Shams stepped inside, shut the door behind her and turned immediately to the picture.

With her right cheek flat against the wall Shams could see the picture was hanging up with a string and she lifted it, pulled it off the hook and placed it gently on the floor so that it was leaning against the wall. Shams studied the area where the picture once hung. Nothing. They must have been delayed, she concluded, bending down to pick the picture up again.

Shams jumped when she heard a loud rapping on the door.

"Everything ok?" Rasha's voice was muffled through the wall.

"Two minutes." Shams tried to sound casual.

As she clasped her fingers around the frame and prepared to lift it, she felt a plastic rectangle under her nails. It was secured to the back with tape and she pulled it away in one motion, ran her fingers across the rest of it to check it was the only one and then hung the picture back on its hook. Where could she hide it? Amin had her bag. Shams pulled the front of her shirt away from her body, tucked it into her underwear then flushed the chain.

"Sorry." She smiled at Rasha. "The chain was broken."

CHAPTER THIRTY-FOUR

Now that Yusuf's computer had been taken away, Shams was faced with the impossible task of trying to access what was on the usb key. The family computer was in the hallway, probably a better bet was her father's computer in his study. It was 4.15am, if she moved quickly, she had two hours before her parents woke up.

Shams knocked slowly on the door, moved closer then knocked again. No reply. The door was already ajar so she pushed it, stepped inside, and scanned the room. On the opposite wall white plastic shelves reached all the way to the ceiling, each holding a fabric box stretching the entire length of the wood. Shams could smell that the room had been hoovered recently.

Under the window was a wooden desk with a black computer screen next to a printer, the keyboard neatly tucked into a second shelf below it. Shams felt the chair creak beneath her weight as she sat on it and heard the runners grind across the metal as she pulled out the drawer. The mouse was on the right-hand side and she reached across and shook it gently. A purple background bounced onto the screen with a white space for the password. She thought for a few minutes and typed something in. It shook, and a red cross appeared on the screen.

Swearing, Shams spun around on the chair and came full circle to face the computer again. She tried each of the three drawers on the right-hand side and found nothing but papers. She slid her hand underneath the third drawer and eventually rested her fingertips on what felt like cold metal. A laptop. She pulled it out so fast the corner of the drawer took a layer of skin off her wrist. She rested it on her knees, flipped it open. Her father and mother stared back at her from the desktop, their arms draped around each other's shoulders and Shams and Yusuf standing in front. She pressed the escape key and the home screen came up in front of her with no prompting for a password.

Shams wiggled the usb into the slot on the side and waited as the file loaded. It was hard to see which one it was, her father had stored so many documents on his desktop. She let the cursor slide over each of them until about halfway down the screen she found a white box with a date written under it. She double clicked. More dates. Shams pointed the cursor somewhere in the middle, pressed and a grid of photos appeared on the screen.

Shams chose the first one. A body. What on earth was this? She clicked onto the next, it was zoomed into the ankles. She could see the flesh had been entirely rubbed away from the bone. Without closing the picture Shams clicked on the next one. This time the body had been flipped over onto its front and there were deep lacerations on the back.

Shams reckoned she had looked at roughly half of the pictures when she reached into the drawer, pulled out a pen and wrote the numbers 1-546 on the back of her wrist. She would start again tomorrow, she thought, throwing the pen back into its place. She looked up at the screen in front of her. One more, she decided, replacing the lid and twisting her feet in circles to encourage the blood back into them. She clicked on 547 and waited as the photo came into focus. She followed the arms and legs, blew up the neck where she could see the hair then zoomed in and out of the picture seven more times. Shams closed the file, shaking, pulled out the usb key and slid the laptop back into its hiding place. She lost her balance as she stood up. It felt as though someone had swiped at her head with a sledgehammer.

Gripping the back of the chair between her fingers, Shams twisted it until it was exactly parallel to the desk, then walked slowly into the toilet, vomited, then back to the kitchen table where she produced her phone.

"I received the files, thank you." Shams keyed in the letters then closed the screen of her phone. Was thank you the right word? She replaced it with a full stop, sent the message then stared hard at the screen. Almost immediately a reply came.

"You're more than welcome. I have thousands more. When do you want them?"

"As soon as possible."

"Of course," came the reply. "Same place. I'll let you know."

Shams placed her phone face down on the table and ran her hands across her eyebrows to smooth them. She would have to find an excuse to go back to Point Café.

CHAPTER THIRTY-FIVE

Sharif stood outside the monstrous grey building and took a deep breath in through his nose. The crowds of people were making his heartbeat faster.

Once he was through the revolving doors, he walked immediately to the reception desk to the right of the entrance.

"I'm looking for Abdullah. On which floor can I find him?"

The man behind the desk had a pile of papers in front of him and the phone was ringing. He held up a finger and indicated for Sharif to wait. He picked up the receiver, spoke for thirty seconds to someone on the other line then looked back at Sharif.

"Which Abdullah?"

"Abdullah Tibi."

"Take the lift to the second floor, he should be behind the first counter to your left."

Sharif nodded and headed for the stairs. Why should he take a lift up two flights? It would be far better for his health get at least some exercise today.

At the top he turned around the corner and saw the first counter. He skipped the queue, held up a hand of apology to the person at the front and poked his head into the booth.

"I'm looking for Abdullah Tibi," he said to the man behind the counter. "I was told I could find him here."

"I am Abdullah Tibi. Who's asking?"

Sharif stared at him. The man was in his late twenties, it couldn't be him.

"Would you happen to know if there is anyone else that works here called Abdullah Tibi. Older than you. Perhaps in his fifties. Works in the visa or passport section."

"Definitely not."

He was overconfident, Sharif didn't like it. "I am from branch 290 and I have reason to believe you are obstructing an investigation. How can you be so sure he doesn't work here?"

"Because the only employees in the visa section are women. This is the passport section, there is only me and two other guys who work here and none of them share the same name as me. I would certainly remember if one of my colleagues shared my name."

"I see."

Sharif rested his notebook on the corner of the counter and clicked the top of his pen. He hovered it a millimetre above the page.

"Address?"

"Excuse me?"

"Address. What's your address?"

"My address? Why do you need my address?"

Sharif looked up and stared at him.

"67 Central Street."

"Age?"

"Twenty-five."

"Married?"

The man paused. Sharif looked up again. Everyone in the queue had gone quiet, all eyes were on him.

"Are you married?"

"No."

"So you wear a wedding ring for no reason? What's your wife's name?"

He looked at his ring, twisted it, then looked up again at Sharif. "Halima."

"Halima what?"

"Halima Riad."

"Phone number?"

Sharif produced his phone, typed in the numbers as Abdullah read them out, then pressed the green call button. "Show me your phone."

Abdullah pulled his phone out of his pocket and held it up in front of Sharif. The screen was blank.

"Look you son of a bitch, it seems you want to pay us a visit at the branch, what's your fucking phone number?"

This time his number flashed on the screen.

* * *

Back in his own office Sharif turned on his computer and opened the internal search engine. He typed in the name Abdullah and hundreds of files came back. He tried again but with his surname. Nothing. He tapped his pen on the side and produced the notes he had taken when he interrogated Ali Miro in his hallway. He had definitely said it was either the visa or the passport department. Perhaps he had been lying, trying to throw him off the scent.

He kept reading, why had he drawn a circle around Amin's name? He typed it into the system, then sat up as he heard the computer beep to say it had found a match.

CHAPTER THIRTY-SIX

It wasn't that Rasha felt guilty about taking a day off, it's just that she had a reputation to uphold. She had a strong work ethic and Doctor Suheir had praised her diligence on more than one occasion. It wouldn't do for five years' worth of hard work to unravel in one single day.

She propped herself up on the pillows and rubbed her throat. Now that she was fully awake, she couldn't feel the razor blades anymore. Perhaps she should go in for the second part of the day. If she left now, she would still be able to see the afternoon patients.

It was the text message Shams had sent that had really got to her. "Sara's dead." So simple, matter of fact. As if that was the daily reality they were living now, as if anyone could be next. She thought back to the day she was in the clinic, the day she had visited. Could she have done more for her?

Rasha closed her eyes and tried to wipe out the memory of Sara. The first person she saw was Amin. It had been so surreal when she saw him in her workplace. Surreal in a nice way, though she had to admit, there were aspects of his personality she found tough. Like when he had appeared at that cafe when she and Shams were catching up, then interrogated her on the way home. Had she spoken to Shams? When would she be able to do that? No she had not, and no she probably would not, she told him. That had made him angry.

Her mind first turned to a white, black space, then she dreamt she had a young daughter and they went together to a restaurant for breakfast but when she tried to order the staff kept bringing dessert. Every time she asked for her main course they would insist that chocolate is actually a starter. Later, she found herself on the ground floor of a shopping centre, trying desperately to get upstairs as gunmen burst into the building.

Rasha opened her eyes, felt her duvet and acknowledged her blue walls. She felt a sense of relief. She lay for several seconds trying to decipher her dreams, the second was more obvious the first more ambiguous. She rolled over. She could see strips of light coming in through her shutters and she reached out for her phone. 6am. She had slept right through.

As she ran up the stairs towards the clinic, Rasha could smell her freshly washed hair. Strawberries. Panting, she stopped at the top. The door was still locked, Aida must have overslept.

"This is Aida, you know what to do." Rasha hung up then called her three more times but each went straight through to the answer phone. The last time she left a message.

"Aida, it's Rasha, where are you? You need to get here before Doctor Suheir comes, she won't like it. I also have a lot to do before the clinic opens. Call me back and let me know where you are… also your voicemail message is weird. Bye."

"Rasha?"

Rasha turned to see a couple in front of her, she hadn't heard them coming up the stairs.

"Yes."

"We're looking for Aida." The woman was roughly ten years older than her husband and about two inches taller. Their arms were interlocked. It looked as though she was holding him up.

"So am I."

"Right. So she's not here?"

"I'm sorry have we met?"

"We are Aida's parents, she didn't come home last night and we're worried. Her phone's switched off. Did she come to work yesterday?"

"I'm not sure. I was off sick."

"I see. Who can we ask? Who knows where we can find her?"

"Doctor Suheir arrives at 9am. She will know."

"It's 9.15am." It was the man's turn to talk, he sounded angry. His wife put her hand on his elbow to calm him.

"She probably just stayed at a friend's place and ran out of battery. I'm sure it's nothing to worry about." Rasha pulled at the skin around her nails.

Aida's parents exchanged a glance. "It's most unlike her. She has never done this before. Then we found this." He held out a twisted piece of paper. Rasha took it and uncurled it. "Somebody posted it through our front door last night." The black ink on the paper was swirling together in front of her eyes. She felt sick.

"Do you know what this is? Do you know what Aida was involved in?"

She folded it down the middle then looked up. "Look, why don't you give me your number and as soon as I hear anything, I'll call you." Rasha could feel her heart racing. She looked at her phone then up again. "I promise I'll call you as soon as I hear anything."

When their footsteps faded Rasha scrolled to Shams' number and hit the call button.

"Rasha." She heard the sound of a tool hitting wood.

"Shams I need to talk to you urgently."

"Is everything ok?"

"Not really. Shams, it's Aida. She hasn't turned up to work."

"Who's Aida?"

"The receptionist. My… our receptionist. Here at the clinic."

"I see. Well she probably went out last night and stayed at a friend's place. It's only one night. What's the problem?"

"Look, can you come?"

"Of course." There was a pause. "Actually Rasha, can you come here?"

* * *

Rasha was surprised when Abdullah opened the studio door.

"Rasha. It's been ages."

"It has."

Shams walked out from behind the workbench and wiped her hands on her apron. "I hope you don't mind that my Dad's here. He overheard our conversation. He wants to help."

Rasha liked Shams' father but he was odd. They had never really spoken though she and Shams had been friends for years. Still, Shams would be happy he was making an effort.

She held her arms out to her friend. "It's so nice to see you."

Rasha lowered herself onto the chair in the corner. The studio was a mess. Wood shavings everywhere, tools spread across the workbenches. It was hard to think in such surroundings.

"So what's happened?" Shams was in front of her now. Her eyebrows were arched. She looked concerned.

Rasha moved her eyes towards Abdullah. Shams nodded. "It's ok. Tell us."

"As I told you on the phone, Aida's parents were at the clinic today. She didn't go home last night and she wasn't there today." Rasha threw herself into the backrest and sighed. "She's missing and it's all my fault."

"What do you mean it's your fault?" Abdullah had pulled up a small stool and was facing the two of them. "How can it be your fault if Aida is missing?"

"Dad." Shams signalled for her father to be quiet. "That's not helpful."

"They thought she was me. Or they wanted to get to me."

"What do you mean?"

"I was writing articles for Al-Thawra."

"You as well?"

"Dad." Shams was shouting now. "Let her finish."

"Somebody posted an article through their front door. Aida's front door." She lowered her voice. "One of my articles."

"Where were you yesterday?"

"I was off sick. Terrible sore throat and headache." Rasha let out a small cough but it sounded pathetic.

"What are the chances of that? You're never off sick. Even at university you were like that."

Rasha hung her head and looked at the floor. "I know."

"Rasha your phone is ringing." Rasha looked up. Shams was pointing at her bag.

"Hello."

"Rasha, it's Doctor Suheir. Where are you?"

"I'm with a friend. I was at the clinic this morning, but Aida wasn't there. Then when you didn't turn up, I didn't know what to do. I couldn't get hold of either of you."

"I know, I know, I had a meeting this morning and I left my phone at home so I couldn't call you."

"Who's that in the background? I can hear a voice?"

"It's Aida. We're both here waiting for you."

"Aida's there?"

"Yes, she apologised for being late. Did you know Aida is epileptic? She went out last night, had a fit and didn't make it home."

Rasha covered the receiver with her hand and moved it away from her mouth. "Aida's ok. She's at the clinic."

"See. I told you." Shams walked back over to the work-bench.

"Are you still there? Rasha?"

"Yes, yes, sorry. I'm here. I'm on my way."

"I think I'll miss you I need to leave." Rasha moved the receiver away as Doctor Suheir exhaled. "Look I need to tell you something. It's about Maryam."

"Maryam?" She pressed the plastic close to her ear again.

"You remember her, don't you? You must remember her, she's always here. Maryam Ashraf, the one whose family live in Homs."

"Of course. What's happened."

"She's dead Rasha. She was tortured to death then her body dumped on her doorstep."

CHAPTER THIRTY-SEVEN

"Nice to see you" Shams raised her arm in the air and greeted the other women. They parted and indicated that she should sit down in between them. She drew out a sandwich bag from her pocket, unpicked the knot and rolled the top down.

She offered the nuts to the woman on her right. "Seen anyone today?"

"Not yet." The woman checked her watch. "It's still early though. No news?"

"Nothing."

It was hot and Shams could feel the sweat on her back. She pulled her shirt out and in again, using it as a fan.

"Amira who used to come here found out her fiancé had been taken to a prison in Damascus. So she set off there yesterday."

Shams moved herself backwards so the women on her left could hear also. "And? Is it good news?"

The women exchanged glances. "We haven't heard from her since."

"Oh dear."

"They say they don't always make it through the checkpoints around the city. They arrest around one hundred people a day as they try to cross."

"I see." Shams looked down at her nails. The polish had worn down at the top and there was a semicircle at the bottom where her nails had grown out. She would have to remove it and start again tonight.

"Look there's one." She looked up as one of the women pointed towards the building. It was grey concrete with pillars holding up the entrance. Above that was a picture of the president, six times larger than life size. Paint was peeling off around the windows but the black iron gate surrounding it looked as though it had just been put in place.

This time it was a minibus. They watched in silence as it pulled up to the gates and waited for them to open. Shams stood up onto the wall to see better but the women pulled her down. "They'll see you, stop it."

She sighed and returned to her seat. Since she had been coming to the police headquarters to look for her brother, she had watched hundreds of cars pull up here and three times as many people get out, but she hadn't seen Yusuf once.

Last week she had walked up to the gate and tried to find someone to talk to, but a tall soldier with a shaved head told her that if she came back, he would arrest her too.

Sitting on the far side of the wall she could see the woman she had talked to last week. She raised her voice so she could hear her. "Samira, did you hear from Ahmed?"

"No." Samira ran her finger round her gums to remove the nuts. "They came back last night for Omar."

"So all three of your sons have now been taken?"

"All four. And their close circle of friends." She looked back towards the building. "I hope they're together."

"How did that happen?" Asked the woman to her left.

Samira paused, took a few moments to gather her thoughts. "When they came to arrest Ahmed, Omar was there in the kitchen. He's six years older than Ahmed and he tried to stop them from taking him. They came back for him the next day."

"And what about the friends, were they all protesting together?"

"Quick, quick, there's someone coming out."

Shams looked up and moved her head around to the side so that she could see past the pedestrians who were in the way.

"I can't see anything, those people are blocking him."

"Come here, we have a perfect view from here."

She stood and crouched to the left, she could see the figure now. The face was obscured with a hat, some sort of cap, but she could make out the thin frame, the outline of the briefcase. She froze and then felt her face flush with the extra blood and she slid her hands underneath her so they wouldn't see she was shaking. The figure crossed the courtyard, pressed a buzzer at the gates and let himself out. There was no doubt about it, that was her father.

She looked up, Samira was elbowing her in the ribs. "Your phone. It's ringing."

She picked it up and stared at it for several seconds. It looked like a foreign object, she couldn't work out what to do with it. "Hi Mum."

"Shams are you there?"

"Yes I'm here."

"What's wrong?"

"What do you mean what's wrong?"

"Your voice. I can always hear it in your voice when there's something wrong."

"Nothing Mum. I'm just tired."

"Shams you're late, I told you this morning I was cooking dinner. Where are you?"

"I'm looking for Yusuf." She moved the phone away and faced the women. "Tomorrow?" she mouthed, then back into the phone, "I'm coming now."

She hung up and waved at the group of women. "Same time, same place."

When she pushed the front door open, she could already smell the food, but it was burnt. She hooked her jacket and her bag on the banister and entered the kitchen. There he was, sitting at the table, his briefcase placed next to his right foot.

"How was your day?" She looked first at her mother and then her father. "This is a nice surprise."

"Sit down, sit down." Her father pointed at the chair.

She smiled and slid into her seat. Her mother left the room so she turned to her father. "So what did you get up to today?"

"Not much, a few errands to take care of."

"Were you working?"

"No. Day off."

"So what did you do?"

"Went for a walk."

"I see. Where?"

"Shams." His voice was raised now. "Too many questions."

She felt her mother's hand on her shoulder. "Don't upset your father. He's had a busy day."

"Not really," Shams looked directly at him.

"What do you mean not really?"

"Why won't he answer me?"

"What's the problem?" Her mother was standing in between them.

"Nothing, she's just being difficult as usual." Abdullah was shouting now.

"Mum why don't you stand up to him for once. Tell him he's wrong."

"Shams." Her mother offered a diplomatic hand. "Let's just all sit down and calm down. We can talk through this together."

Shams stood up and heard the chair legs scrape against the tiles. “I’m not hungry anymore.”

“Shams you have to eat something.”

“I said I’m not hungry.”

CHAPTER THIRTY-EIGHT

'Good morning.' Shams rolled over to check the time and was distracted instead by a message which flashed up on her phone. They had only spoken last night; she wasn't expecting to hear from him so soon.

'Good morning,' she replied and almost immediately she felt the phone vibrate in her hand.

'How was your evening? What did you get up to?'

She pulled the second pillow across and lifted herself up until she was in a more upright position. 'Nothing much,' she began typing. 'Had a look through the photos, it was pretty depressing. Thanks for leaving them.' She read back through the text a couple of times and decided to remove the 'nothing much,' it made her sound boring. After she pressed send, she stayed on her back for ten minutes waiting for the reply to come through but it never materialised, so she pushed the phone under her pillow and went to the bathroom.

Shams usually spent a good fifteen minutes under the warm gush of water but today she felt impatient to get back to her bedroom. Why had Xr not replied to her last message? She gripped onto the side of the bath, side-stepped out of it, and then hung her head upside down, reaching for a towel from the silver rail that hung adjacent to it. She wrapped it around her hair, tucking the corners underneath near the bottom of her neck.

She took another one. It felt rough against her skin and she drew blood as she scrubbed herself dry. Back in the bedroom she went straight for the pillow and pulled out the phone. Nothing. She threw it into the corner of her drawer to avoid the temptation to keep checking it and left the room.

The kitchen looked depressing in this dim light so Shams flicked the switch on and considered the room under the neon lighting. She cursed all the times she had criticised her mother for frying chicken in the morning, she would love to be greeted again with the smell of oil.

Shams pulled the cupboard door open and studied the contents inside. She could see a box of eggs and some dried bread wrapped in paper. Shams bent her knees and tried the fridge. She pulled out a half empty tub of hummus, tucked it under her arm, and with her free hand took some left-over vegetables she had cooked three nights before. Placing both next to the corner of the table she turned, filled the silver pot on the stove with coffee and while she waited scooped the crushed chickpeas into her mouth using the peppers and courgettes as vehicles. She felt the oil drip between her fingers.

Back in her bedroom she dived straight into her drawer to check her phone. She felt a flutter of excitement as she noticed two notifications and she turned to go back to the kitchen. Once the coffee was in the cup, she swilled it around the sides twice, took two huge gulps and then opened the messages:

'You are more than welcome, I know I can rely on you to do a great job with them,' read the first. 'Enjoy the rest of your day' was the second.

Shams re-read the first message at least five times. 'I know I can rely on you.' She smiled, reaching out for the last sip of her coffee. The second she did not read again, she didn't like the finality of it, the way it ended the conversation and indicated that Xr did not want to, or could not, continue the conversation. 'I know I can rely on you' she whispered it to herself quietly, stood up and poured herself another coffee.

She imagined Xr to be her own age, slightly taller with dark waves that were long enough to tuck behind his ears. There was no jewellery or any of those extras that were fussy, just a simple shirt and some faded jeans.

Shams flinched as the letterbox flapped, annoyed that it had disturbed her thoughts. She stood, pulled on a jumper that was hanging on the banister and called through the metal: "Who is it?"

"It's me."

Her hand went up to her head. Amin. She had completely forgotten he was picking her up today.

She scratched her upper lip. "Wait, I'm coming."

In her bedroom Shams was looking for the green dress her mother had made for her birthday last year. She pulled it out, held it by the sleeves and shook it. Did she like this one? The neck was cut into a circle which met at the front of her neck and parted, the embroidery leading down into a rectangle which continued all the way to the hem. This traditional style broke away at the skirt, which flared just below her waist. The excess material ruffled at the bottom to create the impression of breaking waves. She wasn't sure, but Amin hated it, so she would wear it.

Shams noticed the armpits were white from her deodorant and she pressed her nose closer. There was a faint musty smell. She moved from side to side in front of the mirror and smoothed the material across her hips, then pulled a loose cardigan over her shoulders.

Outside Amin was sitting on the small wall which encircled the front patio, his face turned towards the sun.

She pulled the front door shut. "So. What will it be?"

"Coffee? Suggestions?"

Shams paused. "What about that place up by the citadel? Where I was with Rasha when you took us home?"

"Again?" Amin had stood up and was facing her now. "You used to hate it in there."

"Well it's improved. Plus, I feel our visit was cut short the last time." She pulled at his sleeve. "Let's go."

Some of Amin's old school friends had formed a group at the back of the café, there were so many of them a couple had perched on the back of chairs. An elderly couple on the next table were looking across, hoping to catch their eye, hinting for them to be quiet.

"Wait here, I'll go and say hi." Amin pulled back a chair for Shams and walked towards them.

Shams took the opportunity to check her phone again. Some messages with the details of missing family members, some requests to not come near people's homes again, but nothing from Xr. She checked her other phone and clicked on one from Hala, an old friend from university whose brother had been missing for almost a year.

'Mum was told today an amnesty is coming up.'

"What's that?"

Shams looked up as Amin dragged the chair backwards and slid both phones into her bag.

"Nothing. It's my phone, a message from Hala."

"Not that, the other one. It looked like a phone," he pressed. "A really old phone."

"Oh that. It belongs to Rasha. She left it behind last night."

Amin leant back to make space on the table as their coffees arrived. "How was it with you and Rasha last night?"

"It was good."

"You haven't seen her for ages, have you?"

"No."

"How come? You used to be such good friends."

"We've both been busy."

"Don't you think Rasha is just sometimes hard to place."

"Hard to place?"

"I mean, sometimes she's in a good mood and sometimes she is just so melancholy. Like, overthinking everything, always expecting the worst."

Shams rolled her eyes. "Amin. Rasha and I were having a private conversation before you turned up last night. If she seemed unhappy that would be why."

"Are you in a bad mood?"

Shams sighed and looked up. "No. Just answering your question."

"When are you going to see Rasha again?"

Shams threw her spoon into the coffee and the black liquid slopped over the sides. She stood up, clutching her bag. "I'm going to the toilet."

"Leave your bag here," said Amin, reaching out for the strap as she passed him. He lowered his voice and shrugged his shoulders. "I'll watch it for you."

Shams pulled it hard, and he looked up in surprise. "It's my bag, and I will look after it.

Inside the toilets Shams pulled the picture off the wall and without even looking ran her fingertips around the frame. This time there were two usbs and she picked the tape off them with her nail then slid them into the coin compartment of her purse. She replaced the picture, sat down on the toilet and checked her phone again. Nothing. Anger flared in her belly and she flushed the chain and made her way back to the table.

"Let's go."

"We just arrived, ten minutes ago." He looked angry. "And I haven't finished my coffee. What's wrong with you?"

"I'm not feeling well. Take me home. Please Amin, can you just take me home."

Back in her bedroom Shams threw off her dress and cardigan and pulled on a pair of leggings and one of her brother's t-shirts. The flat was in darkness and she knocked on her parents' bedroom door then pushed it open slightly. There was no one there. She went to her father's study, produced the laptop and plugged in the usbs. The same grid of images appeared and she flicked through, looking for any body part that could belong to her brother.

When she heard a key in the front door, she pulled the stick from the computer pushing it up and into her sleeve and slipped out of the door. She stood in the hallway and smiled as her mother and father walked in the door. "You're back," she said, holding her arms out to embrace them. "We can have dinner together, it's still early."

"We're tired Shams and we've already eaten." Her father looked distracted. "Another time."

"The news was good today, wasn't it? For once."

"The news?" Her mother stared at her.

"A new amnesty is coming up. They're going to release a new round of political prisoners from jails in Aleppo."

"Really?"

Shams took her mother's hands in hers.

"Yusuf might be among them."

"Shams." Her father was angry. "Stop spreading false hope. It won't get any of us anywhere."

"It's not false hope. One of my friends told me, everyone's talking about it. Her mother stands outside the police headquarters twice a week to try and get information about her son. One of the officers told her."

"What does your friend know about anything Shams? She's young, she doesn't understand. And her mother shouldn't be doing that. It's dangerous. And she certainly shouldn't be involving her daughter."

Shams turned, entered the bathroom and produced the

phone from her bag. "Who are you?" she wrote, then immediately turned the phone off.

She slipped it into her pocket as she heard a knock on the door. She flushed the chain and opened it to see her father standing there.

"What's the name of your friend?"

CHAPTER THIRTY-NINE

When he saw Shaimaa in his wing mirror he realised he had parked the car too far forward. He looked down at his phone, then up again. She was getting closer, there was no time to reverse. He would have to film her from here and hope she didn't pay too much attention to the car.

He flicked the phone onto video mode and trained it on the mirror. She had stopped, that was good for him. He looked back at the screen, zoomed in on her, then waited. She moved forward, rummaged for something in her bag on the corner, then removed the glasses, pulled a hard case out of her bag and placed them inside.

He put his phone in his top pocket, the camera facing outwards. She had turned around by that point, was heading into the building, and he had to run to catch up with her. It wasn't ideal, that was the best way to attract unwanted attention, but he had no choice.

"Hold the door." She turned around and smiled, held her foot out so it stayed open. He thanked her and took a left as she took a right. He walked through the corridor, up the stairs to the viewing gallery and sat, holding the phone up to the glass.

There were about fifteen of them down there, huddled around one sewing machine. From Sharif's position he guessed it was broken, one of them wandered off and came back with a small metal cylinder. It was Shaimaa who fixed it. He saw her lean in, thread the cotton through the hole. She leaned back and smiled at the others. She still wasn't wearing her glasses.

He stood, rolled his shoulders back, then pressed stop on the camera. He had enough material. He retraced his steps back round, down the wooden stairs and around the way Shaimaa had gone. As he opened the door, they all looked up.

"This is women's only," one shouted. They all giggled.

"I need Shaimaa." He was looking at her now, his arm outstretched. She stood, her forehead furrowed. He could see she recognised him from the entrance, but couldn't work out what he wanted.

"Is there somewhere here we can get a coffee? A tea room perhaps?"

She nodded, turned to face the women and shrugged her shoulders, then led the way out of the room. Directly opposite was a small kitchen with two wooden stools in the corner. She pulled them out and gestured for him to sit down then flicked the kettle on.

"Sharif Halabi military intelligence. Branch 290."

He watched her face, it was paler, but she didn't flinch. He opened his bag and produced the red notebook and laid it down, the pages spread open.

He tapped the second line down. "What does this say?"

She leaned in, squinted. "Shaimaa Rahman."

"Right. But what's next to it?"

"Diabetes, loss of vision, almost blind. Insulin."

"Right."

She straightened her spine. "Is there a problem?"

"Yes." Sharif cleared his throat. "Yes there's a very big problem, you see." He tapped the page again. "Your husband has been claiming insulin for you. Everybody thinks your eyesight is going, that you're suffering." He pointed at her eyes. "But I see you in there, fixing a sewing machine. There appears to be nothing whatsoever wrong with your eyes."

"I'm wearing contacts."

"Right." Sharif rolled his eyes. "So take them out."

"Excuse me?"

"I said take them out. If you're really wearing contacts then just take them out."

He saw her cheeks redden.

"I need you to do something for me."

"And what will you do if I don't?"

"I'll tell your husband you're lying. About your illness."

She paused. "He already knows."

"No he doesn't."

"I'll tell him you're lying."

Sharif placed his phone on the counter and pressed play. There was Shaimaa, folding her glasses and putting them away inside her bag. There she was, leaning towards the sewing machine and fixing it.

She crossed her arms and leant back. "So tell him then. See if I care."

Sharif rolled his eyes again. She was being stubborn, this was taking a lot longer than it had to. He had other places to go to, he needed to get this wrapped up.

"Look." He felt his voice getting louder and Shaimaa got up to close the kitchen door. "I don't have time for this. It's not just your husband who will find out. Using medicine like this when it's not needed, at such a time of severe shortage is illegal. It's punishable."

He leaned closer. "And how did your husband manage to get his hands on it anyway?"

She pushed his hand off her knees and he put it back.

"So this is how it's going to work." Sharif cracked his knuckles on the right hand. "My wife isn't giving me what I want any more. Two children, too many years together. The video stays here. And I'll leave Shams alone. As long as I get what I want."

Sharif heard the door slam behind him and he pulled his sunglasses down onto his eyes. One of the formulas he had learnt very early on in this job was that if you worked for 730 hours you would get fifteen minutes of valuable information, or the golden nugget as he liked to refer to it. Over time he had come to realise that the length of time for such a small amount of information was not something to be disheartened by – in fact this was a joy, something to be celebrated, for we cannot always have exactly what we want without patience and endurance.

This time it had taken 102 hours, his record so far. Sharif couldn't believe his luck, and took it as a sign that he was on the right path. He was doing something good. He was being rewarded for it.

CHAPTER FORTY

Before she could take a deep breath in, Shams' body jerked upwards and in the murky light, she observed that the covers had become twisted around her legs and behind her back. She reached a hand up and ran it down her neck and onto her shoulder blades. When she withdrew it, her palm was soaked with sweat.

Her throat was so dry she could feel the walls sticking together and she leant over and felt around for the plastic bottles she kept by the side of her bed. She shook three of them before finding the fourth was full. She tipped her head backwards and enjoyed the relief the water offered her.

Shams groped around for her phone and lit the screen up. 3am. She lay back on the pillow and tried to calm herself. 4am, 5am, 6am, 7am – she counted four hours she may have to kill before morning if she couldn't find sleep again. The thought of being alone with the darkness made her shake with rage. She was certain she had overcome this insomnia.

Her mind turned to Yusuf. She imagined his face, his knocking on her door and sitting on the end of the bed to talk about their days together. She closed her eyes and she imagined asking him for advice about Amin, or offering hers on Sara. Her eyes opened. These thoughts were becoming intrusive, especially now that they were waking her up so forcefully in the night. And just when she thought she was getting better.

At different times of the day Shams imagined what she would say to Yusuf and he to her if he was here. What they would cook together and the music they would listen to. A couple of days ago she even imagined an argument they would have, playing it out in her head from the moment of relative peace to the time when the shouting became so intense their mother intervened. At the end of it she was shaking with anger.

Over time Shams had come to label this type of thinking as the dead-end road. After she had imagined him to be here, she would spend just as much time asking why he wasn't. She would always end up at the same place: that life was very unfair and whatever she thought or imagined she could do nothing to change the situation. Rather than offer some kind of closure on the issue, this realisation would always give rise to a deep sense of anger.

A couple of times Shams had tried to list positives about what she was going through, similar to the lists she had once made about Amin. Resilience was a word that came up often, as was empathy, but Shams felt that neither did justice to the depth of her feelings.

He was probably dead, she had concluded that more times than she had concluded that he was alive. If she kept telling herself that she would eventually accept it and at least she would have some closure on the issue. But would she?

She checked her phone again, 3.07am, then slid down the bed and pulled the covers over her head. Her eyes and her body felt heavy but her brain was fully awake. She thought of Amin and how in the beginning of their relationship she had missed him so much when they were away from each other for just a day or even a couple of hours in their separate classrooms. She tried to evoke those early, intense feelings but she was struggling.

These days, when he left, she always felt relieved and she never missed him. That is how she knew it was over. Rasha had once told her that the opposite of love is indifference. And what else embodied this more than never thinking about your lover when they are away from you?

Shams lit up her screen again and the digital numbers glared back at her. 3.55am. She sat up straight as she noticed a message from Xr. She clicked on it. 'That is not important now. I have something else for you.' Shams stared at the words with her thumb poised over the top. If she replied now, he may think she had woken up just to read his message.

'What is it?' she tapped out and sent.

'Same place' came the reply. Then: "Shouldn't you be asleep by now?"

'Can't sleep' she wrote. 'Difficult and exhausting few months. Will try again now. Good night.'

She waited several minutes for the reply and when nothing came, she rolled onto her back, closed her eyes and felt the heavy pull of sleep drag her away.

CHAPTER FORTY-ONE

Now that her father was spending so many extra hours at work Shams was doing more and more of her clandestine work in his study. Below the window, diagonally across from his computer table, was an oak desk with two drawers on either side and when she first arrived in the morning, she would carefully move his belongings to one side.

The top of the table was green, it looked as though it was made of foam though Shams couldn't make out the exact material as it was covered in a rectangle of cut glass. In the left-hand corner was a silver lamp which she bent until it spread light over the surface. It was activated by a simple tap on the base.

Shams pulled a pile of papers out of her bag and levelled the bottom edge three times against the glass, then drew out a pencil and her small notebook from her dressing gown pocket, flicked it open and laid it parallel.

At the bottom of the first paper she wrote three numbers, circled them and next to them a list of characteristics. Against the first she wrote "vertical scar next the left eyebrow"; next to the second she wrote, "scar above lips from cleft palate" and finally, against the third, she wrote: "three brown moles underneath the right eye." Then she leaned across and scored three thin marks through the first three lines of her notes.

Shams held her hand up against the light and noticed the circles of her fingerprints were tinged with grey from the pencil. She rubbed her hands against her jeans. She felt proud that this new addition to the newspaper had been her idea. She had first pitched it to Xr two days ago. Every time she saw a distinguishing characteristic about someone, she would note it down, along with the file number of the image.

'How about we add a section to the paper where we list distinguishing characteristics we come across. We can ask readers to get in touch if they have family members who fit this description.'

After she typed out the message, she cocked her head to one side and considered the screen. Was it clear?

'Perhaps it will offer people some closure,' she added, then pressed send before she could change her mind.

It took Xr a whole day to get back to her.

'Great idea,' came the message eventually. She gathered the papers, took her notes out from where they were being stored in her top drawer and prepared to amend the rest of the newspapers.

That evening, after she had roamed the streets throwing the paper into people's gardens, she stopped at a small cafe close to home and ordered a falafel wrap with extra hummus. She had been craving the crunchy, fried exterior of the chickpea balls and the contrast the thin crust made with the soft hummus.

She ate one wrap, sat back on the narrow wooden bench and raised her arm in the air to summon the waiter. "One more," she said pointing to the empty paper wrap that was now screwed into a ball on the table.

She presumed from his age that this young man was the son of the owner of the restaurant and from his demeanour she guessed that spending his Wednesday evenings frying falafel was not his choice. She ground her teeth into the wrap and ate half of it before she felt the chickpeas beans start to inflate in her stomach. She looked down at the swirl of colours the mix of coriander, yogurt, tomatoes, tahini and red pickled turnips had made, then wrapped it in the rest of the paper.

As she was placing it inside her bag, Shams noticed one last piece of paper at the bottom. She looked up and over the glass counter at the young man who had served her the falafel, laid it down on the silver table and walked towards the door. “Goodbye,” she heard, but kept her head down and pulled the door firmly shut behind her.

Back at home Shams checked her phone. After her evening delivery sessions, she had become accustomed to seeing up to twenty messages before she went to bed and tonight she was tempted to leave them until the morning. But if she did that they would simply pile up and tomorrow would be impossible. She flopped down onto her bed and started to go through them one by one.

‘My son had an operation when he was young for a cleft palate, he has been missing for two months now, that photo might be of him,’ read one of the messages. ‘Cleft palate, Abdullah Aziz, call me,’ said another. There were four messages, all about a missing son, father, husband or friend with a cleft palate. Shams scrolled through them, she had no idea how to sort them all.

‘Too many people match the descriptions, I need to send these people photos,’ she wrote and sent to Xr.

‘Fine,’ he replied. ‘I’ll leave you something in Point Café with the next lot of usbs. Two hours.’

Two hours. If she left now, she would be there in forty-five minutes, perhaps she would catch him entering the toilet.

* * *

At the back of the café Shams didn't see anyone. Inside she unhooked the picture and found three usb keys but no telephone. As she inspected the space behind the frame, she realised it would have been impossible to put anything so large behind it.

Shams spun around the tiny cubicle and her eyes rested almost immediately on the toilet. It couldn't be in the bowl at the top, there was too much of a risk that it would fall inside the water. It must be behind. She reached out, grabbed a bundle of brown tape, and fought her way into the top of it to confirm it was a phone, then slipped it into her bag, unlocked the door and walked towards the door of the café.

"Your tea," the waiter shouted after her as she left, but Shams had had enough of tea. She just wanted to be at home.

On the back of the mobile Xr had placed a piece of white paper with her new telephone number and taped it into position. She entered all the contacts from her older phone that had written to her about this particular image and sent the message out to all twelve people. After three minutes one reply came through. "This is my husband. Thank you."

CHAPTER FORTY-TWO

"Hello," Shams looked up over the browning pages of her novel and tried to contain her disappointment when she saw Amin standing there.

"Hey." She placed the book down, pages spread out on the table, and pulled the mug over to her side of the table to make space for him.

"Can I join you?"

Shams nodded.

"I tried to call you. Several times in fact. But you didn't get back to me." Amin paused and looked around the room. "So, I guessed I would find you here."

"Coffee? Tea?" They both looked up, the waiter was hovering at the corner of the table.

"Coffee please."

"And for you? Anything else?"

Shams held up her mug. "Haven't finished with this one yet."

Shams looked at the table for several seconds. "So," she shrugged her shoulders. "What have you been up to?"

"Work. What about you?"

"Also working a lot."

"How are you?"

"I'm fine. You?"

Amin rolled his eyes. "Shams is everything ok? I haven't seen you for so long. You seem different… I mean… we are like strangers."

"I'm fine. I've been busy that's all."

Shams looked down as she felt her phone vibrate against her leg through the leather and tried to decipher between the folds of her bag if it was her new or her old phone which had lit up. Over the past few weeks Xr's messages were becoming more and more spaced out.

'Is everything fine?' she had sent a couple of times. 'Would you let me know if anything happened to you?'

She rarely received a reply and instead tried to busy herself with organising the information and updating the newspaper but she still found herself checking her phone up to twenty times a day.

"You can have this coffee on us," the waiter set the espresso cup down in front of Amin. "Because your wife is such a good customer."

"Is she?"

The waiter nodded and smiled. "Every day she's in here, reading her book, ordering coffee. She's our best customer."

"I see." He turned to Shams. "I thought you said you had been working?"

"I have. But often I work from here." That wasn't exactly a lie.

"That doesn't look much like work." Amin pointed at the book.

"Do I have to justify it to you?"

"No, but don't you think I deserve some kind of explanation? I never see you, never hear from you. Then I find out you spend every day in a café we used to come to as students. By yourself," he added.

"Amin, let's talk about this later." Shams breathed out heavily.

"Later – when, later? Shams we never see each other anymore."

Shams scratched her head and rifled through her bag. When she sat up straight Amin was still staring at her. She picked up her book, turned it over and smoothed the spine so that the pages stayed open by themselves.

"Please Amin, can we talk about this another time? I'm tired."

"Shams I know."

"Know what Amin?" Shams could no longer contain the annoyance in her voice. "What do you know?"

"I know that you've been seeing someone else."

"What?" Shams felt dread rise up in her stomach and she swallowed loudly, then laughed. "Amin don't be ridiculous. Who told you that?"

"I know. I know exactly what you've been doing." He leaned in closer towards her. "Shams let me ask you something."

She looked up.

"Do you really hate the way I eat?"

"What?" She leant back. She wasn't expecting that.

Shams flinched as the sound of his chair legs scraped against the floor and she watched as Amin turned and walked out of the café, pulling the door hard behind him. She spread her hands out on the table in front of her. Why had Rasha told him she didn't like the way he ate? That was really mean. Come to think of it, Rasha had been acting very strangely recently. She leaned back in her chair and recalled the phone conversation they had had after the protest. Had she told anyone else about the cameras she found in the studio? She didn't think so. The footage from those cameras was exactly how they had caught Yusuf.

Shams pulled out her phones and checked the screens. Nothing from Xr, two messages from Rasha. They could wait for another time. She stood and made the familiar journey to the toilets at the back and locked the door behind her. Several times over the last couple of weeks she had checked behind the picture but there was nothing there and neither was there anything sellotaped to the toilet.

Back at the table she produced her phone and hovered over Amin's name. Could she have been softer with him? She pulled at her bottom lip. As the screen lit up, she felt an overwhelming sense of relief followed by a nervous heartbeat. Finally. Six messages from Xr.

She looked up and around her to check no one was close by, then looked at the screen.

'Shams, we need to get the images out of the country. Things here are becoming more and more difficult, we don't have much time. We've had our run of good luck; it won't last forever. I can feel it. Where are you keeping them?'

'I upload them onto my father's computer and then write notes next to their number, including the distinguishing characteristics,' she replied immediately. 'Then I photograph each one and delete them from the laptop until the next batch arrive.'

'Your father's computer? Are you crazy? That's too dangerous. Have you taken photos of everything I sent you so far?'

'Yes.' She hit the send button. Yesterday she had counted 6,876 photographs stored on her phone.

'Make sure everything is deleted and put the laptop away,' he continued. 'Make sure the trash bin is completely empty. Don't use it again.'

In the whole time they had known each other Xr and Shams had never talked for this long.

'Can we speak on the phone?' It was worth a try.

'No.' Came the reply, followed by: 'Is there another computer at home you can use?'

Shams thought of the computer which sat relatively unused in the hallway of their flat.

'You must have a shared computer at home?'

'We have one, yes.'

'Right. Every Monday plug in the usb keys but don't copy any of the photographs onto the desktop. Use this email account and password: shams@shamsnet.com, photos_photos. Attach as many photos as you can to as many emails as you can and leave them in the drafts folder. Don't send them.'

'Next Monday, delete the emails with the attached photographs from the week before and do the same again until there are no more photographs to send. Understand?'

'Yes,' replied Shams. 'Are you sure we can't speak on the phone? I just have a couple of questions.'

She waited for ten minutes and when no reply came, she wrote: 'Who will pick up the pictures?' But she wasn't surprised when nothing came through.

Back at home Shams slid back her drawer and pulled out the usb keys. Each had a black number on the side from where she had marked them in terms of the order she received them in. She held them in her hands, weighing up how many photos she could possibly upload in one go, before taking just the first one and placing it on her bedside table.

She pulled out her father's computer and pulled the screen upwards so that the desktop presented itself to her. It was hard to see through all the documents but she was sure she had left nothing on there. She clicked on the trash bin and waited for it to open.

Amongst her father's discarded photographs and documents was a file labelled 8,971-14,409. Shams deleted it. What if he had seen it?

Outside the room Shams was relieved to find all the

lights off and she walked across to her father's study. She knocked on the door, a force of habit now. Since her father was never there anymore it was just something she did before entering.

"Come in." She was surprised to hear his voice. She turned around to leave but she could hear movement from inside. She looked up to see her father in the doorway.

"I came to return this," said Shams, proffering the computer with both hands in the darkened hallway. "I was trying to go through some of my notes from university."

"Notes from university? Now why would you be doing that?"

"Amin was asking something, I wanted to show him. It's complicated, anyway, I've finished now."

"Why didn't you ask me first?" Her father snatched it from her, he looked angry. "That's what the computer in the hallway is for. I bought that so you and Yusuf" Shams heard his throat catch, he bit his lip and took a step backwards. "So you would have a computer to use."

"I would have asked you first but I never see you anymore. You and Mum seem so. Preoccupied." Shams took a step forward and held out her arm. "I miss you. We never talk anymore."

"Of course we talk," he snorted. "You always exaggerate, take everything too far. I saw you last week at breakfast. In fact, all anybody in this flat does is talk, that's what got us into this mess in the first place." He reached out, slid the laptop out from underneath Shams' arm and shut the door.

Shams stood in the dim light of the hallway. So, that time she was with Rasha and her father was concerned was all an act. That she could deal with, she was used to that. What was bothering her was Xr. She was sure she had never told him her name, how had he found that out?

CHAPTER FORTY-THREE

Amin bent under the table and pulled the black notebook out of the front pocket of his bag, hooked the elastic band under his two fingers and pulled it towards him. It broke and the pages of the book fanned out in front of him. He moved towards it cautiously as though sudden movements might cause it to disappear. A list. 'Cons' read the title at the top of the page. He let his eyes scan the words and then slammed it shut.

Amin placed the palm of his left hand over his right wrist to steady himself. The base of his cup was rattling against the saucer. The blood had drained from his face and he was sure he must be pale. He placed both hands on each knee, lifted his legs up so his feet were raised off the floor, and felt his knuckles throb from the force with which they were pressed into his desk.

When he had regained control over his shaking body, he raised the steaming tea to his lips, sucking it in and enjoying the way it burnt his lips. The anxiety had left his body but it had left him with low blood sugar and he felt exhausted. He leaned back and closed his eyes, the silver teaspoon still between his thumb and forefingers.

Amin thought of Shams and her embroidered dresses.

They never looked fully clean, that was what really got to him. It was like she had left them on the floor overnight, worn them three days in a row and then put them on to meet him. The eyebrows were never quite symmetrical and some days she didn't even bother to wear make-up, the faint line of yesterday's eyeliner forming a semi-circle just above her lashes.

Amin recalled Shams' 21st birthday. He had arranged to take her to a tailor who would sew a new dress for her then onto a jeweller where she would pick out her favourite necklace. Amin had a thing for necklaces. That day Shams was actually wearing a silver locket, his favourite, but she was twenty minutes late to meet him and missed the appointment. Amin felt the rage bubble up in his stomach and he pressed his knuckles further into the table to calm himself.

Of course, it was Shams' carefree attitude that attracted him to her. The impulsiveness he wished he had but which terrified him at the same time. This hadn't stopped him trying to crush Shams into his routine, but she always squirmed out of it. How long would it take for her to understand what he wanted from her?

Amin stood up and retrieved his laptop from its usual hiding place at the bottom of his sock drawer. He called it a hiding place but really it was a safe space. The only other person who ventured this far was his mother, and she wouldn't even know how to open it, let alone log onto it.

His favourite time of the day was what they used to call when they were young: Lights Out, because it was the only time he had for himself to think. His sister spent too long in his room gossiping about work, her friends, and of course about Shams.

Amin heard the faint notification give two beeps and he knew a message was waiting for him. He stalled, feeling his heartbeat quicken and looked around the room for something to distract him. Often, when the messages came through, he would have a shower or finish a chapter of his book before he read them so that he could savour what had been written. Inevitably this meant that when he did get around to opening the messages and there was just one word he felt disappointed. The joy of hearing news was such a brief, joyful emotion yet the comedown from a lacklustre message resonated for hours.

'Hi.'

He rolled his eyes then typed a short reply with his thumb and hit the send button: 'Hi.' Then after thirty seconds. 'Are you there?'

Three long minutes passed. 'I'm here but I can't talk.' Amin exhaled, threw himself back on the bed then lifted himself up again: 'I miss you,' he wrote and hit enter before he could change his mind. There was no reply.

Amin leant back against the pillows, snapped the lid of his laptop shut with his heel and closed his eyes. Ungrateful bitch. After everything he had done for her, she was just using him. He would leave it a week before speaking to her again, that would really get to her.

He threw his blanket aside and reached for his jumper which was twisted into a heap on the floor. He snatched it and held it up by the shoulders, checking for creases. A few bits of fluff were on the back and he picked them off then slid it over his head, holding the neck with his outstretched fingers so it wouldn't mess up his hair. As he stood up, he heard a double beep from his phone. 'Sorry the connection is bad,' read the message. 'I miss you too.'

Well perhaps he had been a bit harsh, he reasoned, kneeling on the floor and tapping out another: 'When can I see you?'

'Soon,' came the reply.

"I don't have time to wait for anyone," Amin murmured

under his breath and scrolled through his list of contacts. 'How's things?' he sent to three other people before falling on Shams' name.

"What are you doing?" He shut the computer and slid it under the bed with his toe. Reem was standing in the doorway in a nightdress at least two sizes too small. From his position he could see where the sleeves cut into the excess skin around her biceps.

Her chunky silhouette against the light from the hallway cut an awkward figure. One shoulder was higher than the other and her right knee was bent which gave the impression she was constantly on the verge of keeling over. Throughout their childhood Amin had often felt the need to stand close to her in case she fell and landed on her nose.

Amin tried to calculate whether she had seen him hide his computer. The narrow bed blocked her line of sight to a certain extent, but she may have been able to see through the gaps between the boxes he used to store his personal belongings. He made a mental note to change the password when she had gone.

"Exercising," he said, standing up to face her and drawing in a few deep breaths.

"You? *Exercising*?" Reem jerked her neck backwards and pulled her eyebrows down.

"I can't sleep," she sighed, venturing closer to the bed and perching on the corner.

Her hair was still pinned up around her ears which were red where the tips had been pressing into the pillow. The friction of the bedclothes had made the wisps around her hairline stand on end as though she had had an electric shock.

From the pocket of her robe Reem produced a bundle of napkins which she laid out between them and pulled at the corners until a star shape spread out before her. In the centre were six cookies and she placed one between her teeth. Amin heard the snap as it broke and looked away as he saw the mixture of crumbs and saliva being forced through the gap.

She still had her mouth full when she started talking: "How's Shams?" She carried on chewing, and with her thumb and forefinger wiped the corners of her mouth then sucked the remaining crumbs off them. "I haven't seen her for ages," she said without looking up.

"Shams is fine, Reem." He sat opposite her and crossed his legs. "Why?"

"Just wondering."

CHAPTER FORTY-FOUR

Abdullah knew he wasn't supposed to be in here and that if he got caught, he would probably be sacked on the spot and in fact a lot worse. But he had overheard his colleagues talking last night about a room where all the files were stored. If he could just have ten minutes to himself in here, he could find what he was looking for.

The boxes were listed alphabetically, and he held out his finger and ran it across the row stacked on the left-hand side of the room, then walked two aisles down and stood in front of the section marked R. There were so many he panicked and couldn't see anything. He closed his eyes for a few minutes then opened them and focused. There it was, right in front of him.

He pulled it off the shelf and then stumbled backwards, he hadn't expected it to be so heavy. It made a dull thumping noise as it hit the floor and he stood as still as possible to see if anyone would enter the room, then bent down and opened the lid.

The first item he came across was a pile of the newspapers like the one Ali Miro had showed him that day in the car. They had been stapled in the top right-hand corner and were protected by a plastic sleeve. There was a pile of photographs that had been printed off, a picture of himself, Shaimaa and the kids standing together then one of Yusuf with that girl he saw outside the studio.

In the same pile was a business card, though from what he could make out there was nothing written on it, just the outline of what looked like a cafe with the picture of a coffee cup in bright red. He flicked it over. In the bottom right hand corner Neon Cafe had been printed in bold typeface along with the address and phone number. On the left someone had scribbled in biro: meeting point, Al-Thawra.

Abdullah memorised the address then returned it to the box. He was about to put the lid on, haul it back onto the shelf, when he saw a phone hidden underneath the papers. That was odd. Maybe it was a mistake and it wasn't meant to be there. He turned it on, the battery was glowing red.

He tried the messages, there was a list longer than the screen, all to the same number. It looked familiar; he opened the first one. It was an address, sounded like a hotel. "Meet me here on Friday at 7pm." He closed it and looked at the next one. "It was nice to see you." He scrolled down, so he was almost at the bottom of the list. "Shaimaa if you don't come, I will tell everyone."

He felt his heart rate rise and the blood pulsate in his head. He pressed on the photo icon, there was a single video there. He pressed play immediately. The footage was blurred around the edge from where it had been zoomed in, but it was her. It was definitely her standing there on the corner. He pressed pause, went back again. Had she taken off her glasses? Yes, he watched her put them back in the box then walk towards the building.

There were several minutes where he couldn't work out what he was looking at then the video opened out, there was light again, and he was staring at a group of women.

There she was, in the right-hand corner of the group. He used his two fingers to enlarge the image. She was fixing the sewing machine, feeding thread through a tiny hole. She still wasn't wearing her glasses.

The screen went blank and he threw it into the box, replaced the lid and slid it back onto the shelf. He walked to the door and placed his ear against it. He couldn't hear anything, better to take his chance and run for it. He opened the door and held it with his foot so that it wouldn't slam.

"Abdullah."

He spun around and looked at the tall man standing in front of him with his arm outstretched. "I'm Sharif."

"How do you know my name?"

"You signed in at the door. May I ask what you are doing here in this building?"

"I was called to a meeting. But it got cancelled."

"Cancelled?"

"Yes."

"Why did such an important meeting get cancelled?"

"I didn't say it was important."

"No but your very presence here in this building suggests it's important."

"One of the big bosses was sick."

"So you got all the way here to be told that one of the big bosses was sick?"

"Yes."

"I see."

Sharif cleared his throat.

"May I ask his name?"

"Whose name?"

"The big boss. Who cancelled at such short notice."

"Can't remember. Jamal I think."

"Jamal. I see."

"It was great to meet you." Abdullah held one hand in the air, he was already at the end of the corridor.

Outside on the street the noise of the traffic blurred around his head. He stepped out onto the road and then jumped back as a car swerved around him. A taxi pulled up alongside him, asked him where he was going, but he wanted to walk home. He wanted to think.

When he reached the end of his road he circled around the back and sat on the small wall outside. There must be a rational explanation, she must have been wearing contact lenses. Or perhaps she was starting to feel better.

He pushed open the front door, he could see her silhouette from the end of the hallway. She was bent over the sink, wearing a long nightgown. She turned as she heard the sound of the door and walked down the corridor, her arms outstretched.

"I missed you." He could see she was wearing her glasses.

"How are you feeling?"

"I'm ok."

"I mean your eyes." He waved a finger between them.

"My eyes?"

She turned and headed back towards the kitchen. "They are the same as always. I'm struggling."

"If you take them off what happens?"

"Take them off? Abdullah you know I can't do that."

"Try it."

He was getting aggressive, he could see in her face she was scared.

"No."

He reached out and pulled at them by the bridge where the two lenses connected. They became tangled in her hair and she reached up her hands to pull them back. He heard the plastic snap.

"I know you don't need to wear them. I know you've been

lying." His voice was raised, he was shouting. "Are you even ill? Do you know what I had to do to get that medicine? Why did you do it?"

She was crying now, the glasses on the table between them.

"I didn't mean to hurt you. It started with a small white lie and then escalated."

"Why?" His voice was loud now, out of control. He grabbed her by the arm and pulled her towards him. His teeth were clenched. "I asked you why you did it."

"Abdullah you're hurting my arm, let me go."

"Tell me why or I'll break it."

"I was enjoying the attention. I mean the attention you've given me since all this started. It's like I had my husband back. It's like we fell in love again. You have to admit, things have started to get better since I told you I had diabetes."

He loosened his grip. "I thought you were dying. I thought you were never going to see again."

"Well so did I. In the beginning at least. That's what the doctor thought also, he told me that it was ninety per cent certain that that's what it was."

"So what happened?"

"When the blood tests came back there was no sign of diabetes. They didn't know what it was, they thought it was all in my head."

"It was all in your head."

Abdullah pulled a chair out and put his head in his hands, rolling his eyes in circular motions. "And what happened about the school?"

"Well the school didn't want me anymore. They told me I was too old and out of touch with modern teaching methods. They forced me to take redundancy and hired someone far younger. I was too ashamed to tell you."

"Too ashamed? I could have done something about it."

"Exactly. That's why I didn't want to tell you. Because you think you can solve everything through your contacts and where you work. And I wanted to solve this by myself."

"I hardly call lying about a life-threatening illness, solving something. Is there anything else you want to tell me?"

"I had no choice. I guess if you saw the video then you've also seen the text messages."

Abdullah stood, turned around and walked out of the kitchen.

CHAPTER FORTY-FIVE

Xr wasn't usually one to give in to fear, but he had to admit that when his telephone had beeped this morning – his day off – asking him to attend an emergency meeting at the office he had walked over to the drawers in which the hard drives were stashed, pulled out a section of his skirting board and sellotaped them behind it.

In the cupboard just above, he took out a tranquilliser and put it on the end of his tongue before bending down and letting the gush of cold water from the tap wash it down.

Inside the morgue the corridor felt cooler. Xr was tempted to walk back to his locker and retrieve his hoodie but in the end, he decided it wasn't formal enough for a meeting. He stopped at the hatch in the wall and was disappointed to find the space behind it still in darkness.

Xr looked down at his fingers and saw that the tranquilliser had done its job. They looked steady, even if on the inside he felt his organs were melting. He thrust them deep inside his pockets and craned his neck around the side of the hatch to see if Ahmed's coat was hanging on its hook.

"Amin." He turned to see the pathologist with his brown teeth bared. They had known each other for seven years now, he wasn't aware that he knew his real name.

"We're all waiting for you in the main office." Amin nodded stiffly and followed him up the corridor, the smell of rust, rot and sweat encasing the outline of his body. Every so often, when he would turn to check if Amin was there, the smell would waft in his direction. Amin reached out to the wall to guide him.

When they were no more than one hundred paces from the office the pathologist turned around and faced Amin, pulling him by his overalls into the shadows.

"The big boss is here, head of the centre" he snarled, when he was sure no one was behind him. Amin was surprised to hear his voice soften. "I need you to back me up." Amin was puzzled and straightened his face to hide it. His eyes flicked to the floor and then up again when he felt the pathologist squeeze his elbow. "Can I count on you?"

"Yes."

Inside the office someone had laid out a white tablecloth on Amin's desk and put a silver pot of coffee, a tea pot, a tray of sugar cubes and a plate of baklava. Amin could see the liquid sugar glistening and he looked away. Such an unhealthy food to eat, and such an unhygienic place to leave it given the proximity of the dead bodies.

"Have a baklava, my wife made them." The pathologist waved the tray under Amin's nose. "Thank you." Amin scanned the plate for the smallest one then popped it in his mouth. It was dry and the rose water was overpowering. He felt the sugary inside squeeze into his mouth and he thought of pus leaking out of the wounds of the dead bodies next door in the morgue.

Amin couldn't believe this man had a wife. Who would feel comfortable sleeping next to him at night and washing his underwear? It was almost impossible to believe.

"Amin," he heard the level voice of the boss behind him and he struggled to swallow the rest of the baklava but the flakes of pastry got caught in his throat. He coughed, thumped his chest with his fist and took a slug of water. He turned and extended his hand.

"Abdullah. It's good to see you." He pulled a chair back. "Please" he said, moving towards the coffee pot. "Let me get you a drink."

"Do you have tea?" asked Abdullah. "I don't like too much caffeine, it clouds the mind." He tapped his temple with a wrinkled finger. "I have a lot to do today."

"Of course." Amin secured his fingers around the second pot then placed the cup onto the saucer. The noise rattled around the empty room.

It was always disconcerting to see Abdullah out of his studio overalls and in a smart suit. There was something about his small frame that never quite filled out the shirt and trousers in the way it should and this took away from the authority such an outfit was supposed to exude.

As they sat down at the table all three of them pulled their chairs towards the table at the same time and the sight of them going up and down together made Amin want to giggle like a schoolboy. He bit his bottom lip to stop the corners of his mouth turning upwards.

"How have you been Amin?

"Very well thank you. Yourself?"

They looked across as the pathologist cleared his throat. "Abdullah, I hope you don't mind me interrupting," he began, "but we have a lot to get through and Amin still has work to do."

"Of course," said Abdullah. "Tell me, why am I here."

"There is… was… a problem in the office." The pathologist struggled to find the right tone. Amin had never seen him look nervous before. "And I felt it only right to make you aware of it."

He popped a baklava in his mouth. They sat in silence as he finished it.

"Sorry. Couldn't resist. Anyway, where was I? Oh yes. Some… items have gone missing. I mean items have been going missing on a regular basis."

Amin felt his heart expand in his chest. His head was racing and his hands felt clammy. He looked down at his shoes and counted the lace holes. One, two, three, four, five on one side so if he multiplied that by four that was twenty lace holes. On the row furthest to the right something dark was caught around the plastic coating and he made a note to remove it when the meeting was over.

He wanted to stand up, run down the thin, grey corridors and out of the front entrance but he knew he would never make it. They would catch him at the door and even if they missed him, he would still have to get past the soldiers guarding the checkpoint.

"I discovered it two months ago, quite by accident," the pathologist was warming up now. "I was in the kitchen making a hot drink and I noticed that a whole packet of coffee was missing."

Amin looked up. Coffee?

"I knew it was there the day before because my brother-in-law gave it to me as a gift. I brought it into work because I cannot stand the stuff they provide here. It's like drinking dirty dishwater." He paused to take a sip of his drink and Amin looked at his cracked, pink lips. He had never heard him speak so much before.

"This happened a couple of times, not just with coffee, but with everything. Milk, sugar" he leaned closer towards Abdullah. "My wife's baklava." Amin didn't believe anyone would steal his wife's baklava. "I thought I was going mad at first but then a camera went missing and some of the valuables we had taken off the dead bodies. Rings, necklaces, a watch here and there."

Amin and Abdullah watched as the pathologist lay his

cheek on the side of the table so that he could bend down and pluck a photograph out of his battered leather bag. He laid it out on the table before them, letting the corner slap down for effect. Amin stared at the image.

"Ahmed," he said, shaking his head. "Of all people."

Amin looked across at Abdullah who was nodding his head. He felt tears sting his eyes, he had undoubtedly been sacked. How would he support his family now? Amin cursed himself for not finding out his address. He would search for it in the office later, then pay him a visit and offer to help.

"You see Abdullah… I… we… wanted to let you know that this happened, but that we resolved it," he looked across at Amin, who nodded. "We resolved it," Amin repeated mechanically.

"Mustafa you really didn't need to bring me all the way here just to tell me that." Abdullah was impatient. He drained the last of his tea and waved away the plate of baklava that was being wafted under his nose.

"If you have a problem, just deal with it and move on." His voice was rising and he brought his cup down onto the saucer so hard Amin thought it would shatter into tiny pieces. "The less involvement from higher up, the smoother operations run. Just solve the problem and move on. Everybody is busy."

"Of course," said the pathologist, visibly annoyed at being reprimanded in public.

"Goodbye gentlemen," said Abdullah, his chair letting out a low grind as he stood up. As his footsteps faded the pathologist hissed at Amin: "Get your camera and get moving, there is work to be done. I want a photograph of whatever is in there."

Amin stood, straightened out his trousers and wiped the stray pieces of pastry that were caught in the creases of his overalls. He walked back to the hatch in the wall, let himself in the side door and helped himself to a camera. He opened the door of the morgue and stepped inside, grateful to be away from the heat of that conversation. As the light flickered into action, he was surprised to see one single body in the centre of the room, wrapped in plastic sheeting.

He moved closer and peeled back the corner of the covering. He turned his face away, dropped to his knees and rested his head on the cool white tiles feeling his mind drift in and out of consciousness. It was Ahmed.

CHAPTER FORTY-SIX

There was something ceremonious about the way Amin stared back at his reflection in the circular mirror above the sink, brought the silver razor up to his cheek, stretched the skin and created the sharp line which mirrored his jawline. Usually he would go to the barber, the result came out neater, but today he was in a hurry and anyway, he didn't like the way they burnt the ends of the hair, there was something inconspicuously dangerous about the whole process.

Amin looked straight ahead to admire his handiwork. When they first met, Shams had run her fingers down the bone that formed the side of his face and whispered in his ear, "you have such a beautiful face structure," her breath tingling his ear. He couldn't remember the last time she had done that.

Amin tapped the razor three times on the side of the sink, then ran it under the tap to release the remaining stray hairs. He dried it on the towel, opened the cupboard and placed it beside the stack of soap his mother had collected over the past year and let the handle rest on a plastic stick of deodorant.

Inside his bedroom Amin pulled open his underwear drawer, reached his hand right to the back and pulled out a ball of blue and white socks he had wrapped tightly together. Inside was a wad of notes and the gold watch his father had given him. He kissed the face of it then slipped both inside a travel belt, unbuttoned his jeans and clipped it around his waist. With the denim pulled back over it, he checked his profile in the mirror but there were no obvious bulges.

"Amiiiiin." Reem's voice was so high-pitched Amin had to put his finger in his ear and wiggle it around to release the whirring sensation. She must have been waiting for him. "Amin are you coming down now?"

Reem had squeezed herself into a pink and white dress, across the hips the material had stretched until it was almost transparent and when she walked, he could see the flicks of her black velour heels which were far too high.

Amin rubbed his forehead. Reem's birthday. He had completely forgotten.

"I just need to pop out quickly," he offered, trying to keep his voice light. "I'll be back soon."

"Oh Amin" Reem brought the corner of her lips down, fixed her hands on her hips and bent her right knee so she was slanted in the air. "Everybody's waiting," she leaned towards her brother and lowered her voice. "Sofia is about to start playing."

Sofia was the worst guitar player Amin had ever had the misfortune to listen to, she could neither hit the right notes, nor could she keep a tune together. As much as he could, Amin tried to avoid her because she was overly flirtatious and trapped him for hours on end in dull conversations that he could never wriggle out of.

"Look Reem" started Amin, then stopped abruptly. "I'm going to get you a surprise, I can't explain it now otherwise it will be ruined."

At the word surprise Reem's face flushed and her eyes darted from side to side. "Oh, Amin you must tell me what it is… ok no don't… oh Amin that's so thoughtful of you."

Amin put his hand on her shoulder. "Back soon," he called as he slipped behind the front door.

Outside the sun was disappearing and Amin found the shadows it left behind disconcerting. He checked his phone for the twentieth time, an attempt to look natural.

"Amin."

That was quicker than he had expected. The voice behind him was low and the phlegm rippled across it from too many cigarettes. He turned and was surprised by how normal he looked. His beard was also closely shaved and his thick black hair formed waves over the top of his head.

"Do you have the money?" He looked backwards over his shoulder. Amin reached into his jeans and pulled out half of the cash inside.

"That's not enough." His voice was high now and Amin could see that he was agitated. "Don't waste my time. If you don't have the money, I can't take you." He grabbed Amin's t-shirt and pulled him towards his chest, spit flying out from between his yellow teeth.

"Ok, ok," Amin raised his hands and tried to calm the man but he was twisting his t-shirt with his fist, the material ripping at the neck. Amin looked around him, a few people were starting to look from the other side of the street.

"Here's the rest of it." He pulled it out of the belt and shoved it into the man's chest. He released Amin and deflated like a balloon.

He crumpled the pile of notes into his pocket. "I'll see you tomorrow. 9am."

"Can we make it 10am?"

"9.30. Otherwise I go without you."

Amin nodded, turned away and ran his fingers across the outline of his watch. At least he hadn't had to give that away.

* * *

The next morning, as he lowered his head into the car, Amin leaned in between the two front seats and instructed the driver to take the road up to the left of the citadel, then directed him using his hand through the adjacent streets until they drew up next to an unassuming apartment block on the corner.

The driver had been smoking, probably for years, in this car. Amin suspected he had been doing so with the windows shut because the smoke had seeped its way into the soft seats. A cloud of it reached his nostrils as he leaned across, opened the door, and swivelled and brought his face level with the driver.

"Wait for me here," he breathed through the front window, then turned and took the short path which led to the front of the building. He stopped halfway to kick at some weeds which were protruding from the cracks of the concrete, then stood and pushed the buzzer and asked to be admitted inside.

On the first floor of the dental clinic Amin politely refused Aida's pleas to keep him in the waiting room. Rasha was sitting with her back to him, looking out of the window, just as she had the first day he came to visit her. The light was bringing out red streaks in her dark hair. He liked the way it contrasted with the light blue of her scrubs.

"Rasha," he held out his hand to steady her as she jumped off her seat at the sound of his voice. A flash of red crossed her cheeks. As she stood, he could see she was eating the same breakfast of flat bread and boiled eggs that she had the last time he was here. Some butter had smudged itself onto her chin and the neon examination light was reflecting off it.

The other day in the coffee shop he had been surprised when Rasha had run away so quickly when he mentioned

Shams. Of course, he had always suspected that Rasha had deeper feelings for him than just the best friend of his fiancée, but he had thought that over time this would have faded, or she would have met someone else. The day she dropped that spoon in the university canteen and asked for help carrying her tray, it had been too forced, there had been none of the wonder that comes with the recognition that fate has played its hand.

That day he was not looking for love, but it was an almost immediate feeling with Shams. His feelings for her consumed all of his thoughts and directed his actions every day. Amin felt frustrated by the fact that he was no longer in control and that his life was suddenly dependent on what somebody else was doing and feeling. How can extreme happiness and sadness be at the mercy of another person? At the beginning he had seen this as a wonderful thing but over time this helplessness had converted itself into frustration at the distance that grew between him and Shams and her inability to be what he wanted her to be.

Rasha was sitting again, her hands clasped together and resting on her lap. He moved closer to her, unsure of how she would take the news. "I'm leaving." He sounded arrogant – he hadn't meant to. He stood awkwardly next to the lamp and waited for her reply.

Rasha used her feet to swivel the chair around, bring her breakfast to the front of her and place it on her lap. "I see." She nodded without making eye contact, then continued eating.

"I will go first and Shams will join me later. There is a car outside." He gestured to the door. "We can go together."

"Go where?" shrugged Rasha, returning the plate to the table behind her and letting it fall noisily on the surface. She wiped her mouth with a napkin, scrunched it, then threw it on top. "I have work to do."

"Rasha we have a chance to leave now, let's go," Amin's voice was rising and he turned around and pushed the door shut. "Get your things."

"No. I want to stay here. I have a responsibility towards my patients, who will look after them if I leave now? Amin, what will I do with you and Shams away from here? My life is here."

"You don't have a life here." He corrected himself. "No one has a life here. It's not possible to have a life here, not anymore."

"Yusuf is gone, Sara is dead, you and Shams are leaving," sniffed Rasha. "If I go also there will be no one here to contribute to the paper, no one here to document the stories. Somebody has to stay behind. My family is here, I have no need," she paused; "or desire to leave."

"The paper is over, Rasha." Amin was pacing the room now. "The paper is over, everything is over. We tried our best, now we have to see what we can do from the outside. Shams has all the material with her, we'll take it with us and distribute it once we're out. Rasha there isn't much time, let's go."

"No." Her voice had levelled now but there were cracks in the words as they came out. "I don't want to. I want to stay here in this room, with my patients, listening to them, treating them and doing what I love. I want to continue documenting their stories and continue delivering them to the café, it's what I want – it's what I need – to do."

"Rasha you're crazy." He reached out and took Rasha's elbow. "All that, it's over. They know who I am, they know that Shams is involved, they killed Maryam to get to you. If you continue, they will kill you also. Move, let's go. We're leaving now."

"No Amin, I'm staying here." Rasha pulled her elbow out of his hand and moved her body in a circular direction towards the window so that he couldn't see the tears form in her eyes. When she turned back around, Amin was gone.

CHAPTER FORTY-SEVEN

Amin was late, he must be upset with her. Shams sat back in her seat and sighed. For all his faults she still cared for Amin. She hoped there was a time in the future they could be friends.

Shams' phone vibrated and she lifted the screen into her vision. Reem. She placed it face down on the table. The last person she needed to speak to right now was Reem.

It rang again and then a third time.

"Where's Amin?" came the tearful bleat on the other end of the phone. Even by Reem's standards Shams was taken aback by how wrecked her voice sounded. She heard crying – sobbing – on the other end of the phone.

"Reem, try to calm down." Shams could feel herself getting flustered. "I can't understand what you're saying. Tell me what happened."

"He was supposed to… last night it was my birthday, I was having a party with some friends and Amin was supposed to come. I mean he was at home and I thought he was preparing himself and then he just took off when everyone arrived." She took a huge gulp of air. "He said he was going to get me a surprise… a present for my birthday but he never came back."

Shams leaned back into her chair and listened as the sobs grew louder on the other end of the phone. Why hadn't she been invited to the party? Amin hadn't even mentioned it.

"Are you listening?" Reem drew the mucus up through her nose and swallowed it.

"Of course. Amin never came back."

"Yes, I saw him at home, he was going out to get my present but he never came back."

"What time was that?"

"Around 7pm."

"I'm sure there's a perfectly rational explanation. He probably just bumped into a friend and forgot about the party." Shams bit her lip. Amin was never late for anything and he would never have missed his sister's party. Reem would never let him forget it.

"Are you there?" Reem's voice was getting more and more high pitched, she was hysterical. Shams was starting to get irritated.

"Look." Shams tried to keep her tone authoritative. "I need to have a think. There must be an explanation, I'll call you back… are you at home all day?"

"Yes" snuffled Reem. There was a pause. "I might go and get my eyebrows done later."

"Keep your phone next to you where you can hear it." Shams hung up and pressed her mobile into her bottom lip. She withdrew it when she felt it vibrate again and saw a message from Amin. She slid the green bar across the screen.

'Shams. I had to leave. Try to join me if you can. I will wait for you on the border with Turkey. Someone will come for you and then I will tell you everything. Don't tell anyone – not even your family – where I am or about this message. You have to trust me and come. I love you. p.s. delete this message as soon as you've read it.'

"What the hell" Shams slammed her phone down on the table. First Amin disappears, then a phone call from Reem, and now this message. What on earth was Amin doing leaving without telling her first.

"Shams." She was startled to see her father towering over her. He was holding his baseball cap in his right hand, the thumb clamped around the base.

"Have you seen Amin?"

"Amin?" she replied.

"Yes." She could hear anger in his voice. "Amin."

"He was supposed to meet me here but he obviously got delayed." Shams looked down and saw that the message was still exposed on her screen. She tried to hold her father's gaze.

"He's not answering his phone," she added, shrugging to fill the silence. She picked up her mobile as if to emphasise the point and pressed the button on the side. The screen blackened.

"Let's go out for lunch." He was holding a silver pen in his right hand and was obsessively clicking the catch. She could see that his nails had grown too long and curled as they went up over the fingertips.

Abdullah placed his hand on the small of her back and steered her through the uneven paths of the souq. She tripped at one point and felt her toe reach right to the end of her shoe. She kicked at the floor with her heel. She felt the temporary release of her father's grip but as she straightened herself up again, she felt the strong clamp of his bony fingers on either side of her spine.

"Where are we going?" she turned, trying to naturally lose the connection between them.

"You'll see soon enough."

They walked for quite some time in that pose, Shams walking in front trying not to fall, her father behind with his hand outstretched.

They turned left and she looked up. The Neon Cafe. Shams swallowed but there was no saliva in her throat and she could feel the swell of a cough build up in her chest. Both hands came up to her mouth and her chest convulsed. She swallowed the phlegm that eventually landed on her tongue.

"I thought we could eat here, it came highly recommended from a friend. Apparently the shawarma is excellent." Abdullah peered through the boards that were covering the entrance. Shams heard the crunch of broken glass. "The only problem is it appears to have been closed down."

"Have you heard of this place?" Abdullah turned away from the cafe and faced her, pausing for several seconds. "You know where we are, don't you Shams?"

"No. You said we were going out for lunch. Why have you brought me to a rundown café? I'm hungry and there's nothing here. Let's go."

She felt her body jerk back as her father caught the neck of her dress and pulled it. Shams had to put her hands out to steady herself on the wall. She felt the broken stone dig into the palms of her hands. She straightened herself up and pulled at the hem of her dress where it had ridden up.

Shams tipped her head to one side. Her father's trousers were ironed into a point that started at the thighs, went up and over his knees, and ended somewhere just before his ankle. Shams noticed that the wrinkles around his mouth had become deeper, as though someone had scored them with a knife.

Shams recalled a story Rasha had told her when they first met. It was the admission that sealed the friendship in the way that secrets shared for the first time do between friends. Her mother and father had been married in what appeared to the rest of the family relative harmony for thirty years, until their last year of marriage when Rasha's father started beating her mother. You never really know someone, Rasha had told her that day in the college cafeteria and Shams had agreed.

"Go inside and sit down." Abdullah was shouting.

"Inside?" Shams gestured at the boards and broken glass. "How?"

Abdullah reached across, covered his wrist with his sleeve and pushed away what was left of the window. "Go."

"Where is Amin?"

"I'm telling you, I don't know. I mean, I know he's missing because his sister called me to tell me, but I don't know where he is."

"Why do you want to know?" She sat back on her hands. Her head was throbbing and her mouth felt so dry. "I need water." She looked up at her father.

"Why do I want to know… why do I want to know?"

Shams looked at the ground.

"Amin and I have known each other for longer than you might think."

Shams felt a story coming. A story which she hadn't asked for. A story that would no doubt be long, winding, and one which she would have no control over where it began and ended. She crossed her legs and straightened her spine.

"Amin is a military deserter and there is a warrant out for his arrest."

"A deserter? What are you talking about?"

"You see Amin and I work together." Her father was pacing now. "Not in the studio, not in some dull office job." He paused to look at her and inhaled deeply. "We work for branch 248."

"Branch 248?" Shams looked up at her father to check his expression.

"It's true Shams. Both of us. In fact, there are many of us that do so secretly without telling anyone."

"Why?"

Her father sighed and began to circle the room again. "It's not because we have to. It's because we choose to. It means we can keep an eye on things that might otherwise escape our attention."

"You mean spy on people?"

"In a way, yes."

"So it was you who gave up Yusuf."

Shams felt a rush of blood rise to her head. She chewed some excess skin that was protruding from the side of her nail and felt it come away in her mouth. She rolled her tongue and spat it out.

"It doesn't make sense, with what happened in the studio that day. When they came for him. Why didn't you stop them? Why haven't you been able to get him back?"

"Shams, if I had tried to stop them, they would have killed me too and probably you and your mother also. But it's more than that, I was warned they were coming and I agreed." He stopped and stood in front of Shams.

"What Yusuf was doing was contrary to the good of this country. Yes, he's my son but he had to be stopped. He was using my studio to film." He spun around and raised his voice. "My studio. Do you know how hard I've worked to build that business up? You both disrespected me."

He lit a cigarette and walked over to the window. "I found the cameras in the books on the windowsill and wrote them a letter informing them of his activities. It was a good job I did, they had just found out themselves that he had been filming from there, can you imagine what would have happened to me – to us – if they thought I was trying to cover it up? I agreed with them on a time and a place when we would be there together."

"You agreed." Shams was screaming now. "You agreed to your own son being taken away?"

"Shams," said her father, interlocking his hands behind his back and circling her. "You can't get emotional over these things. This is politics, it's black and white and there is nothing in between. What is best for this country comes above all family ties and if someone doesn't agree with that it's my role – or the role of any respectable head of the family – to educate them until they do understand."

"You have to see it like this" he continued. "Yusuf is now in a better place, a place where over time he will come to realise the mistakes he made and he will be able to repent for those mistakes. Only then can we see the best of the country shine through."

"If you work for them, why did they beat you so badly?"

Her father had been in hospital for three days, his rib was shattered and his nose broken. She and her mother had cooked his favourite dishes and brought it to the hospital twice a day. She should have spat in them.

"Shams... Shams…" his voice had taken on the tone of a father explaining to a schoolgirl why she had to go to school every day and could not just stay at home and watch television. "It had to look genuine."

"Is he still alive?"

"Shams." She wanted him to stop saying her name. "It doesn't matter anymore. What matters is that Yusuf is in a better place."

"Is he still alive?"

Her father paused. "Honestly. I don't know."

"Why didn't they take me also?"

"Because that was the deal I struck. I managed to convince them that you were not really involved. I mean, I knew you were because I saw you hiding in the bathroom that day I went to Yusuf's room but I didn't tell them that."

"Why did you go into Yusuf's room that day?"

"Evidence. I knew it must be somewhere."

"Did you find the articles?"

"No. Not by myself." Abdullah took a pull on his cigarette. "But the one I found in your pocket the next morning was enough."

Shams felt a weight drop inside her, somewhere around her rib cage. She stood up, wiped the dust off the back of her dress and stepped towards the door.

"Shams." She stopped and turned. "I need to know where Amin is."

"I don't know. He didn't tell me anything."

"You've always been a terrible liar. Abdullah reached out and snatched her handbag with such force Shams cried out and cupped her shoulder. He plucked the phone out of her bag and held it up in front of her. "I saw in the cafe that he had texted you. It shouldn't take me long to get into this and find out."

Shams turned, squeezed herself calmly through the gap in the wood. Let him find Amin, he deserved it. "1960" she shouted her passcode into the air, embarrassed that it was her father's date of birth.

CHAPTER FORTY-EIGHT

Shams felt her knees begin to ache and she shifted her weight to try and relieve the pressure on the bottom of her spine. From her position across the street she had a clear vision of her flat from in-between two rubbish bins she had wheeled to obscure the end of the alleyway, but the smell emanating from the plastic was overpowering. Shams looked over her shoulder. There was a patch of grass which would be more comfortable but she judged that moving backwards would risk her missing vital activity.

Eventually the front door creaked open and she saw her mother and father turn to pull the door behind them. She checked her phone. 4.30am. She counted to 50, rose from the floor and let herself into the family home. She felt like an intruder. These walls – or what was inside them – had been her comfort and resting place for so many years yet it had only taken thirty minutes with her father for that to come shattering down. The air felt cooler and the shadows in the corners were darker.

Shams refrained from turning on the lights, just in case anyone was watching. She went into her bedroom and looked around the room. What could she take with her? It was impossible to pack the last few decades of her life into a small rucksack. She opened the top drawer of her bedside table and felt a surge of relief when she saw her old Nokia sitting there, partially covered by tissues and old batteries.

She knelt down to take her bag from under the bed and began to put her clothes inside, sandwiching the phone in the middle of them. She pulled out the bottom drawer of her bedside table and placed it squarely on the carpet then reached for the usb keys she had taken from Point Cafe. She nestled these in between a pair of jeans.

Shams moved towards her parents' bedroom. She had never noticed how bare it was inside, as if they considered it an afterthought compared to the lavish decorations that adorned the rest of the flat.

Like Yusuf's room the bed was completely neat, the corners of the blanket pulled taut across the mattress. Shams walked towards the wardrobe, pulling the sleeve of her cardigan over her hand. She opened the drawers on her father's side and found the leather envelope with the takings from the studio. One, two, three, four notes Shams peeled off the pile, folded them and tucked them into her bag. She heard the thud of the pouch as it hit the bottom of the drawer and she pushed it shut with her knee.

Down the hall Shams opened the door of Yusuf's room, leaned against the door frame and sucked the air in through her nostrils. Smell was something we took for granted when confronted with it every day. How many times had Yusuf come down for lunch bathed in cheap oud he had bought from the market, dotted behind his temples, then rubbed down the sleeves of his shirt. One of their cousins, who they later found out had been two months pregnant at the time, had once shouted at him, kicking and screaming, until he went into the bathroom and scrubbed it off.

What would Shams give to stand beside her brother again and smell his cheap aftershave one more time? Would she give her own life? Shams cocked her head to the side and contemplated that question. Here in the empty flat, there was no one to hear her thoughts. She felt the floor creak beneath her feet.

Shams stood at the entrance to Yusuf's door and took in everything within it. It seemed like years since she had frantically searched his room and found the papers inside his mattress. Perhaps she just didn't look hard enough or find everything. She hesitated in the doorway for several seconds, then crossed the threshold.

As she took up her position in the centre of the room, Shams felt something hard beneath the ball of her foot. She lifted her leg backwards and looked over her shoulder so she could see what was stuck to it. Pieces from Yusuf's solar system had fallen from the ceiling and were now scattered around the floor. She gathered them together then stood on the chair next to his desk and pushed them into the ceiling where they belonged.

Dropping to her knees Shams peered into the space under the bed. There was a pair of trainers which would have been white at one time but had turned grey with dirt. She smiled as she identified the second object and reached her hand out, hooking it around a wooden box and pulling it towards her. How could she have missed that last time?

Shams lifted it, placed it on her lap, and wiped the dust off with one swoop of her hand which made the shape of a rainbow on the lid. It was the first wooden box Yusuf had showed her how to make. She flipped it over, felt the contents move around inside and studied the bottom. Yes, there were the lines from where they had practised and she struggled to control the chisel and there in the bottom right-hand corner were her initials. She scraped her nail across the inverted wood to check they were real, then cursed as a piece of splintered wood drew blood from her finger. She smeared it across the flat of her thumb and then made a print next to the letters.

Shams lifted the lid tentatively, as though if she opened it too wide the happy memories of her and her brother would escape forever. She placed her thumb in the corner of the papers and flicked through them. What was she even looking for, she asked herself as she snapped the box shut and manoeuvred the brass catch into place.

Shams lifted the box to her nose and sucked in the smell to draw inspiration from it and as she did, she heard a faint thud as if a piece of loose wood was rattling around inside. Her brother had taught her to make the inside layer fit exactly within the outside wall. If it didn't, it would rattle when a customer picked it up and would ultimately be considered a bad design.

Shams tipped the contents onto the bed so she could inspect the inside. She leant the front of it away from her at a forty-five-degree angle then back towards her again. The base of the box looked like it was loose, that must have been what was making the sound. She held it in place with her thumb then shook the box again, but the thudding sound was still there.

Inside the drawers of Yusuf's desk, Shams found a metal ruler which was thin enough to slip between the outside wood and the loose rectangle at the bottom. It was thinner than it looked from the outside and it didn't take much force before a corner of the panel had raised enough for Shams to pull it out completely. There, where the base had once been, lay a piece of paper folded once down the middle. Before she even opened it, Shams could see the imprint of Yusuf's handwriting from where he had applied the force of his pen.

The sound of the paper fluttering between her unsteady fingers was distracting Shams so she laid it down, circled the room once drawing deep breaths to calm herself, before sitting at her brother's desk and unfolding it out before her.

Shams,

On the morning of the 3 May 2012 I was caught distributing newspapers through people's front doors by a government official who had received complaints about it from his neighbours. He gave me an ultimatum. Either you work for us and report on all those who are involved in the newspaper or we'll arrest your Mum, your Dad and your sister.

They told me to forget about Sara, she was already under surveillance and practically in prison anyway. Since there was nothing I could do for her I warned her to get as far away as possible and became an informer.

For the next four months I wrote down all of our group's activities and movements, where we hide the documents, how we organise the protests, how we communicate with each other. I swear to you Shams, all of this was just to protect you, Mum and Dad.

As soon as I made the decision to do this, they wanted more and more information from me. Where were we meeting to produce the newspaper, who else was involved, would I help them get to the other contributors. They said the only way that all of this would stop was if I was willing to join the army and fight "the terrorists."

Shams, just remember how much I love you. And be careful – he told me he was first alerted to my role in the newspaper by someone close to me.

Forgive me.

Yusuf.

Shams turned and pulled the door of her brother's bedroom softly behind her. She paused for two minutes outside with her palm on his door handle before turning to face the darkness.

She curled her toes into the balls of her feet, away from the chill the floorboards had collected overnight. She moved forwards on her heels, trying to limit her steps to the areas that were covered by the rug but sometimes it was impossible, so she held her breath and manoeuvred herself over these patches as quickly as possible.

When she and Yusuf were young their mother would call them for dinner and they would race to the kitchen, but you would only win if you made the journey without touching the floor. The only time she beat Yusuf was when she ran from the front door, jumped, and landed squarely on the woven material at the end of the hallway. She breathed in and out again. How cruel that such a happy memory had become so painful.

When Shams reached the kitchen, she found one of her father's shirts, ironed, folded neatly, and placed in the centre of the table. She didn't really have much room and she would rather take something that reminded her of Yusuf but the size would be useful. Amidst the soft fabric she pushed in a gold bracelet on the left-hand side and a pair of earrings on the right.

Shams twisted the tap, which let out a low whine as the water flowed through the pipes. She threw her head back and winced as the freezing cold water slid down her throat.

She wrapped her passport and bachelors' certificate in a plastic bag and inserted it into a plastic folder, then tucked a wad of notes and her phone into another. She opened her backpack to check she had remembered everything – her brother's waterproof jacket, a spare pair of jeans, a t-shirt, a cardigan, some underwear, aspirin, dramenex, a notebook, two pens, three packets of cigarettes, a lighter and a box of matches. On top she placed three lemons, some bread wrapped in newspaper and a packet of cheese triangles, before drawing the strings of the bag to conceal the contents.

As she slipped on her trainers and pulled the front door quietly closed behind her Shams felt that familiar, burning feeling of guilt flare up in the depths of her stomach and she stood on the step, one hand on the doorknob and screwed her eyes shut.

CHAPTER FORTY-NINE

Wind blew into a rip in the back of Shams' jeans and she buried her head into the neck of her jumper and turned towards the road. Small stones on the pavement crunched beneath her trainers and she kicked three of them out into the road with the tip of her shoe.

Shams raised her arm to flag down a taxi. She couldn't remember Rasha's address but she would be able to direct the driver there. On the backseat, as she bumped along the uneven road, she turned her phone on. To the only contact saved she began to type, 'I need to meet it's urgent…'

"Which way?" the driver interrupted, using alternate hands to point in the possible directions.

"Right" she said, still looking at the phone. "Then first right."

"This one?" he asked, and she sighed, locked the screen and slid the phone into her bag. She held onto the seat in front of her as the car flew over a speed bump.

"Sorry" came the voice from the front. "Didn't see that one." He cleared his throat.

Shams tapped on the window and the driver slowed down so he could pass the handle through the front seats. Shams fixed the plastic onto the metal knob, wound down the window and squinted to try and recognise Rasha's apartment building.

"Slow down a bit," she instructed. Shams counted the blocks until she saw Rasha's.

"Slow down," she repeated, the annoyance coming through in her voice. Was it this one? It was so hard to tell, they all looked the same. She narrowed her eyes and craned her neck to look, then abruptly sat back down in her seat. Her father's car was parked outside Rasha's apartment block.

Shams felt her heart begin to beat, her limbs went limp. The phone thudded against the floor of the taxi. She leaned down to collect it, hoping to conceal her face. "Speed up, I got the wrong road. I'll get out at the next corner." She shaded her face with her hand, her elbow resting on the windowsill.

* * *

The bells on top of the beauty salon jangled as Shams entered. She hadn't been able to see inside as the windows and doors were covered in pink posters so that the interior was completely concealed. It was the perfect place to wait.

To the left of her vision were two white basins with black leather chairs in front of them, worn at the head rest. The shower heads were coiled around the taps and Shams could see that the remnants of products had crusted onto the surface.

To the right of the room two women were deep in conversation. Shams felt uncomfortable standing in the doorway and took her phone out to check it. She slid it back into her pocket and pushed the door shut with a bang which forced them both to look at her.

"I need to get my hair done." She pointed towards the ceramic basins. "Wash, cut and blow dry please." She made the actions with her hands. One of them dragged herself up and waddled over to the sink. She pointed at the chair and Shams sunk into it and closed her eyes. They were burning again, only this time she could feel water begin to build up underneath her eyelids.

As the woman's fingertips massaged her scalp and the warm water dripped down her ears Shams felt herself moving in and out of sleep.

She felt her hair being tugged from behind, the towel went up and around the outline of her face before she was led to the chair. One of the things that put her off about coming to the hairdresser was having to spend an hour staring at herself in the mirror. Today was no better. She had deep, black circles underneath her eyes and dry skin forming on her scalp.

Shams moved forward in her seat to retrieve her phone from the dresser in front of her. She had forgotten to send the message to Xr and she found it with her thumb and pressed send. She placed it back on the small shelf.

"Busy day?" She tried to make eye contact with the hairdresser in the mirror, shrugging her shoulders and raising her eyebrows.

"I can't remember the last time business was good." She had a sweet in her mouth and she moved it across to the other cheek. "You're our second customer all week. My family is starving."

She pulled over a small stool on wheels and sat down next to Shams. "In the beginning of this… all the protests… we had more customers than ever. People wanted to feel good about themselves, despite whatever was going on out there." She waved towards the door then lowered her hands and pulled each side of Shams' dripping hair down to see it was even. She snipped a bit off the side.

"But now everybody is leaving." She reached for the hairdryer. "I suppose that's what they want isn't it. For everyone to leave."

Shams felt her scalp burn as the hairdresser pulled it with a round brush and brought the hot air over it. She had an itch so she lifted her hand out of the black protective gown and rubbed her forehead. With one hand free she took the opportunity to check her phone. No reply. She threw it back onto the table and the hairdresser looked up as the force rattled the mirror. Her hair was nearly finished. She would have to go back to Rasha's.

Shams stood up to leave, brushed the hair off her knees and pressed one of the notes she had stolen from her parent's bedroom into the woman's hand. "Thank you," she said and tucked it into her back pocket. The bells jingled again as Shams left the salon.

Outside Rasha's apartment Shams had to ring the buzzer three times before anyone replied. The voice that came through the intercom was tentative.

"Yes?"

"Rasha?"

"Yes." There was a pause. "Who is it?"

"Shams." The receiver clicked.

Shams shut her eyes and groaned as she turned away to leave.

"Shams," Rasha hissed, stepping out, holding the door with one arm and pulling at Shams' sleeve. "Come inside quickly so no one sees you." Inside they stood looking at one another in the dim reception.

"Your father was here," she said immediately. "He's so angry Shams, he made us promise to call him as soon as you arrived. Shams he was so aggressive, I'm afraid."

"I need somewhere to sleep" pleaded Shams. "I need to stay here for a while. He won't know, he won't come back."

"Here?" Rasha's eyes widened. "Shams you can't, my parents are here and they're terrified. Your father smashed a lot of things in the apartment and..."

"Smashed? My father?" Shams looked away.

"He didn't believe I didn't know where you were. He said..." they stopped as they heard footsteps on the stairs. Rasha tugged at Shams' arm so that her face was towards the wall and she looked upwards, smiled weakly at her neighbour and held Shams' hand. They heard the door creak open then bang shut again.

"He said he was watching the flat and that if I did anything to help you or if you came here and I didn't tell him he would take my younger brother. Shams please," Rasha looked desperate. Her eyes were round and she had red patches on her neck.

"Rasha I'll go now, but there's one last thing I need to ask you."

"Quickly Shams."

"Why did you tell Amin what I told you."

"What you told me?"

"You know that day in Point Café, when I told you I had met someone else."

"Of course I didn't tell him. Why would I do that?"

"You told him I didn't like the way he ate. Why?"

"Shams are you mad, why would I do that?

"Are you sure it wasn't you?"

"Shams, are you crazy. I think you're mean to Amin, he's a good person. But you're my best friend, I didn't tell him anything. Now go, please."

Shams went onto her tiptoes, kissed Rasha on the forehead and turned to leave. When she looked back Rasha had already disappeared.

Shams dribbled a stone along the pavement with her big toe. She thought of when she was young and used to argue regularly with her parents. Those days she would pack a bag and threaten to run away, though she would only get to the end of the street before turning back.

She pulled her phone out of her pocket and lit up the screen. Finally, a message from Xr.

CHAPTER FIFTY

Amin pulled back the red curtain which was obscuring the doorway and gathered the material onto the plastic hook that had been driven into the wall. It was similar to the ones in Shams' father's studio, only the white circular pattern printed onto it gave it an ethnic feel. Shams would like this, he thought, rubbing it between his thumb and forefinger then pulling down the metal latch to release the handle and using his shoulder to push the panelled door and let himself inside.

The room opened up before him in the shape of a square. He liked the way the width and the length were totally in proportion, it gave him a sense of tranquility.

Whoever had lived here before him had covered the floor with a huge rug that was green and pink and faded in patches. This had less of a calming effect. In the corner was a foam mattress, a cream blanket laid out over the top of it. It was that cheap fleece material that Amin hated because it always left strands of fabric that looked like cat hairs over his clothing. He kicked it away with his foot and dug out his phone from the bottom of the bag. There was only one bar of battery left.

The plug and only source of electricity in the room had seen better days. The first time he had released the charger a chunk of the wall splintered around it and the silver wires elongated out, some sparking with red. The next time he plugged the charger in he muttered a prayer under his breath and left it there figuring that was safer than constantly putting it in and pulling it out.

Directly opposite the door, just under the window, were six cushions laid as a resting place for receiving visitors, instead of a sofa. Amin leaned into them, picked up an enamel mug he had abandoned that morning and sipped the cold coffee. Scrolling through his phone he found Shams' name and clicked to read her message. It had come through this morning when he had been at the souq but he wanted to wait until he got home, to read it in privacy alone with just his thoughts.

'Thanks for your message. Where are you exactly? I'm planning to leave this afternoon and come and find you. I haven't told anyone. I miss you xxx.'

Amin threw his head back onto the wall and felt tears begin to form in his eyes. Perhaps the hardest part of this whole ordeal was the worry that Shams would not believe him and would not come to meet him. He couldn't imagine doing what he was doing alone, but with Shams by his side he felt he could do anything.

He took the phone and with his thumb carefully punched out directions for where she could find him. He described the street and the exact location of his room including the red and white curtain that hung over his front door and the brass handle which had become tarnished over time but which was so distinctive he was sure Shams would be able to pick it up. How long would it take Shams to get here? Really, they should have done the journey together but he wasn't going to waste his energy feeling guilty. There had been no time to waste, it was the difference between staying alive and perishing there in the city in which he had grown up. If anyone could survive that journey alone it was Shams.

Amin looked around his lodgings and decided he would clean before Shams arrived. He could move the mattress outside on the porch and sleep there. He had seen some gas cookers at the market that had three hot rings, he would get one of those and cook a proper meal for when she arrived.

Amin yawned and rolled his shoulders back. First, though, he would have to sleep for a couple of hours, his whole body was aching from the drama of the last few days. He pulled the front of his t-shirt out and tugged at the string around his neck. The usbs carrying thousands of photographs were still hanging there. He lay on his back and began to count the cracks in the ceiling until his eyelids drooped and the steady sound of snores rattled through his sinuses.

When Amin woke five hours later his muscles felt stiff and his head was beginning to ache. The pain was concentrated in a circle close to where the tips of his ears reached. His mouth was dry and sticky so he groped around for water in the dark but all he could find was the dregs of his coffee. He sat up, washed it down, then shivered as the caffeine hit him.

He had fallen asleep with the phone in his hand and now that he was up, he could see the screen was glowing. A message from Shams to Xr. He had forgotten to wrap that particular part of the work up, there was no need for it now that he had escaped. With Shams on his way to meet him he could shut down that line of communication with her. He clicked the name in the bar and read the message. 'I need to meet, it's urgent. Where is best for you?'

Amin sat upright. How could Shams meet if she was on her way to the border. There was no time for this, she had to hurry before her father found out where she was going. 'Where are you and when and where do you want to meet?' he replied, staring at the screen. The response was almost immediate. 'Tonight in Point Cafe at 8pm. I'll wear a red dress."'

Amin froze as a message from Shams' real number came through almost simultaneously. 'On the way. Not long and I will see you. Can't wait. Xxx.' Amin rubbed his forehead and stood up.

He noticed a strip of light coming in through the corner of his window and he edged towards it, his back close to the wall. He could hear the growl of an engine outside. He dropped to his knees and crawled to the front door, opening it softly and tugging the red curtain to free it from the pole. It wouldn't move so he rolled it from the bottom and tucked it into the top.

Back in his room he looked around for something to secure the door. It only had a small metal lock that slid across, the kind you find in public toilets, and he pushed it, then bent down and wedged a notebook in the space between the bottom of the door and the floor. He took a reel of string out of his bag, tied it around the handle then onto the top hinge. He tested it with his hand – it wasn't tight, but it might buy him a couple of minutes.

Inside he tried to breathe calmly as he gathered his belongings, throwing them into his rucksack. He looked about the room to see if he had missed anything. His charger. He held the wall with his left hand and eased it out with his right then slipped it into his right trouser pocket. He walked back towards the front door and checked through the cracks. He could see the outline of a man knocking on the door opposite his, the car that had once been outside the window parked beside him. In his right hand he was holding a black hat. Amin paused for several seconds to see if he would reveal his face and then spun and scanned the room, his eyes resting on the window opposite.

He hadn't tried to open it since he arrived several days ago and he pulled the handle upwards but the lock was firmly shut. On the third yank it let out a high-pitched creaking sound like a cat dying and he stepped away and returned to the door to check again. He couldn't see the figure anymore.

At the bottom of his bag he found a paperclip, and with his shaking fingers lengthened the thin metal then wiggled it into the lock, pulling at the handle again. Then he heard the knock on the door. He turned, closed his eyes and dug the paper clip in and felt the window become loose in his hands. The knock came again, louder this time. The door was rattling, someone was pushing it from the outside.

Amin leaned his stomach over the window frame, dropped his bag outside then as gently as possible pulled himself up, swung his legs over the side and jumped down, a broken nail protruding from the wall ripping into his leg.

CHAPTER FIFTY-ONE

Shams checked her watch. 6pm. She could head to Point Cafe now and waste two hours inside reading her book. She put her hand out for another taxi, hesitated then patted the notes in her pocket. It wasn't too far she was better off just walking.

As soon as she opened the door her cheeks were flushed. Was she really about to meet Xr? She felt out of breath but the volume of voices that met her calmed her nerves. Good, she thought, squeezing herself between the crowds and sitting at a free table by the window. She would blend in more easily.

Shams draped her cardigan over the seat, produced her book from her bag and placed it on the table. She took a step back and considered if that was enough stuff to save her table. She added a notebook and pen then hooked her bag over her shoulder and headed for the toilet.

Inside the tiny space she looked for a place to put her bag. The floor was wet and had mixed with dust from outside to create a kind of sludge on the floor. She placed it over the hook on the door and it immediately came crashing down. "Shit," she said between her teeth, lifting the bag above her head to inspect the damage. There were two circles of brown underneath and she wriggled her hand inside to see if any of the contents were wet.

When she had sent the message to Xr telling him she would be wearing the red dress she hadn't considered the fact that she would have to find somewhere to change into it. She had sent it because it seemed like a line from a movie.

Shams gathered some of the toilet roll and used it to shut the lid of the toilet, threw it into the corner and pulled more to clean the surface. On top of this she placed her bag, pulled out the red dress and held it up to check for damage. She could see the hem at the back had become grey from where the damp floor had soaked into it.

Turning to face the mirror Shams managed to pull off her jumper and jeans and fold them, placing them carefully on top of the bag. Had she brought leggings? She surveyed the pile, which was getting higher and higher on the toilet and decided to first try the dress. Standing there in her socks balancing on top of her trainers, Shams pulled the dress over her head, down past her stomach and let it fall at her ankles. It was wrinkled so she turned to inspect her side profile. There was nothing she could do about that now. Shoes. That was something she had definitely forgotten.

Someone outside banged on the door and she ignored them, opening the tap to release a stream of water and washing her hands then running two fingers underneath her eyes to tidy up where the kohl had run. What about her hair? Xr was going to think she had had it done especially for him and the thought embarrassed her. She took her hairband off her wrist and tied it up into a messy bun on top of her head. That was more casual.

As Shams opened the door, she saw a line of five women. She smiled, turned her chin towards the ground and navigated her way back through the tables and back to her chair. She tucked the bag underneath the seat, draped her cardigan back over her shoulders and opened her book.

Two hours later Shams checked her watch again. 8.10pm. He must have been delayed, she thought, placing her book face down.

Shams looked at her outfit. The cardigan was partially obscuring her dress, perhaps he had already been in and missed her. She shrugged it off her shoulders and swapped chairs so she was facing the door. A young man in his early thirties walked in, a laptop under his arm, and she tried to catch his eye. But he walked straight past her and as she turned, he joined a group of three other young men. She tapped her finger on the table, drew her mouth to one side and surveyed the room.

Shams lit up the screen of her phone with her hand. 8.45pm. He obviously wasn't coming, was he. She looked down at her clothes. She felt embarrassed to be dressed like this with no one to meet her.

She bent down to pull her bag towards her and on the way up banged her head so hard into the table the people next table stopped their conversation to look. Xr was ringing. She looked around her, pulled the hairband out and ran her fingers through her hair.

"Hello?"

"Hello?" she said again, louder this time.

"Shams it's Amin, don't hang up, just don't hang up."

There was a long pause.

"Amin is that you?"

"Shams I know who your father is, I worked with him but I've been collecting evidence to smuggle out of the country," Amin sounded out of breath. "Shams it was me sending you the messages all this time. Shams you have to listen to me carefully, I will tell you where to go. Shams?"

Shams gripped the phone tighter and felt all the blood rush out of her head.

"Why did you pretend to be Xr?"

"I'm not pretending. I am Xr. I mean that's the name I have to use at work."

"You know what I mean Amin." She could feel tears beginning to form. "I mean why didn't you tell me it was you sending the photos?

"Shams there really isn't much time, can we talk about this later?"

Shams didn't respond.

"Shams are you there? Shams you have to listen to me, this is important. Shams?"

"Why did you keep your job hidden? Why didn't you tell me?"

"Shams we are not allowed to tell anyone what we do."

"But I'm not just anyone am I Amin?"

"Look I need to tell you something else. Shams your father was here, he came looking for me."

Shams shut her eyes. "He took my phone. Where are you?"

"I will explain later. Shams you have to keep this phone hidden, don't let anyone take it. Ok? It's our only line of communication."

"Amin?" Shams tried to catch him before he hung up. "Amin I have nowhere to sleep tonight where shall I go? What shall I do? I can't go home."

"No. He replied. No, you can never go home Shams. I will think of something, ok?"

"Ok."

"Amin?" She wanted to hear his voice one more time. He breathed, waiting for her.

"I love you." There was a pause. She bit her lip.

"I love you too."

CHAPTER FIFTY-TWO

As Sharif opened the front door, he could smell coriander. Of all the herbs his wife used when she was preparing food it was his favourite. When he was young and his mother was cooking, he and his brother used to fight over the stalks then sit and chew them for hours.

He kissed her on the forehead then bent his knees so that his eyes became level with his two daughters. They had been playing a game on the kitchen floor and had scattered tiny pieces of cardboard everywhere. He felt one dig into his knee.

"Daddy, come and play with us?"

"Play with you? Looks like you've been doing a good job of playing by yourselves."

He tried to stand up but they were pulling at his collar.

"Daddy come back. Come and play with us."

Sharif fell backwards onto his hands then rolled onto his side. He could hear his daughters giggling and he felt his cheeks redden.

"The place is a mess." He stood up so that he could look at his wife. "What have you been doing all day?"

She ignored him, turned and fiddled with some plates in the sink.

"Rabia, are you listening to me?"

She didn't turn around.

"Rabia?"

He sighed and walked out of the room. He spent so much time trying to keep his family safe, the least they could do in return was show some gratitude. He would wait in his study until they had finished their dinner and she had cleared the kitchen.

He walked into his study, shut the door and sat down at his desk. The file was just as he had left it in the centre of the table. He opened it and scanned what was written inside – had he missed anything? He didn't think so.

Sharif wasn't really supposed to bring his work home with him but he always made copies of the files once he had finished with the people inside. His wife had once called them trophies but he didn't really see it like that. It was his work, he had to support his family, and he was proud of himself for fulfilling this to the best of his ability.

He ran his thumb over Yusuf's name then closed it. With a red pen he wrote on the front cover "file completed," then stored it in the grey filing cabinet to the right of his desk. He pulled out the drawer below and retrieved another.

Back at his desk he opened the front page and looked at the information inside. A network of volunteers had been delivering aid to villages in the countryside outside of Aleppo. He ran his finger all the way down to the bottom of the page and there he found a list of ten names. Next to one of them an address had been written by hand. He squinted; the door number was hard to make out. Sharif produced his notebook from the inside pocket of his jacket and copied the address into it. Tomorrow, first thing, he would get started.

CHAPTER FIFTY-THREE

From where she was standing Shams could see the river. She closed her eyes, breathed in, and tried to remember the days the ebb and flow of the cascade soothed her nerves.

In the past, whenever she felt down, it was towards the river she went. Whatever was happening internally the water always made the same steady gush as it hit the black rocks and continued its journey downstream.

The bridge was built out of concrete, with slopes on either side to contain the water. It was an unsightly view at odds with the beauty of the river. Nevertheless, when she swung her legs over the side and closed her eyes the flow of the current helped her think.

She thought back to the last day she sat on the concrete edge to process her thoughts, 22 January 2012. Before the café, the newspaper, her father. Before the violence and before the arrest.

That day the wind had ripped up the current and the rain had dampened her seat. She tried to picture herself sitting there on the water's edge, a few hours before she understood her life was about to change and her understanding of who she could trust was completely upended. The moment before and the moment after.

Shams opened her eyes and focused on the present. Now she felt as though someone had tied a rope around her rib cage and when she looked at the water, she was certain someone would pull so hard she would suffocate.

There were few buildings overlooking the water's edge where Amin had told her to wait so Shams sat on the curb and pulled her hood over her hair. She pushed her legs out in front of her and the gravel scraped along the ground. She considered how relieved she was to have changed out of that red dress and thought of it in the tight ball she had rolled it into before dropping it at the bottom of the bin. She had thrown away part of herself with it.

Since Xr had started messaging Shams he had awakened in her feelings she believed she'd buried long ago. By contrast her life with Amin was familiar and safe but it lacked passion and since their communication began, she had often sat on her bed with the lights dimmed and her forehead screwed up into a frown, trying to recall those very same feelings which she knew she had once felt for him.

The eternal question orbiting relationships was how to keep the flame of those initial feelings alive. She considered how people spent their whole lives searching for continuity and stability but once they had it, all they longed for was change. Now she had discovered Amin was both of those things. That was very confusing indeed.

All of this left Shams with the unbearable task of answering the question, who was she in love with – Amin, or the idea of him he presented through Xr.

Shams shifted her weight forwards and hugged her knees into her chest. She realised she had no way of knowing whether Amin was telling the truth but at the same time she had no one else to trust. It felt as though someone had taken a balloon, stretched it out and inserted it just below her ribs so that it rested tentatively on her stomach. Shams knew it would burst later and leave behind a residue, loose ends that fluttered around her body. She would feel more relaxed but ultimately exhausted.

"Shams?"

She looked up and saw a man around the same age as her, his hand outstretched. She offered hers in return and he pulled her from the ground and in one movement led her towards the car.

Inside the vehicle Shams arched her back against the seat and fed the strap of her rucksack through her leg, gripping onto the looped handle.

"Music on or off?" He was looking at her in the wing mirror.

"Depends what it is."

"Radio."

"Then off."

She shut her eyes. She wanted to remember the fading bricks that formed the walls of the citadel and the mother of pearl that decorated her family boxes so she leaned her head backwards and let the low growl of the engine send her to sleep, rather than stare out of the window and let her last image be what Aleppo had become.

When she woke the first thing Shams saw was Amin, one hand on the roof of the car, his forehead pressed against the window.

"Shams."

She couldn't hear the word, but she saw the way his mouth moved and was surprised when the sight of him evoked faint waves of electricity in her stomach and she felt the corners of her mouth turn upwards into a smile. He walked around to the other side, slid in beside her and the familiar scent of his aftershave filled the air.

The vehicle lurched forwards until eventually mountains rose up before them. Shams heard the handbrake screech and watched as the driver held onto the roof of the car and swung his body out of the door, landing on both feet. Shams stood, stretched her legs and pulled her bag onto her back, then began to walk. She had imagined unloading everything onto Amin as soon as she saw him and had looked forward to the lightness she would feel after doing so. But they had the whole journey ahead, it would come out slowly. Perhaps they could savour it like that.

"Wait Shams," Amin called out from behind her. She turned as she heard his hurried footsteps on the path. He held out a padded envelope that had been sealed at the top and bottom with brown tape. "The rest of the usbs. Put them in your bag." They stood for several seconds, with his hands outstretched, and Shams staring at the package before her.

"You're not coming?" Shams snatched them out of his hand feeling a flare of anger rise up from her stomach.

"No Shams. I will go back for my parents and Reem and meet you later." Another man was standing to the left of him and he turned slightly to introduce him. "This is Ziad, he will look after you."

Shams looked at the ground – she had had enough of young men appearing from the shadows. She turned away from both of them and stumbled over the rocks that lined the base of the mountains.

"Shams" she heard him call into the wind but she ignored him and pressed ahead, too proud to turn in case he saw the tears. She heard the sound of feet running and was relieved to feel a hand on her shoulder. She turned to face Amin but it was Ziad.

"Wait for me," he hissed and she could feel the spit in her face. "It's not safe for you to walk into the darkness alone." He gripped her wrist "Wait, I said." She moved her head to look beyond him but the car carrying Amin had already left.

Ziad, who can't have been more than twenty-five, had a muscular physique and Shams wondered how many times he had gone back and forth over this no man's land.

"More than a hundred," he told her when she asked.

He smelt of olive oil and had a nasal voice, which he used to tell her about his family, who lived on the Turkish side of the frontier. "In early 2011 I had a bad feeling about where all this was going to go. So I took my family and put them there."

"Your family?"

"Mum, Dad, wife, two sons." His mouth broke out into a smile. "My wife is pregnant again. We think it's a girl this time."

"I hope so too." She stopped, looked straight ahead of her. "Is this it?"

"It is."

The border consisted of a set of concrete posts that had been driven into the ground to hold up the sheets of wire mesh. Several lines of barbed wire ran the length of it and at the very top six or seven pieces had been twisted together to block anyone who wanted to climb over.

On the horizon military trucks roamed the uneven ground and Shams could hear continual gunshots. Sometimes they popped, just like a burst tyre or a firework, but at other times they released a constant barrage of sound that burrowed into her ears. When the noise subsided, she could still hear it faintly, her ears pulsating in the aftermath.

Shams had lost the ability to comprehend anything around her. Her hands were clammy and she tried desperately to get rid of the excess moisture by rubbing them down her jeans. The lights were fuzzy and there was a strange buzzing sound in her head. She took some deep breaths in and out to try and bring some calm to the situation, but there was no time.

Ziad pulled hard on her arm, pointing to the ground where someone had hollowed out the earth beneath the wire and Shams lay on her stomach and clawed herself forwards, hidden stones within the earth ripping craters across her palms and tearing her fingernails.

Ziad buckled his legs, fell onto the palm of his hands then glided under the mesh, barely disturbing the structure as he pulled his limbs underneath it in one graceful move. Shams willed his jacket to get caught up in the wire to give her time to gather her breath, and her thoughts. She still hadn't recovered from navigating the terrain of her feelings for Amin. Over the course of her journey she had slipped and fumbled in the darkness trying to find a physical foothold among the rocks that littered the path.

Emerging from under the wire Ziad nodded at Shams, grabbed her wrist and they ran for perhaps thirty or forty minutes without stopping. Her lungs burnt in her chest and she could feel liquid moving up from her stomach and out of her mouth as she threw up into the wind. Her thighs tightened and her feet burnt from the repeated smashing into the ground.

Each time she wanted to collapse Ziad pulled on her arm. Not a friendly encouraging touch, rather a brutal uncompromising grip. As the sound of the guns got louder a second set of concrete posts and wire mesh appeared in the distance and she collapsed on the ground, huge chunks of earth entering her mouth as she sucked in whatever air she could find. Ziad left her panting on the dirt and crept along the fence, studying it closely before turning around and motioning for Shams to join him. Together they stepped through a hole in the wire.

ONE MONTH LATER

Amin ran his fingers in between the gaps of the sofa cushions and felt the grit force itself under his nails. No matter how many times he lifted the cushions off the seat and brushed the dirt onto the floor, whenever he felt down the sides it was always filthy. He stood and removed the cushions, cupped his hand at the edge of the sofa, then scraped what was there into his hand and emptied it into the bin. That was better. He always found it easier to concentrate once he knew his environment was clean.

When they had found this basement room there had actually been a television in the corner but Amin preferred to watch the news on his laptop, that way he could bypass the various blocks put in place and live stream the international news in four different windows at once. It had become addictive, watching and waiting to see if Syria came on the news and when it did, how the rest of the world dealt with the crisis he was living through.

One of the presenters was talking about a power cut in a city he didn't recognise in Europe, people had been stranded on the metro for three hours. He stood up, stretched his arms in the air then hung his body over his waist and felt his spine click. It was getting to him, being inside this basement all day, but until he found a way out of the country, he couldn't really go outside. He felt one of the cats press its nose into his leg and he leaned out and ran his palm down its tail.

As he pulled himself upright, he caught the sliding bar at the bottom of the screen in the top right-hand box. Syria: Breaking News. He clicked to enlarge it and sat on the floor with his back leaning against the sofa. Then a photo. Was that him? The pointed nose, the sunken eyes, the yellowed fingers. And there in the background were the white tiles of the morgue and the outline of three dead bodies.

The camera cut to the presenter: "Photographs smuggled out of Syria have been published across major news outlets this morning as evidence of war crimes in the country. In particular investigations have been launched into the whereabouts of this man, believed to be involved at a senior level in the torture of protesters. Investigators believe he may be hiding in Germany."

Amin stood up and circled the room. Germany? How had he got out of the country and got to Europe? He bent so that his head was level with the computer and pulled up the other screens. They were all showing the image of the pathologist. He reached for his phone, everywhere he looked on social media the image was there.

He heard a knock on the door. He reached forward, pulled his socks on, and walked as softly as he could manage to the door. He heard the knock again, louder this time. Three short taps and the sound of nails scraping. He put the metal chain across the door, then pulled it open. He smiled, shut the door just enough so he could pull the chain off, then side stepped to let her into the room.

"How are you?" Rasha smiled as she reached up on her toes to kiss him. "I missed you."

Amelia Smith is a recognised name within the human rights and global issues sector. As a columnist and author of features she works closely with communities facing the most serious challenges within the UK, Egypt, Syria and the MENA region. She has edited two non-fiction books about Egypt and the Arab Spring and interviewed scores of political prisoners and their families. Her work has been translated into many languages.

Printed in Great Britain
by Amazon

78185340R00183